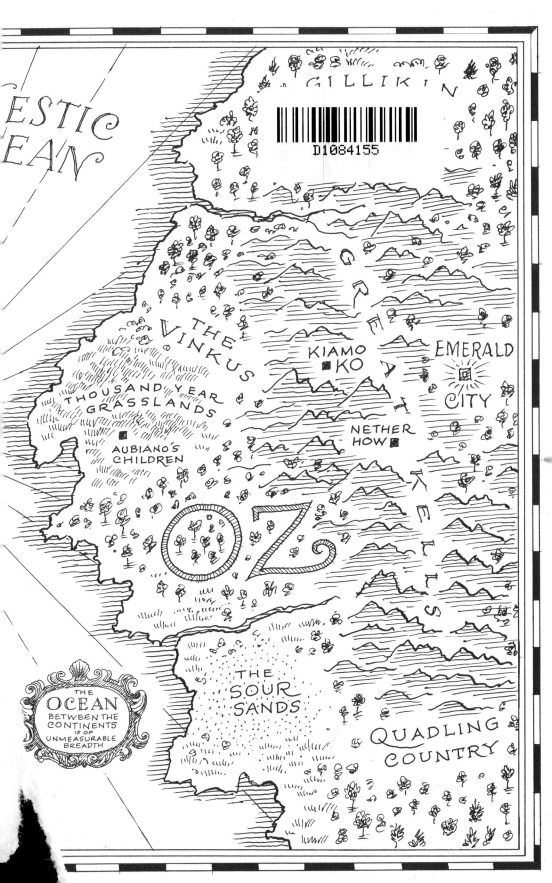

THE WITCH *of* MARACOOR

ALSO BY GREGORY MAGUIRE

FICTION

A Wild Winter Swan

Hiddensee

After Alice

The Next Queen of Heaven

Mirror Mirror

Lost

Confessions of an Ugly Stepsister

The Wicked Years

Wicked

Son of a Witch

A Lion Among Men

Out of Oz

Another Day

The Brides of Maracoor

The Oracle of Maracoor

NONFICTION

Making Mischief: A Maurice Sendak Appreciation

FOR YOUNGER READERS

Cress Watercress

Matchless

Egg & Spoon

What-the-Dickens

Missing Sisters

The Good Liar

Leaping Beauty

THE WITCH *of*
MARACOOR

A Novel

GREGORY
MAGUIRE

wm

WILLIAM MORROW

An Imprint of HarperCollins*Publishers*

HarperCollins books may be purchased for educational, business, or sales promotional use. For information, please email the Special Markets Department at SPsales@harpercollins.com.

FIRST EDITION

Designed by Bonni Leon-Berman
Illustrations by Scott McKowen

Library of Congress Cataloging-in-Publication Data has been applied for.

ISBN 978-0-06-309406-2

23 24 25 26 27 LBC 5 4 3 2 1

HB 08 02 2023 0626

For Michael Steinberg

. . . Keys ever remoter

Lock our friend among the golden things that go

Without saying, the loves no longer called up

Or named.

. . . And in the final

Analysis, who didn't have at heart

Both a buried book and a voice that said

Destroy it?

—James Merrill, *The Changing Light at Sandover*

For the rain it raineth every day.

—Shakespeare, *Twelfth Night*

CONTENTS

AUTHOR'S NOTE

Clarity on the reproductive practices of cranes was kindly supplied by Kim Boardman of the International Crane Foundation, Baraboo, Wisconsin. I have muddled the matter for my own narrative purposes.

PART ONE

ITHIRA STRAND

1

ny witch worth her ginger is at least somewhat immortal. Trust the word on the street. So much easier to kill her, should it come up—she'll bounce back, one way or the other. They always do.

The Witch of Maracoor. That's what some called her, whether or not she was actually a witch. The Witch of Wherever-It-Is-This-Time. A slur or a compliment, depending. The easier to identify, the easier to dismiss; who cares about *her*? Let's go get our hands on a jug of beer.

Easy enough to see where the witch label came in. Hardly any deviation from stereotype. That green skin, the self-possession, even the take-no-prisoners manner of walking. ("She stomped herself across the Wool Exchange in that way she has—just so *aggressive!*") Someone had heard her cursing once in an unladylike way—as if so-called ladies were ignorant of barnyard vocabulary. But was she a witch? How so? Language? Okay. And manners. Attitudes. Little attention paid to her clothes, for instance. Society forgives a woman everything but lapses in taste.

The Witch of Maracoor had appeared as if from nowhere, with her green-apple cheeks and that twitchy broom. Intent on some intrigue. Always unseemly and possibly seditious. Well, but when does a witch go in for community organizing? The singularity of her. She was like no one else.

Or she was like that Elphaba, revived. Perhaps? No? Maybe she *was* Elphaba, after all, come back from wherever she'd disappeared to. Few remembered the original Wicked Witch of the West from personal experience, but hardly anyone in Oz was agnostic about her. All those stories.

Her name was Rainary, this Witch of Maracoor. Her friends, when she had any, called her Rain. She lived under a cloud, and had done so for a long time. It was beginning to tell on her, though. That's also where witchiness comes in—when temporary scar tissue turns into carapace.

It was the Goose, her familiar, who'd named her the Witch of Maracoor. Possibly it had been a joke. Or he'd been annoyed and in one slip of the beak he'd tarnished her reputation for good, forever. Or maybe he did it on purpose, setting her up to be able to clomp through a mob without having to trade in small talk.

The Goose had a lot to answer for. His name was Iskinaary. He'd flown with her in from—well, from wherever they'd originated. No one was sure.

2

A trim little windswift vessel called *Ocean Heron*, out of the Maracoor port of Tonxis, was headed for Great Northern Isle by way of Ithira Strand. Captain, crew, and three passengers: a middle-aged guy named Lucikles, this Rain, and the Goose. The crew was only four—no need and no room for more. The Captain managed all right. She claimed she was a former bootlegger up Regalius way, but her manner was more like an auntie glad for the liberty afforded by widowhood. Stalta Hipp; she refused to answer to "Captain Hipp" because she said that made her sound like the chaperone at a geriatrics' picnic.

"You're not going to find much on Ithira Strand," she warned them. "It used to be a pretty enough haven, but since the *Hind of the Sea* imported a plague from Lesser Torn Isle, Ithira Strand has been avoided like—well, like the plague. We'll anchor off Toe Hold first. It's just across the strait. Reconnoiter from there. You, Goosemeat, you can goose yourself across the water and have a gander. Ha ha."

"I flew across the damn Nonestic Ocean," said Iskinaary, "and I'm planning on surviving to attempt the return journey. If I must make a sortie, it'll be brisk. I'm not interested in carrying a fatal disease back to Oz. Except in a few dedicated cases that I won't go into."

ITHIRA STRAND had long been home to a species of bird called the border crane. Lazy, the cranes preferred sorting through village garbage to fishing. At the moment, though, few border cranes remained on the island, the rest having migrated when the human population disappeared from disease first and then panicky exodus.

One such creature had been known as Silverbeak for, in a biological misfiring, her bill gleamed like polished weaponry rather than the ordinary muddy pewter. Like all her kin, her eyes were encircled by a bright red cap that cupped her head. A robber bird in a party mask. The effect lent her an air of keen intelligence that was possibly unmerited—otherwise wouldn't she have left with her tribe?

Little can be said about what an animal perceives. Without spoken language, a creature's concepts of time and history, or of consequence on any scale beyond the flock's immediate well-being, remain unknowable. The habits of animals: instinctual and emulative. To be sure, animal personalities emerge. That brindle cow is the ornery one; this duck alone seems to be scared of the water. But is there such a thing as a lazy spider, a songbird gone mute on a hunger strike, a puppy born with a radical instinct for guile? Few humans can ever say. And animals aren't talking.

For whatever reason, Silverbeak held to her sentry post on Ithira Strand, unflinching as a bronze, when Iskinaary arrived across the strait from Tea Stone. The Goose carved his first circuit above the harbor. The crane didn't appear to follow his flight path by tracking him with red-circled side-eye. The dusky hour was coming on. Better for fishing. Dinner took precedence.

After the Goose had flown on, Silverbeak moved into the water. The line where light and shade met on the sandy bottom made movement easier to distinguish there. It wasn't long before she spotted a glint some ways off. Her legs angling in slow, splashless movement, she paused as if to pose no threat, and then she lunged. A nice-size stickleback. She stood with it pinched midway up her beak. It flapped noisily enough that two seagulls came in at an angle, hoping to scare Silverbeak into dropping her catch. She didn't flinch. She lifted her head and let supper drop farther along her bill toward her throat. Then, one gulp and down the gullet. Distending the elastic skin of the crane's neck, the meal thrashed in protest.

Silverbeak stopped eating when the Goose descended into the water in that collapsing way geese have. The Goose folded his wings upon his dorsal feathers and ruddered his tail feathers ostentatiously. He neared her. She kept her eyes on several horizons and didn't acknowledge him.

"I don't suppose you have a word of welcome for a traveling stranger?" he said.

It seemed she did not.

"You won't mind if I help myself? I prefer insects and weeds, but the offerings on board a seafaring vessel are, shall we say, limited. Something fresh from the shallows would do nicely."

The light lowered; a cloud trailed its hem across the sun.

"After weeks of human society, I was hoping to kick back with my own kind, or near enough," he added. When Silverbeak showed no interest in him, the Goose gave himself over to supper. In elegance of execution he was no match for the crane. He caught a tarnished item quickly enough—his male pride satisfied in front of this female from another tribe. He thwacked it on the surface of the water, worried it about, dropped it three or four times, bloodied his beak. This was normal procedure. Iskinaary wasn't self-conscious about it until Silverbeak spotted a morsel with which to finish her meal, and took two patrician steps forward before securing a much larger specimen. With the calm of a priestess she stood there letting it thrash, its moment of sacrifice extended—was

she showing off, wondered Iskinaary—before she smoothly gobbled it down.

"You have the look of someone who knows more than she's saying," said the Goose.

When the border crane took off, it was with a single step forward
into the air. Her wings extended eight feet—a third again the span
of Iskinaary's. He followed her with the traditional dashing-on-
water takeoff that could look stupid even to him. When he was
younger he could do it in only six steps. Now it was more like
twelve. He'd be lucky to make it back to Oz—at the rate he was
aging he might have to walk home across the ocean.

He followed the lean pretty thing at a distance, not wanting to
frighten her, not ready yet to go back to his companions on the
ship. Could she be a Crane—a talking creature? Regardless, the
company was welcome, even if she didn't have much in the way of
social graces. Her habits might teach him something about the
island it was useful to know. That's what he said to himself.

The town of Ithira Strand strung itself out along two roads
running parallel to each other and to the sandy verge. For a place
eviscerated by plague not so long ago, it was kempt, as if the
breeze had taken over the job of sweeping the streets. The doors
were mostly closed, the windows shuttered. One might have expected packs of wild dogs, but perhaps the Ithirians had taken
their dogs with them. Or had the hounds succumbed to plague,
too? The thought of this made Iskinaary distinctly queasy, and he
was about to turn back when he saw three old cats reclining on a
flagstone plaza in front of a padlocked café of some sort. Cats can
be sort of eternal, like witches, but these looked too disaffected to
bother to die and come back. Iskinaary found this a little encour-
aging. Though it was a stretch.

And the Silverbeak—the same name came to Iskinaary, it was
inevitable, an obvious and reductive name like Gimpy or Shrimp or

Carrot-top—Silverbeak lived here too. For there she was now lifting, upon those white wings as pure as faith, and settling athwart
a bracken nest perched upon a listing chimney stack. Maybe she
had some stork in her lineage. Or maybe she was wary of old cats.

Where there was a nest, there would be eggs, or even baby colts.
A sign of life. If not now, soon. Iskinaary didn't realize he'd been
holding his breath. He decided to visit Silverbeak by flying up to
land on the roof-beam just beside the shoulders of the chimney.

"I suppose you're wondering where I've come from," he said.
"Can't be too many Geese making their way from any mainland to
this northern isle."

Silverbeak set to work revising the fringy edge of the nest. She
didn't reply but she didn't fly away either. So Iskinaary told her
about the long trip from Oz, and his companion, Rain, and their
hopes to make it back home safely. The border crane listened without making snarky remarks. When the Goose finished, he sat in
silence. She was regarding him with a level look, neither vicious
nor welcoming. He'd never met anyone so serenely herself.

The others bobbing off the shores of Toe Hold, or maybe col-
lecting fresh fruits on the island itself, would be waiting for a
report. Let them wait. What an unexpected vacation, to sit in
complacency with someone who didn't answer back. Look at that
slender neck against the burnt-orange sky.

3

On Toe Hold, while they waited for the Goose, Rain wandered away to find a pond shielded from the eyes of her companions. Lucikles, the nominal ambassador of the court, now at loose ends, began to rehash his recent adventures to the affable Captain.

Stalta Hipp relaxed with a beaker of sour ale and smiled her appreciation for a tale of woe that for once hadn't happened to her. "I'm a good listener," she said. "If our friend the chatty Goose is taking his time over there, spin out the tale as long as it takes. What else are we going to do? You don't want to hear me sing a tiresome roundelay of my life as a smuggler."

Much of what had happened in the past several months Lucikles considered privileged information. State secrets, if you wanted to go that far. The devotions practiced by the brides of Maracoor, and their untimely interruption. (Or was it, precisely, timely?) The cross-country pilgrimage to visit the Oracle of Maracoor, out in the unmapped western regions of the nation. The disposing of the lethal item known as the Fist of Mara. The abdication of the Bvasil from the throne.

So Lucikles talked instead about the return to the western slopes of High Chora by the subdued party of adventurers. Only five of them left by that point. Filthy, dispirited, hardly speaking to one another. Rain and the Goose. Lucikles with his newly adolescent son, Leorix. And finally, the palace representative, a handsome young man named Tycheron, who'd shown a romantic interest in Rain until he'd seen her fly, at which point his skepticism about romancing a witch got the better of him.

And on the way back cross-country, the travelers saw only glimmers of the secret world of the homegrown Maracoorian spirits. Where once there'd been apparitions of piskies and minor deities, scraps of Maracoor's fabled past, now Lucikles could detect only a sweet decadent odor, as if something questionable had recently passed by. A quiet had begun to settle upon the land. Evidence of repair and restoration, Lucikles hoped, rather than an indication of some sort of final coma.

And why not? He savored any signs of revival. Look, while harboring in the enchantment of the western woods, even Rain had made some recovery. Her drowned broom had been restored by the so-called Oracle of Maracoor; she'd proven her ability to fly in front of them all. With less commotion than the Goose could do, she'd mounted the air. She'd swept the tops of the trees with the business end of her broom, raising clouds of powdery pollen. She'd swung back in a loop to collect it, using some old seashell as a kind of scoop. Quite a sight, Lucikles did admit it.

"I don't know about this witch business. Are you talking the get-up, or the make-up, or the giddy-up with the broom?" asked Stalta.

"Can *you* fly on a broom?"

"No. But piloting a ship and plying the waves doesn't make me a mermaid. Just what is it that seals this girl's identity in your mind?"

A good question. A witch was a concept—like most concepts— with forgiving outlines. But a witch was more than a certain kind of ornery one-off, to be sure. A witch possessed a capacity for rawness coupled with a strength of charm—the ability to cast a spell of sorts.

True, many old wives could do much the same with their fingered portions of ground herbs and oils. The muttered chants, the candles and incense for atmosphere—that was histrionics, surely. (Surely?) The real proof was in the person. And Rain, for all her confusion, her amnesia and recovery from it, was a live thread of capacity. A sprig of green lightning in stout boots and a walking cape.

Lucikles said, briskly, "She promised our hosts to bring their unspent pollen to Ithira Strand and to try to sow it there before she continues her trip home."

"This *Oz* that she keeps mentioning." Stalta belched; the brew was rough. "What do you make of such a thing?"

"I never knew there were lands beyond the ones it was my obligation to oversee—the Hyperastrich Archipelago, the Great Northern Isle, and so on. I thought that was as far east as the world went, and the Sea of Mara stretching beyond was too vast to be knowable. We all did. The Bvasil did, and all his factotums and courtiers beside. This notion of a possible Oz makes me feel—crowded. The policy from the Crown, so far anyway, is to keep the matter very hush-hush-hush-a-bye."

"So tell me, do you even believe in Oz? I mean, how trustworthy is this off-color girl-thing anyway? With her trick Goose being so chatty and all that? It's true she has an accent, but so do the Skedelanders and the Pomiole clans and most people who are more than seventy years old. Anyone can fake an accent." In a parody of up-country drawl. "Oy coin dyoo its moisef, whens Oy heff thay moind tyoo."

"I don't know what to believe, I don't even know what belief is," said Lucikles. "A few months ago I'd have said I hardly believe in the Great Mara except as a relic of our cultural identity. But in the past few months I've traveled with a couple of annoying harpies. I've met up with a giant who emerged from the earth like a laborer waking up from a drunken stupor. So I've retired my skepticism and replaced it with—a more refined skepticism, I guess. Oz may be, or may not be. Does it make a difference to me now?"

"Following your interview with that Oracle, you left him and started back, scaled the cliff to High Chora," Stalta reminded him. "But what happened next?"

"It's easy to telescope. We hot-footed it cross-country toward my mother-in-law's farm at the eastern breast of the plateau. We sidestepped a few Skedelander contingents, lingering remnants of the invaders, who were still on the hunt for that treasure removed from the capital. Once, they surprised us on the path of a roister-ing brook. The noise of a cataract had cloaked the sound of our approach, and theirs too. They raised their weapons until they got a good look at Rain. Then they stepped aside and let us pass. I think the steam was going out of their search."

Stalta Hipp arched an eyebrow. "You're not telling it all to me, are you."

Well, the Captain was on to him, and no mistake. It *had* been an encounter, all right. Lucikles hardly liked to envision Rain, sud-denly enraged, like a cat seeming twice its size. Holding slantwise on to her broom, she'd lifted in the air a few feet. The Skedelander contingent—some soldiers in breastplate and helmet, others shucked free of their heavy chained mail and sweating in their torn and greasy tunics—had quailed and then rallied. Rain had no fire-balls to fling, no curses to lower. But in her flashing eyes Lucikles had caught sight of an instinct toward lethal vengeance. Probably over the Skedish murder of one of the harpies some weeks earlier. Rain had pivoted in the air, stirring like a ladle, and a coil of wind at her heels updrafted a cone of straw and last year's leaves. She'd issued a single note, a trumpet voluntary, as if calling to her side, to her aid, all the shrikes and flying spiders, the boreals and zeph-yrs, the anemoi both malign and conciliatory. What had caused the soldiers to turn and run? The ferocity of her singular aspect. It was all of a piece—her raised voice, too angry to be a word; and her skin flushing green; and the impossible height of her outrage. He'd been terrified himself—and he was on her side.

"I knew a mountain witch once, a Morgwera, who was a kind of den mother to hedgehogs. At least I think they were hedgehogs. They didn't come out of their cave often. And I also heard tell of a trio of river witches, near Olion, who shared an eye among them. But they were always fighting. You know why?"

She was trying to ground him; panic must be showing on his face at the memory of Rain, enraged. "No, why?"

"They could never see eye to eye over anything."

He grunted without much appreciation. The Captain continued. "You know enough to be careful, don't you? There's nothing more dangerous than an enraged woman, Kerr Lucikles."

"Because she has too much to lose?"

"Mmm. Or because she has too little."

At his mother-in-law's farm at last, Lucikles had been reunited with his wife and daughters. The flying monkeys, who'd been holding down the fort, gabbled some unconvincing tales of their derring-do. That first evening his son, Leorix, had gone to bathe in the duck pond at dusk. Still wary of the boy, whom he loved, Lucikles wandered to the stone wall under pretext of having a smoke, to make sure nothing happened to Leorix. The father watched the son strip in the brown dusk, and saw how the lad's lengthening limbs had bulked themselves up in travel, how the little nest of his genitals was beginning to boast the beginning of wolf-fringe. The father turned away then, and for good, saying goodbye for all practical purposes to the little boy he'd adored. He listened to Leorix splash, though, and he kept ready to turn back should the world subvert itself once again, and some deranged Nereid of the pond emerge to try to drag the boy under.

"What was your Tycheron fellow up to all this while?" asked Stalta, bringing Lucikles back to his storyteller's role.

"He had jettisoned whatever fondness for Rain he'd been nursing," said Lucikles. "When the Bvasil began a further, solitary pilgrimage that promised no quick return to the capital, Tycheron's obligations shifted from romantic affairs to those of court. He had to deliver to the palace the news of the Bvasil's defection, or at any rate unannounced absence. He took back from me the jeweled pendant that only the Bvasil was privy to wearing. Proof, you know, that the king had departed."

"Wouldn't this Tycheron be put in prison and executed for Bvasilicide?" asked Stalta. "I mean, showing up and saying 'Look at me, I have the throne jewels and by the way the Bvasil has disappeared.'"

"A chance he had to take," replied the overseer, "but one that he'd been raised to perform. I suppose he knew the risks. Palace command is likely sending out scouts to hunt for the Bvasil or his body, and to see if there is any way to prove or disprove Tycheron's assertions. He'll be fairly comfortable under lock and key until they come back with some news or no news."

"He didn't think having Rain at his side would be a convincing witness?"

"Are you paying attention? She'd already been indicted on a charge of possible sedition, since her arrival in Maracoor Abiding had coincided with the invasion by the Skedians. Hardly useful for Tycheron to return to the capital city with her at his side saying, 'No, she's fine, she's clean of insult to the nation; and by the way the Bvasil has disappeared.'"

"But it was more than that."

Canny woman, thought Lucikles. "When Rain was still suffering her loss of memory, she was timid. Finding her way. Tycheron has a certain sweetness to him, and you know what the young are. But once she regained her power to fly, he shrank back. She began to scare him. The thought of an independent woman with such capacity—you can imagine. Especially if he thought there was some chance he'd be hailed as the new Bvasil, thanks to his service to the nation. Why jeopardize the possibility of advancement? After all, the Bvasil and the Bvasilina have no issue."

"So once you returned to your starting base, what—you and Tycheron turned your sandals toward the capital to file your reports?"

Hardly as smooth as that. Lucikles wanted to go immediately to Maracoor Crown as part of the reporting committee. Tycheron *would* have benefited from corroborating testimony. But Oena, Lucikles's long-patient wife, had had enough. She could see the risk: if Tycheron was not believed, no more would Lucikles be. Irritated as she was at her husband for all this heave-ho, lurching yonder and otherwise during a state crisis, she nonetheless didn't want him to be slammed into prison or put to death. Besides, Oena had insisted, you haven't finished with Rain. She's still in your custody.

Stalta raised her eyebrows again. Constantly startled by domestic equations, this seagoing woman. Here on Toe Hold for a breather, she seemed less certain of herself. "Your wife took to the green stranger? Ah, the state of modern marriage. Glad I never tried it."

Indeed, Lucikles had been surprised at Oena's identification with Rain and her troubles. But perhaps he oughtn't have been. Rain's being so obviously from somewhere else made her travails hard to deny. And Oena was a mother of two daughters—the little scampions, Poena and Star—as well as of Leorix. Her parental instincts were acute and enflamed. "You'll go with Rain as far as you can until she's ready to launch on her own. If she's determined to scatter foreign seed upon the danger ground of Ithira Strand, bring her there. Deliver her to her departure point. We'll take up everything else when you return."

"Even with this foot?" he had said, because on the journey, a scarab had gotten embedded in his instep, and he'd been sore and halt ever since. "I've been told to see a sawbones of one type or another."

"You leave here for ten or twelve weeks every year and you survive *that*. You've made it to the back of beyond and all the way home. So see this child on her way safely, Lucikles, and when you come back we'll consider what happens next. There's a country physic who pulls nails out of the hooves of horses, and if she's not skilled enough, there's always the Groves of Salanx."

"I want to come with—" the boy had started, and both father and mother rounded on him so fiercely with "No!" that he determined to run away that night—a plan upon which he didn't follow through. So he really was growing up, then.

Tycheron had left, on foot, all alone, to brave the return to the palace and to find out if the barbarians were still holding the capital city, Maracoor Crown. The flying monkeys who'd been hunkering at the farm insisted that the Skedelanders were in retreat. Word was getting around that since they'd dropped the trail of the pernicious Fist of Mara, they were cutting their losses and pulling out. Not to mention that vigilante bands of Maracoorian citizens were sabotaging the occupation. Gossip had been rife, and contradictory, but no one could deny a certain return of calm.

Stalta said to Lucikles, "All that time, I was in berth in the harbor at Pasken Next. We've had our own channels of information. Yes, the Skedelanders seemed to be mobilizing for a retreat. But if the flying monkey thingies had come in from Oz, why didn't they want to return with Rain?"

"The monkeys weren't her private entourage," said Lucikles. "They'd been sent here by her father. They were to locate her and rescue her if possible. They did their best, but if she was about to start home, they had no further interest in the matter. The chieftain, a creature named Tiotro, thought they'd only survived the outgoing journey because the circling winds of that great storm had sped them along. So they've chosen to stay in High Chora. Apparently they're good at scouting lambs lost out on the escarpment. They've made themselves useful to the local farmers."

Stalta grinned. "Maybe they just don't want anything more to do with our wandering witch, who's tiptoed away for her bath. Very la-di-da of her. She seems a bit forlorn without that Goose at her heel, doesn't she? I hope the plague that did away with the natives of Ithira Strand doesn't have Goose-kill in its nature, too."

"Little but the smoke and burn of forest fires can kill everything at once," said Lucikles. "But I agree. Rain seems bereft today without her familiar."

Bereft—but stronger than she had in the months since they had first met.

"She's not really a witch, it's all public relations," he added, uncertainly. And then, falsely chipper, "What do you say, how long should it take a witch to bathe?"

"A woman's bathing is only incidentally about water."

4

Her thinking had become choked—a mere testing of theorems. Was this uncertainty of hers, Rain wondered flatly—without the usual up-lift of emphasis in a question—just the normal myopia of late adolescence. Or was it the continued aftershock of her accident. Yes, she'd suffered a loss of memory. She remembered dropping the Grimmerie from a great height, but couldn't recall any terror at herself tumbling from the sky against the hard stone of the sea. Nor the moment of impact. Now she wondered if more than her memory had gotten scrambled. She'd misplaced her sense of her own self in some interior way.

What did it mean to be green, for one thing. To be the only one of your kind in all the world. Or was that a universal feeling. The wisp-lipped kid on a leatherball pitch, mocked for a fouled goal, the girl dubious about her new swelling breasts—did any young person ever feel anything other than alone in all the world. Rain didn't know. She'd had too few friends her own age. A servant girl named Scarly, back in St. Prowd's School. And the jack-of-all-trades, Tip, her first love.

Maybe green skin does paint you marginal in a deeper, more irrevocable way. Or maybe every one of us, you too, are mere maggoty pupae behind the hard lacquer of your family ways—your mother tongue, your father silence.

What Rain had awakened to, and to which at dawn she had gone off alone in an effort to accommodate, was the fullest sense yet of her first romance, her lad Tip as he was then known.

In her earliest stages of recovery from amnesia, her sense of him had been imprecise. An impression. This morning she'd come around to the clarity of his presence. His outline against a sunrise. So precise as to be nearly cut in ice. It hurt her mind to look at him again but she knew she must.

At a vernal pond, behind a blind of reeds and clacking palm fronds, she undressed and dropped into the water to her shoulders. Her green nudity at home in the algaed shallows. There he was, in her mind, almost as if shedding his own clothes in order to bathe with her. She couldn't ignore him any longer, even if he didn't exist. Her Tip, her boy. What a name—not just at the tipping point between boy and man, in his fresh molded form, creased only with muscle and joint and not with any tightening or loosening of age. But also, she now acceded, at a tipping point between boy and girl. His penis had been more than ornamental, she knew from a certain amount of personal experience—but in deeper qualifications of identity, in the vagaries of metamorphosis, he was mystery.

The fineness of his steel-cut profile; the lollop of pale brown hair on his brow. The eyes, turning to her—a kind of pitiful grey with tawny aureoles. His lips even—what a joke, to think about the loveliness of specific lips. The top curve proud as the prow of a ship, the lower lip indrawn, as if the fleshier part was inside his own mouth, hidden, for seeking. And then, oh—she began to laugh at herself, and she hadn't laughed in a hundred thousand days, perhaps—what to admit of a sexy boy but a torso like turned oak, well-shaped thighs and tender vulnerable backs of knees and insteps, and a coy ignorant bum, and fingers like musical instruments that could be played but also knew themselves how to raise a green melody in her skin. Did any young woman ever see her own beloved in any other way. Why didn't he have a goiter, an overlarge pair of ears. A single twisted digit that threw his symmetry out of whack. He didn't. He was so beautiful she might have invented him. And he was too beautiful to last, and her love was too consuming.

Then the magic spell that had kept him incarcerated in flawless youth and ignorant of his charm had been lifted by that old witch, Mombey. And his perfect form had shriveled away, orange rind, bean pod—revealing in his place an equally beautiful girl. The unfortunate Ozma, released from her enchantment. Splendid, both ancient and new. Stuck in a destiny that, as far as Rain knew, no one in history had ever suffered before. Ozma, yoked to her own fate, one that had no need of a green-skinned girl who had loved her when she was still a boy.

As Rain was emerging from the pool at last, a snake unfurled from the cleft of a rock and raised its lissome head. Rain had had congress with snakes before. She was leery. Still, she became intrigued when the greyed head scraped its lower jaw along a sandstone ledge and opened its mouth. Not to speak—for which she was grateful—nor to hiss—but to widen the sleeve of dusty transparency from which it began to emerge. A more verdant green underneath its overused clothes.

"Oh, please," said Rain, "could you be any more obvious?"

The snake had no interest in how effective a metaphor it might be, serving to show Rain the story of Ozma emerging from Tip, or of Rain herself recovering from the paralysis of her grief. It kept at its job of wriggling out of its own past. Rain watched with a certain amount of envy, so intent that she didn't notice another voyeur was lurking nearby too. When the snake was nearly free, going the green of young grass in wettened sunshine, a hawk swooped down with a crash of wings. Its talons struck as Rain yelped and wheeled her arms. She needn't have exercised herself. The bird veered off with only a clump of papery detritus, and the snake disappeared into the water, camouflaged by the currents. Rain withdrew her feet and headed back to search for her traveling companions and her Goose aide-de-camp. She was wrinkled and she was famished. She'd been lost in longing most of the day.

5

Lucikles watched Rain coming up the shoreline of Toe Hold. Her hair was fanned out to dry on her shoulders, an aspect of copper oxide as the sun slid horizonward. Stalta Hipp chose this moment to haul herself to her feet. She'd go talk supper with her crew, who were hunching on board playing with dice. The contagion that had wiped out Ithira Strand had made the sailors squeamish about coming ashore even here, given Toe Hold was so near to Ithira Strand.

"Chowder at moonrise," said Stalta to Lucikles over her shoulder. "I wouldn't loiter here after the sun comes down; evening mosquitoes can raise a relief map of the Hyperastrich Archipelago on your forearm before you scratch the first itch. I'll leave you the bigger of the two coracles."

Lucikles bade her goodbye and hailed Rain. "What's Iskinaary's report?" she asked him.

"I don't think he's returned. Unless he circled around to the ship when my back was turned."

"I hope he hasn't become the next victim of the plague."

"When has *he* last had a night off?" asked Lucikles. She shrugged. Sitting on a stone for modesty, she lowered her head to her knees and used the amplitude of her skirt to finish drying her hair. The overseer was ensorcelled by her growing confidence. He'd met her first in the throes of her amnesia, which had conferred upon her an appearance of guarded innocence. Only a few months later and she was very much a young woman with presence and, yes, even allure.

Being a man of the open sea—at least for a couple of months every year—he'd known the appeal of women other than his wife. Up until now, Rain had seemed some halfway creature—the green a kind of disguise, a costume of such otherliness that she'd scarcely come across as feminine. He sat up, squared his shoulders. Professional custom or instinct. He felt the rotation lengthen his spine and broaden his upper chest. "You're nearly late for chowder."

"I saw the most arresting thing," she said. "A snake in the act of shucking off its skin. It just rolled back like a worn old stocking off a fresh young foot. And in so doing—there was a hawk on the prowl—the snake escaped death and became born at the same time."

"I've seen plenty of old snakeskins left to crinkle up in the sun."

"Well, yes, who hasn't, but this was the moment of makeover. I always thought snakes were alarming but I had to give this creature credit for beauty. And smarts."

"A green snake. Perhaps a distant relative?" Oh, that slipped out, and what a mistake. Yet she grinned at him, as if knowing he was merely male, clumsy with social patter like all his kind. She patted the pocket of her skirt and, finding it empty, went to where she'd left her apron. From its folds she withdrew a box covered in some sort of worn grey fur. It was familiar to Lucikles, but took him a moment to place it.

"Zesto presto, behold: the pack of cards the Oracle of Maracoor uses for fortune-telling," he said. "Did he give them to you?"

"Let's say they were handed down from generation to generation, whether he meant to or not. I remember that there is a snake on one of the cards. I haven't examined all of them closely yet."

"Reclaiming your powers, I see. I mean as a witch." Trying for a joke.

"The witch thing, that's your notion," she said, but added, "mostly," and laughed.

"Read a little future for us, why don't you, and we'll see?"

"You know, I don't believe in that boneheady guff." Still, she tipped out the worn cards. What had the Oracle called them. The backs were worked with the same device, the versos particularized with arcane symbols, each one different. "Tarot cards, that's it. Sham, guesswork. Assist to the rogue."

Rain flipped through a dozen or more cards before she found the one to show him. She held it up. A great godly hand came out of a mound of clouds gesturing to a floating loop of snake. It had slipped a knot around the end of its tail. It looked supple enough to bite its own head off at the neck. "This tells us precisely nothing."

"I take it that the skill is in—discerning—adjacency?"

"Snakes are adjacent to everything in this world." She slid the card into the pack, snake in hiding once again. "I already know about that."

"Maybe you're just not so good at reading cards yet."

They both laughed. She slapped the deck back into its fur-covered box. "I don't imagine the alphabet of magic is denied anyone, how could it be?" she said, as they gathered their things and tipped the barque into the shallows.

"Some sing on key, some are pitchy as hell," he replied, and demonstrated his own uncertain strengths. They laughed so hard that he nearly overturned the dubious skiff that Stalta had left for their return to the *Ocean Heron*. Their hands met as they both lunged to stop the oar from jumping out of its oarlock.

6

But when she learned that Iskinaary hadn't returned to the ship, Rain got worried. Her gaze trained on Ithira Strand. A range of pine-forested ridges growing indistinct. The sky above the headland a lurid maroon-blue as the night came in.

"Put that broom down," said Stalta. "You're not going anywhere at this hour."

"You're the captain of the water, not the air," said Rain.

"I don't brook mutiny. My brief is to take you as far as Great Northern, but mutiny me and I'll leave you to wing it on your own from here, quick as flipping a pancake. Watch your way, girl. Were it up to me, I'd just as soon swing about for home port before dessert is served. If you're going to abandon ship against my say-so, say so and let me get a head start. Otherwise, wait till the morning to make your foray."

Cowed by the authority of her host and captor, as it were, Rain spent the night in a swivet. The cards of the Oracle whispered to her in their mouse-fur, tauntingly; she resisted looking at them again. A couple of sailors up deck brought out a mandolin and a squeezebox and sang lurid chanteys to the stars. The Goose-shaped absence within reach of her call, well, goose bumps. She felt more alone without him than she had felt without the memory of her own childhood, girlhood, and youth.

"You're worried," said the overseer. He was suddenly near, arms folded, his shoulder leaning up against a post at the foot of her hammock. "You can't sleep, and I find I can't, either."

"What is known about the ailment that carried away the residents of Ithira Strand?" asked Rain. "Or drove the survivors away?"

"Very little. I heard tell of it on one of my expeditions. A vessel foundered and broke up on the rocks just beyond the harbor break. Ithirians went out to investigate and to rescue survivors, but there were none. The ship was peopled with a skeleton crew—skeleton in both senses of the word, ha ha."

Rain threw him a baleful look and he cleared his throat before continuing. "The ship's log detailed the start of it, how the blighted ship must have picked up a virus at some port, but the entries trailed off. Its sailors apparently sickened and died. The first deaths were buried at sea, but by the end, no one had the strength to haul the last of themselves overboard. The ship foundered off Ithira Strand, and the Ithirians burned the remaining corpses on land. Maybe the virus survived upon the dead flesh of the crew, and made the leap from rot to vivid flesh? That's all we know. With no human host upon which to breed, perhaps enough time has passed for the sickness to have wasted away. On the other hand, maybe now it's carried by saw grass, or seagulls, or the very wind."

"If seagulls, then Iskinaary could have caught it too."

"Yes, but we've seen gulls glide back and forth between Toe Hold and Ithira Strand. So it can't be fatal in all instances. Iskinaary is a tough old bird. Don't be alarmed."

"I've never known it to be useful to tell an alarmed person not to be alarmed."

"You're right. What I mean to say is this: it's sensible to be alarmed, but don't give in too hastily to it. Sense what you feel, and let it find its level. There are other ways of knowing things besides feeling them."

"That's a seasoned older person speaking to a younger one." But she smiled in the dark at him.

"I was already like this when I was your age," he said, a little stiffly. "If I can be of no comfort, I'll withdraw."

She nearly said "No, don't go" but stilled that sentence. Now in the dark, adjacent the vacuum caused by Iskinaary's absence, hovered a second absence, the shape of a standing man. That shape became Tip, became Tycheron, became Lucikles, in turn, as he turned away. Absence was contagious, too.

IN THE MORNING she refused Lucikles's offer to row her from the *Ocean Heron* to the sandy verge of the stricken island. "If a plague is still rampant, I'll want you to be free of it," she insisted. "You have a wife and children to go home and take care of. Anyway, I may need to explore. With your bad foot you'd hold me back."

"I promised Oena I'd see you safely launched."

"Safely expelled from Maracoor Abiding, you mean."

"Same thing. It's indecent of me to let you go into danger alone."

"Your attraction to doing the decent thing seems, um, variable at best."

"I'm a king of prevarication, which makes me a fully human being, no less."

Her ascent was anything but clean—she hadn't regained much confidence in the air yet. Sailors spoke of sea-legs, but what did she need. A sky-soul, that's the gist of it. She didn't fly with her arms but with her intentions. An appetite toward lift. But you couldn't order one up to go. It took practice.

In her satchel she brought the pack of cards and the seashell holding most of the tree pollen she'd harvested in the west of Maracoor. Even if she fell prey to infection, Rain might still make good on her promise to Tesasi, the humble-mannered queen of the

Caryatids. Spread the future, Tesasi had required of Rain. Rain would try to oblige. A limited amelioration to the world, could it be done.

Seen from up high, the ocean that elbowed its way between Toe Hold and Ithira Strand looked more active than she'd expected. She made swift enough passage, though. She corrected for the cross-grain breeze by steering at an obtuse angle against the prevailing. The soft approach took some time, but the biscuit-crumb sands of Ithira Strand came nearer. The closer to the island, the slacker the wind, at least at this hour. To her right, the ship was lost in the winking of sun on green-glass water.

The island seemed larger than Maracoor Spot, but she easily spied the harbor town strung out along a cove. She could make out windmills upslope. A brave and defensive look to them. Banking, she began a descent, pulling up on the broom to slow it, so she could scrutinize the rooftops of the harbor town more carefully.

Making a first pass over the terrain, she tried to regard it the way a dot of fertile pollen might. An arid aspect due to lime wash applied to stone lintels and thresholds. Beyond this proud campaign of antisepsia, though, the earth seemed vigorous. Cedars and cypresses, and old, battle-ready, full-canopied oak trees. Kitchen gardens gone to seed; beach roses in ramble; fields needing haying; vines and ivy a-clutch upon garden gates. It seemed Tesasi may have selected Ithira Strand as the possible ground for the pollen of the Arborian trees due to some instinct about its fecundity. For flora, anyway. But this place already so rife with life—how could a sowing of seed find its own foothold. When does life make room for more life. Life is too greedy.

Rain looped out over the water and back, returning from the south. This time she saw what rampant blossom had distracted her from: a cemetery behind some kind of chapel. Ceremonial gravestones tilted on one side of the yard. They gave way, farther upslope, to a barren allotment. Here, no time for stone markers or even wooden ones. No grass had yet grown back over the turned soil. Twice the width of the original cemetery. A mass grave.

When she'd passed that by, the chill in her green skin lifted, but she became more aware of cold patches. Her wind-wet eyes stewed her vision with phantasms. A curled child's form with her lifeless forehead upon a living dog. The dog was still there, looking at Rain; the child was history. A set of evacuees who sat down to rest their spines along a stone wall and died there before being able to get up again. Workers collapsed at the side of a rack where fish or seaweed could be dried or smoked in the sun—evidence of blackened coals beneath. A woman having hanged herself on a rope tied to a bracket used for raising supplies from street level. The bracket and rope remained, and the rope still swayed; the woman was gone but her suffering and despair were not.

Rain nearly gave up, it was too much, but she remembered that her charge was twofold—to find Iskinaary and to dispense the pollen. She could do all this on one trip if she was lucky, and return to the crew and passenger of the *Ocean Heron*. Then they could set out for Great Northern Isle, the last port on their journey in Maracoor before setting out for Oz. But she had to find the Goose first. She made a third circuit over the roofs of the town, this time trying to see not as a tree or as a human being. She was, after all, flying. Think like a bird, she told herself.

Was this witchiness she endured just a . . . a heightened apprehension of sorrow. The immortal sense of mortal loss. Was it. Was it.

Immediately the ghosts of sickened and deceased humans faded away. The colors of vegetal vigor dimmed as well. The port town of Ithira Strand became a collection of stationary wings—the planes of tile and thatch angling from central roof-beams. Now she noticed that the place was threaded with birds. Wrens in the corn. Robins at wrestle over worms. And nesting birds, mostly small ones. Upon the chimney stack of one of the grander buildings, Rain spotted the nest of a heron or a crane. Only then, in the shadow of the chimney, did she see Iskinaary. His head was leaning against the stones. Rain's heart skittered in a knucklebone toss.

The bird, probably a crane, regarded Rain with no alarm but with little welcome, either, when Rain managed to steady her broom enough to plant her feet upon the roof's ridgepole. Iskinaary didn't notice her arrival. "You're indifferent to me after one night away?" she said tauntingly, knowing that would rouse him. He liked nothing better than an exchange of temper. He didn't lift his head.

He wasn't dead. A dead bird would have slid off this perch and down the roof tiles. She could see his breast moving. She ventured nearer.

"What is your problem?" she said. Hardly the manner of a ministering angel, she knew. "We have to get out of here, Iskinaary. Shake yourself together, Goose!"

At last he seemed to come around. "Oh, is it that late already, so late," he said. A voice of gravel, uncertain. "Silverbeak, my fine consort." Rain noticed the nacreous sheen on the crane's bill. "We've become attached to each other. She's the unusual creature who keeps her own counsel."

"Iskinaary, you're not yourself. What's the matter?"

"I'm mature and I'm in love. Is that a contradiction in terms?"

She shook her head, as if to clear her own vision if he couldn't clear his. "Why are you listing about like, like—a glove without a hand in it?"

This was a different Iskinaary, a new one—less acerbic. Which was worrying. Devoid of sass or mordancy he replied to her. "I know I may not make it back to Oz, Rain. I've gotten old. This good dame crane seems to be welcoming my company in the absence of a male crane. But we aren't suited to mate. Incompatible equipment."

"I don't need to know—"

"Squeamishness in humans is so artificial." That sounded more like the Goose she knew. "Cloacal frottage works for crane reproduction, but for geese it's the classic method of penetration. Bluntly put, we need a little marital aid."

"It's something in the air," she said, "it's gotten to you. You have a mate back in Oz, and scores of offspring, no doubt. Would you risk that—"

"When you reach the end of *your* life, you can ask yourself a question like that. Meanwhile, don't judge me by your customs. I need your help, and I think I know how you can give it."

"What are you talking about? I want to seed the soil with this pollen and get back to the ship. Snap out of it, 'Naary." She'd never tried a nickname with him before. He flinched—a sign of life, anyway.

Then he shifted his tail feathers and moved a few inches. He was sitting upon a piece of parchment, worn, and torn, and the worse for wear due to his droppings. But in an instant she knew what it was. "Bloody hell. It's haunting us," she said. She clutched at the broom for balance to keep from sliding off the roof.

A page torn from the drowned Grimmerie. Here on Ithira Strand. Aged but legible, covered with language and ornamentation. "Where did it come from?" Her voice husky, low, cold.

"Silverbeak had rolled it up for packing her nest with. When I arrived, she either tossed it out at me coincidentally or she had read what she wanted of it and was passing it along like a used newspaper."

She tried not to look at it but the title of the spell insisted. *On Vagueness and Variety.*

"Can you make use of that?" said the Goose. "I want to leave my seed here. This will be my last brood, and Madame Silverbeak has no other callers at the moment. Due to the plague."

"I think you've gone mad," she said, feeling faint herself. Though *On Vagueness and Variety* would probably allow for sanity in madness, and the obverse. "Can all my effort to shuck off the menace of this magic have come to naught?"

"Perhaps this page doesn't want to be lost. Or not lost entirely. Who does?" replied Iskinaary. "It wants to keep going. The same impulse that powers a father to want some eggs to watch over. Time is passing but the future is in the young. Isn't that also why we're here, you with your pocket full of pollen? It's the identical urge of the Caryatids and of those weird lusty gods the Maracoorians tolerate."

Such life on the lip of death. Iskinaary looked green around the rims of his eyes, and not in a good way. "I can't remake anatomy to suit your randy mood," she shouted at him. The one he called Silverbeak ruffled her feathers with equanimity. Maybe she was deaf. Dizzy with rage and maybe even despair, Rain fell a few feet down the slope of the roof. Then, to give him some space, clutching her broom she dropped farther, not quite feather-light but without jarring impact. Grounding herself in front of the building upon which the Goose and the crane were perched.

The double doors to this larger house were slightly ajar. To get a moment to herself she pushed in, hoping that there were no ghosts of plague victims disported around the furniture or kicked up against the baseboards.

The only item of furniture, a single table in the center of the room, waist-high. Ah, of course; the largest building in the village would be a chapel of sorts. A few benches along the edges of the room, to whose light her eyes were becoming accustomed.

Most of the room was plastered in a color, perhaps once blood red but faded now to a genial rose, swags of greenish mold looping from the roof seams. The back wall was silvered with hundreds of small tin cutouts tacked into place. Knees, and feet, and heads.

Petitions for healing, or thanks for miracles performed? Or maybe this was no chapel but a doctor's theater of sorts, and the table not an altar but a counter for surgery.

That she could sense none of the suffering population *here,* of all places in the village, seemed queer. Rain walked along the intaglioed wall, touching the hammered testimonies of suffering. One came off in her hand. Rather than drop it on the floor—the tinny noise of nothing else—she pocketed it. The room was beautiful and vacant. A place of congregation wanted memory, didn't it? This vessel was null.

At the other end of the room from where she'd entered, Rain saw two louvred doors. One was warped and didn't fasten tightly. She pulled it inward, and then its match, revealing a rusted wrought iron screen of simple design. A gate of sorts. The fretwork was screwed tightly into the doorjamb. The center an open circle four feet in diameter. Vines with orange trumpet flowers had colonized most of the grillwork. She pushed the trails of greenery to peer beyond.

Oughtn't have been surprised, ought I.

The aperture in the wrought iron gave onto the older tombstones she'd seen from the air. Beyond that, on a gentle upslope, the rough-torn wasteland of graves so new they hadn't yet grown over.

Or perhaps the disease that had wasted the population of Ithira Strand, and chased away any survivors, was so dreadful that the very earth in which corpses were sunk had been rendered inert.

She knew what she had to do. If the contaminating virus—or the spell of malice—was still live, she had no time to waste. Goodbye, the table, which only now she recognized as a staging area for arranging the dead in their winding sheets.

Goodbye the bright wall that winked mockingly at her. Cutouts of arms, heads, ears, noses, breasts, and legs. Abandoned prayers in tin and pressure.

Once outside, she rounded the corner of the funeral house and barreled up the lane toward the graveyard. Tucked her broom in her armpit, as if afraid it might take it upon itself to flee of its own accord. Struggled in her satchel. A strange hard purse, a spiny, voluted seashell, but it had been a canny enough bucket to drag through the clouds of pollen she'd swept up from her broom. Would the shell be just as swift to disgorge the cargo she'd carried back across the River Seethe, over the High Chora, down the coastal plain and across the open sea.

No need to use the broom. The seed wanted soil and her hands were low enough. Running among the graves, she tilted the shell just so, allowing the pollen to trickle and puff behind her. She was doing the work that the butterflies of the great forest had failed to do. She was carrying out the bidding of Tesasi, untitled queen of the Caryatids. Glancing behind her, Rain saw the rolls of dusty future uncoil, lift, settle. In the fresh light—the sun had only just surmounted the morning mist—the dispersal shimmered, mica-like glints in the creamy scatter. They eddied and settled upon the scarred earth, newly turned and fresh for a broadcast of pollen.

What the seed might manage here, or not manage—that was beyond her. She just hurried back and forth, shaking the shell to roll out the pollen packed in the curves of porcelain sleeve. When she was done, she glanced up. Iskinaary and the crane he'd named Silverbeak were watching her. She had to get him out of here or he'd succumb to whatever was threatening him—exhaustion and a lack of ambition for the future. Maybe it was no more than that.

She barely made the lift back to the roof. Iskinaary was holding down the page of the Grimmerie with one mildewed foot. *On Vagueness and Variety.* "Look at this," he said. "You've just done so much for that tree person you met once, and you've known me your whole life. You owe me. At least see what it says."

Rain picked up the page with reluctance, half expecting it to sting her. It did not. One side showed a kind of map or diagram of sorts—curving lines and obscure symbols. She couldn't make it out and didn't try. The other side was more ornate, a pretzely sort of writing in a language she didn't know beyond the larger manuscript of the heading. "Of vagueness, that could be anything. Not to mention variety," she said. "Short on specifics. It might as well say, 'Of this, that, and the other.'"

"Maybe it does," said the Goose. "It's all in the interpretation. Can you chant some of it aloud?"

"You want me to play some sort of wicked go-between and find a way to make it possible for you to be a sexual predator," she said. "It's heinous."

"Silverbeak is not rejecting me," he pointed out. "There are no other cranes to be seen, and she hasn't raised cry or slapped wing against me, neither has she driven her silver stiletto beak through my aging skull."

Rain was beginning to feel weary. The miasma of the place. "I need to land on the ground or I'll tumble off the roof and smack my head on the cobbles and go back into the amnesia I'm just finished with. Or worse."

"Before you lose focus," he begged her. "I came all this way with you whether you asked me or not. This can be back pay. Just try."

She leaned over to worry out four or five lines.

> *Aupo, aupo, insansa morphexa*
> *Aupo, aupo, tinn fihlo, fihlo*
> *Bessuna bessahmer traumina aulexa*
> *Traumina bessuna, aupo echoso*
> *Traumi, traumin, traumina aupo . . .*

As far as she could go. She barely managed to clutch her broom as it pulled her off the roof and gently lowered her to the earth. There she sank to her knees in the dusty seeded wasteland, vomited, and keeled over.

7

As the sun dropped upon the ocean horizon, Lucikles took issue with Stalta Hipp's authority. "The witch knows we were curious and even frantic about Iskinaary's absence," he said. "She'll know that our concern extends to her. She's not showing up because something bad has happened. We can't let her stay the night on that pestilential shore. No, you'll not stop me, Stalta. You won't deny me a small boat for passage to Ithira Strand. This is what you've come for, to help us in our passage. If you won't release a sailor to take the other oar with me, I'll launch on my own across the strait and take the risks upon myself. I've handled oars on the open sea."

"You're not sweet on that child."

"She's a young woman and that is neither here nor there."

Stalta Hipp looked anything but jealous, but she shrugged. "We'll sail midchannel and let you launch from there. You'll have a better chance of making it. But if I can't find the perfect place to drop anchor off the coast of Ithira Strand, we'll return to Toe Hold. I won't berth at Ithira Strand, not with the trouble they've had. I promised to try to help, but not to endanger myself and my crew."

The *Ocean Heron* drew anchor and pivoted while there was time and useful light. Stalta Hipp came to stand by Lucikles as the coastline of the larger island drew near.

"Do you have any reason to suspect you may be better protected against a virulent illness than a green girl and a Goose might be?" she asked. "Not to mention the poor sods who brought the germ to this shore and infected the human colony here?"

"I have none," he said.

"You have a wife and children to return to," she told him. He didn't reply. It was none of the Captain's business that Oena had signaled to Lucikles that something had snapped, and that their marriage was in disrepair and possibly unsalvageable. Lucikles knew that the good woman had endured too much in one year, with the disappearance of her oldest child, Leorix, into pestilential adolescence. The boy had apprenticed himself to his father, submitting to several dangerous excursions. True, so far Leorix had returned safely—in better shape than her husband, with that foot wound that refused to seal over and heal—but Oena had found the fear for her son's safety a punishment nearly beyond bearing. She remained in an uncertain frame of mind.

"My wife and children," he said to the Captain, "have been provided for. By dint of my efforts this year I've saved them twice. First, from the Fist of Mara and the invading Skedelanders. Second, I bargained to lift the threat to my daughter of being impressed for life into service as a bride of Maracoor. I've left my kin whole and as secure as any of us can hope to do in this treacherous life. What remains to me in Maracoor Crown is the writing of reports and the chairing of committees and eventually, maybe being elevated to the status of a Boor in the courts of the House of Balances. And that surely will kill me in the end. So I consider this a last service to perform for my country. I'd rather risk a premature death while trying to complete a mission than to shrug and abandon the uninvited guest of our nation to her unknown fate."

"You know," said Stalta, "one of the reasons I decided to take to the high seas was my chronic distaste for the rhetoric of people who regard themselves too highly. If you're going to go, just go. Spare me the self-congratulation. I'll put it about in some wharf-side public house that you were a decent enough fellow, so far as I could tell. Not my type."

"Mutual, that," he muttered, which was shabby of him, and he knew by that comment that he must be feeling less brave than he was making out to be.

"If you don't return by morning, I'm not sending crew after you, mind. Not unless there's some signal of need. I'll wait a day or two by Toe Hold, advancing during the daytime to loiter offshore of Ithira Strand and make out what I can through the spyglass. If you or Rain don't hail us to come in, I'll count you both as deceased. I promise to salute your memory and foolhardiness with an extra pint."

He accepted a firkin of wine and some food tucked into oiled muslin. The coracle dropped slapping onto the sea. The waves were surprisingly high; it felt as if he were rowing the boat down a set of broad descending steps. In the west, the sun gave up, pink blot in bolsters of rouged cloud. The shores of Ithira Strand had an air of betrayal. But this was the normal aspect of dusk, its purpling shadows the portent of any and every night, including the final one.

For many years of his life Lucikles had paddled to this or that island haunt on his own, while the mother ship waited offshore for him to return from an inspection. One day he'd become too old to govern even a small skiff without an assistant. As he pulled on the oars, his left foot, braced against the small boat's central thwart, ached from the pressure. By the time he drew up to the gravelly verge breasting Ithira Strand, he was almost spent. "Let's go, Cur," he said to his dog, but the friendly creature—ah yes, of course—wasn't sitting behind him as usual. Cur was back in High Chora with Oena and the children, standing guard in the overseer's stead.

"Island of goodbyes," he said aloud, and stepped out of the boat.

He secured the little slipper of a boat to a grip of storm-proven bracken. Then he picked his way up a breakfront of tumbled stones. The main street ranged off to his right, bending around a make-shift quay that came and went, irresolute—sometimes blocks of marble, sometimes skips of sand. That couldn't have been a problem, he thought. Ithira Strand had nothing of especial value to trade. Wool from highland sheep, he remembered. A certain local honey from the apiaries.

Some doors stood open to the elements. As he passed, cats and rats slithered into shadows, already unaccustomed to human footfall. The Minor Adjutant strode on, missing Cur more with every moment. What a little agent of normalcy that dog had always been, freaking at the harmless sand beetle and overlooking the deadly scorpion. But company throughout.

Shops, homes, a weaving collective, perhaps. Here, a doctor's surgery, to judge by the stone and metal bowls and implements left out to sanitize by sunlight, and a heap of bloody cloths overrun by ants. Here, a nursery with a dozen bassinets hanging from a beam in the center of the ceiling. But never sound of human sigh or even, by now, scent of human suffering. Only that faint sulfurous expiration of stone and the clammy scent of mold that undergirds everything, you go down deep enough.

At one of the larger buildings he paused, guessing it was a town meeting center or a chapel of some sort. He peered into the doorway that fronted the street. The room was steeped in darkness but for a glowing door at the far end. He saw at once it was barred by iron, and heard a warning squawk from above that he recognized all too well. Retreating, he tilted his head. "You up there, Iskinaary, or some impersonator?"

"She is in the graveyard. Out back," called Iskinaary's voice, weak and troubled.

He raced as fast as the damn foot would allow.

Hardly recognizable as a human form, recumbent on the ravaged earth, in a state of undress, her clothes taken off her. At first he thought she'd been raped and left for dead, but her ocean boots, a parting gift from Tycheron, stood neatly heel to heel, as if on display in a cobbler's window. Her vestments were somewhat folded, too, weighed in place by the seashell she'd carried with her since he first met her those several months ago on Maracoor Spot. Her broom lay next to her, formal as the sword at the side of a chevalier's corpse.

He dropped to his knees, felt her cheeks, lifted a wrist to hunt for life. His blood was running so wildly he couldn't determine what was his pulse or hers, if any. Her color didn't look bad—but how would *he* know when green was going off? Especially at this evening hour, as the sun was fully swallowed and the sea turning blue-black, losing evidence of distance.

"Rain, Rain," he said, not knowing what to do. He ran his hands along the outside of her arms, hoping to help blood along by manual pressure. The nakedness of her, the green bosom and strong-muscled abdomen and the female apparatus in its clutch of hair, wearing its own modesty as if modesty were anointed by biology—it didn't have the usual effect on him such as he'd experienced upon seeing the occasional women of easy acquaintance. He wasn't unaware of her glorious youth and peculiar charm, but her life and breath were of more urgency. He couldn't determine if she had either.

"Iskinaary," he called over his shoulder. "Come down here, tell me; what's happened? You'll have to go get help from Captain Hipp—I can't maneuver in this dark, and haven't time."

"Not possible," replied Iskinaary. "Stricken too. I can't lift my wings even to come down from here. It's a palsy, a wasting away."

"I can't fly a broom! You have to do this! Is she dead?"

The Goose quawked, but his voice was too low for Lucikles to make out what he was mumbling. Maybe Iskinaary was complaining to himself about being bossed around.

Rain's skin wasn't cold but he couldn't agree it was warm, either. She was still as a corpse on a bier. The night breeze off the water was picking up. He was afraid of her losing whatever vigor she might still have left. Without reasoning it out, he found himself unbuckling his tunic and shucking off his own clothes, all of them. He lay down on the stony ground next to her and spread his seagoing cape across them both like a shroud. If she would die, he would die with her, and they could sleep in this foreign graveyard together forever, the only comfort in permanent exile he could imagine to offer her.

At once a racket of wings and the thump of a heavy body on the soil. Lucikles saw the scattered ivory pollen from the Arborian trees rise with the impact. But it wasn't Iskinaary making one final valiant effort. It was a larger bird with a peculiarly shiny bill. Had it landed in this scoured graveyard by mere chance? Then it stalked over to the small neat mound of Rain's clothes. With surgical deftness the creature reached out its ominous beak and managed to wrestle between upper and lower jaws the tapering end of Rain's seashell. Not an easy thing for a bird to balance, but such creatures often tussled with fish as large, and the seashell was at least immobile. The bird, a sort of crane now he could see it in the dusk, secured the seashell farther along its bill, closer to its throat where the pinch was stronger. Then the crane with the luminous beak lumbered in a run upslope and managed to lift off into the air, carrying the seashell. Lucikles watched as the bird cleared a row of poplars at the far end of the cemetery. A thin curtain of pollen wafted from it. The most evanescent of sparkling veils. Hung against the first stars clicking to life in the sky.

The bird disappeared out into the dark. Lucikles tried to cry out a goodbye to Iskinaary, to the night and the world, but he hadn't the strength. His bad foot was bleeding again. He set it on the top of Rain's naked feet, as if his blood could run into her between her toes. He threw his arm around her, was too beaten to sob or sigh, and pulled the cape up to both of their chins. "You don't die unloved," he managed to whisper, as from his vision the stars began to soften and wink out nearly as quickly as they had appeared.

8

The border crane made the crossing from Ithira Strand to the deck of the *Ocean Heron* with some difficulty. As Silverbeak flew against west-moving winds, the shell caught the air like a sail. It buffeted and unbalanced her. Had it been a fish she'd have swallowed it by now or let it fall. Not in her nature to endure this amount of trouble. In some circles a border crane is a symbol of serenity, which is another way of saying such creatures are clueless and blasé. But tonight, Silverbeak flew on, shifting the shell forward and back by tiny degrees, and patiently taking the time needed to fulfill this task.

How she knew this was a task for her to fulfill must go unverified. It could be that the scrap of spell that Rain tried to read aloud from the page of the Grimmerie—*Of Vagueness and Variation,* or something like that—had some tricky influence upon the working of her own animal mind, an instrument both docile and subtle, pertinent to her kind and her needs. Certainly she'd demonstrated capacity for variation already, merely by having remained in Ithira Strand when the rest of her flock had departed. Maybe she understood the needs of Iskinaary and the human.

Though little documented, the means of communication across the species divide is subtle and certain. As for discourse between the cognitively adroit Animal and the natural animal, the latter being bereft of apparent memory and language and capacity for projection or prediction, communication is indisputable if unqualifiable. It still occurs. Otherwise how would a mother of any loquacious species be able to tolerate and communicate with her day-old infant, and it with her the same way?

Iskinaary may have sent Silverbeak on an errand, or, with her own idiosyncratic wisdom, she may have figured out something for herself. She might have been able to see that Rain and Lucikles had come from a ship settled in the strait between Toe Hold and Ithira Strand. She may have determined the seashell was a foreign object with a taint of something unrecognizable about it, and become determined to remove it. In any event, she came in with an ungainly flump upon the deck of the *Ocean Heron,* alarming the small crew and causing Stalta Hipp to drop the brass barometer. "Merciful mother of leviathan," she said. "Look at the bit of spindrift that crazy bird has brought home to us."

The crew saw Silverbeak as an omen and her return of the seashell as bad, bad news indeed, and they began to lobby for a swift departure for the mainland at once. Captain Stalta Hipp cut that off with ruthless dispatch. She declared that in the morning they'd take the other of the two small boats at least into the cove, if not to the beach, and see what they could see from there. And she'd go herself to prove her valor. And she'd keep the astrolabe with her so there could be no abandoning mission by the two sailors left on board the *Ocean Heron.* Not that two sailors alone could crew a ship of that size, three being the minimum, by concurrence.

Upon the island of Ithira Strand, night stole in with its ceaseless sequence of lamentations and jeremiads, bat squeaks, rodent scurryings, and the invisible vegetable crawl that nets earth to sky. Iskinaary had summoned just enough strength to lob his carcass up three or four feet to the nest that Silverbeak had abandoned. He sat upon the four or five eggs the way a male crane might when the female goes to feed. The eggs were warm, which was agree-

able. He couldn't feel the settling upon his back of his own dorsal feathers—usually a calming routine when roosting. If he was
losing his life, and the realization of egg life beneath him was to
be his last thought, he was grateful for it. You could do worse.
He'd raised and dispatched goslings for more years than he knew
how to count—all of them sweet and adorable, if they made it out
of the baby pool, none of them particularly memorable. Even the
wife, whose name he had never really mastered, was only a warm,
affectionate wife-like idea in his head. Yes, Geese might mate for
life, but they don't go on and on about it over supper. Just because
an Animal can talk doesn't mean they must, or that they have anything memorable to say.

His perceptions spun out toward the character more crisp in
his mind than his wife—yes, his wife's name was Eskadonna, he
did know it after all—and this was Rain, the green human gosling
of his old human chief, Liir Thropp. Perhaps she'd been no less a
conundrum of a human than any other, but she stood out from a
crowd, even for a Goose with a fairly dull color sense to start with.

He swiveled on his behind, rubbing affectionately against the
eggs, polishing them in a sense, so that he could look in the direction other than where Silverbeak had flown. The low hills that
lifted behind the town, rising in gradations of dark ink, began at
the foundation stones of this very chimney stack. He made out the
patch of earth he'd come to realize was a graveyard. He saw the
heap of cape and the pairs of human legs, knees to ankle, revealed
from its hem. From here he couldn't tell if it was sleep or death,
but it wasn't sex, or not right now anyway. Marmoreal stillness,
while the stink of decay rose from the ground.

As he waited for his own final breath, loving these eggs as if
they were his own kin, the surface tension of the graveyard seemed
to seize fractally into increments smaller than motes of dust. Life
breaking up. He smelled nothing but the sea, the salt sea, and the
wind from beyond the back of possibility.

9

The air was redolent with expectation. She rolled onto an elbow and lifted herself up. The dead man beside her gave a fluttering of eyelids for a moment but sank back into eternal rest. It was a moment as might have happened before dawn, back when dailiness was to be counted on. The man was Lucikles, she remembered. She felt his leg and hip against her own and saw that he and she were lying naked in the graveyard together. Which was perhaps not so startling. It had always seemed bizarre to her that some circles buried the dead in their best garments, where rot would claim them within the season.

She sat up, recognizing Lucikles's seagoing cape and letting it slip down her front to her waist. Yes, she'd removed her boots and clothes yesterday, she remembered that. On the notion that if she was dying, some passing survivor eventually might make use of them.

She tested her senses one by one like a baby waking for the first time. The air was salt and sweet alike, verdant, potent. Her fingers felt the itch of woven wool, its hairiness and its rough warmth. Her ears could hear this world seething rhythmically. No, that was Lucikles—he was breathing as if one of his nostrils was obstructed, a mucousy whistle. Slowly her eyes adjusted to the dark, and her heart to the chance that she was not, after all, deceased.

Lucikles seemed now to be sensing her stirring. He tried again to open his eyes, and this time he managed it though she could see it was a struggle, like the revival of someone drugged or drunk. She couldn't work her own throat yet, but she reached out and touched his shoulder to welcome him back, in case he, too, thought he was now dead.

He gave a shudder like someone in a thrombosis, and a faint wail of alarm as if something from very far away in his past issued through his throat. Then he bolted upright and wept, fiercely, for a minute. A few feet away from her, naked in a way she'd never seen a grown man naked. He stumped through the ground cover to the edge of the allotment and relieved himself against a tree trunk. He shook himself off, came circling back, his feet ankle-deep in the overnight growth, and lay down beside her. They fell into sex before they remembered their words. The crushed stems and leaves lent a fragrance as of basil and lavender. By the time they had come back to the world, the dawn had begun. The grave-yard was tumescent with aureoles of blue bud nested in spread hand-widths of oak-green leaf.

On her nest, Silverbeak had turned toward the sea. Iskinaary was back on the roof's ridgepole, his head still sagging against the chimney, as if his neck was made of wet clay. If the Goose wasn't dead, Rain thought, he was kindly pretending to be dead a little while longer, to afford Rain and Lucikles privacy while they proved themselves, again, alive.

10

The *Ocean Heron* had ventured closer to the shore than before. Lucikles and Rain watched it bobbing at anchor beyond the cove. They saw the stout figure of Stalta Hipp
climbing down the netting to the second of the small boats that,
roped and trussed, traveled the seas against the side of the ship to
serve when needed to serve for ferrying or lifeboating. The overseer and the green stranger pulled themselves upright. They were
still too weak to shout across the noise of tide to alert the Captain
that they were alive. When her rowers pulled their oars up and
Stalta Hipp turned to regard her passengers with a hand held over
her eyebrows, she looked annoyed. She came within thirty feet of
the shoreline but no closer.

"You've lost your clothes in some sort of bizarre accident," she
called. Rain was draped only in Lucikles's cape, and he was disheveled still, though decent. They stood shoulder to shoulder,
untouching.

"We survived the night," Lucikles replied.

"So I see. And flowers in your hair. It's a bit much. Are you performing in a tableau of some sort?"

Yes, there were blue petals in Rain's tresses, and a few at the wispy
crests remaining on the brow-edge of Lucikles's natural tonsure.

"These are the blossoms from the seed we carried from the

mainland," said Rain, running her hands against her scalp. The petals fell out, looking quite a bit like blue butterflies.

"Planted seeds don't sprout and bloom overnight, what are you on about? You found a bottle of hooch somewhere? You both look a bit wracked and wasted."

Neither of them was inclined to venture an explanation, but Rain gestured over her shoulder. The empty chapel was glowing in the sun as if freshly whitewashed, the effect of being backlit by a low meadow of blooms and greens rising behind it.

It was only now that Iskinaary seemed to shake off his own lethargy and notice the conversation going on. He flapped his sore wings with an effort, lifted himself from the roof, and descended in a wide loop, coming to land by Rain's naked green shins. "It seems she's done what we came here to do," he remarked.

"When that shiny-nose crane delivered your seashell to us, we took it as a sign you were in trouble," continued the Captain. "Why didn't you come back last night instead of making me miss my second coffee and wend my way over here?"

"We were in trouble, I think," said Lucikles. "But the witch has cast a spell that seems to have saved us. Whether she meant to or not."

He looked at her with a slanted, appreciative, wary expression. Rain shrugged. "The witch stuff is pretty bogus," she said, without bothering to raise her voice. "I happened to read aloud someone else's advice. There was hardly intentionality in it."

"That speaks of power to me," said the overseer.

"Don't get any ideas," said the Goose. "I mean any more than you've already had."

"How do I know you're not infected, and won't infect us?" called the Captain.

"You don't, and we don't," replied the overseer. "But we survived when, last night, I thought we wouldn't."

"That much is true," agreed Rain. "And the pollen has taken root. It's from strong stock to begin with, as you and I knew, Lucikles, but maybe that muttered spell from the page of—" She didn't want to continue with the sentence.

Stalta Hipp seemed to be considering things. Planting her feet far apart for balance, she stood, and indicated that her crew member should row her closer. She studied Lucikles and Rain from twenty feet out. "Well, I always knew it might come to something like this," she said. "You have a look of rude good health about you that's not much like a final illness. Of course something could steal upon you in time, and we could all be dead by home port. But this is what I'm being paid for, to take risks like this. Get in your boat and come back to the ship. We have another port of call or two before I say goodbye for good."

"Wait," said Iskinaary to Rain and Lucikles. "You'll have to find a ladder somewhere. We are going to take two of the six eggs in the nest."

"Steal the heron's eggs?" Rain was appalled.

"They're part mine, and it's not stealing. Wait and see: she's not going to raise a fuss. She wants her kind to live as much as Tesasi wanted her family seed sown. You and I brought seed and maybe health back to Ithira Strand, and we're going to bring a pair of border crane twins to Oz. If we can manage it." The Goose looked proud and a bit pompous. "You're not the only ones who went to town."

"I don't want to picture it," said Rain. "Cloacal frottage or vaginal penetration—it doesn't work between herons and geese, as you explained rather too vividly."

"You don't know much. But I expect that phrase you intoned had more than a touch of enchantment to it. What was it—'aura, aura, fauna and flora,' something like that? Whatever, you've got a more powerful delivery than you imagine."

"And one other thing," said Stalta Hipp. "Put your clothes back on. I don't want the rest of the crew to get ideas that you're some sort of a loose woman. Bad enough that these buckos at the oars here have already had something of a glimpse."

Lucikles and Rain glanced at each other. Whatever they'd done, a waxy sort of venture, neither quite welcomed nor wasted. To the witch, the overseer looked both strickened and strengthened. To Lucikles, Rain's green skin, smudged with a blue stain of immediate blossom, had gone less turquoise than, perhaps, ruddy. He ripped a few dozen blooms from the ground and handed them to her. Not so much a bridal bouquet as a token of her inviolate genius. She stuffed them in her satchel where, in time, they proved resistant to fading away into brown dust.

OFF THE COAST OF
NORTH ORGOLE

1

The pressure was letting up some. It was hard for Rain to put her finger on what exactly had changed—though wasn't everything changing, all the time, if you paid enough attention. Wasn't it enough to sense it without necessarily sorting it out.

Something about twining and untwining strands of memory, while the interwoven strands of feeling were pulling, too. Maybe. Or maybe it was nothing like that at all.

Light summer cloudbursts, as if the world were having sympathetic gusts of feeling, swept over the open water. The *Ocean Heron* plowed stubbornly on toward the island of North Orgole. Here the crew would refresh stocks—the hold of the ship wasn't generous enough to carry supplies to last more than a week. Then, the final leg, to Great Northern Isle, where Rain and Iskinaary would bid everyone adieu and continue on their own. Home to Oz.

A downpour upon the surface of opaque seas; a ripe unsettling of air at gunnel level. It was as if the ship were wading hip-deep through wisps of moving damp. Was it sea, was it rain, was it evaporation as hot drops hit cold ocean. Rain didn't know. One thing or the other, who could tell. She was learning to live without looking up the definitions. Registering the animal presence of weather rather than formally baptizing it.

She tried on the thought that experience counts as more than material to be anthologized. You've changed even if you forget how and why. She was thinking of Lucikles, sure, and that she'd slept with him; but also that she was essentially independent even having stumbled into this liaison.

Something was widening in her mind, but she hoped she wouldn't lose the instinct to characterize the particular. *Openness of heart*—such a sad and hopeful expression. Drawn lamely out of the preacher's portfolio, often delivered to the poor sod standing beneath the gallows tree, waiting his turn. Nonetheless, she found something nervy in a theory of such openness, even if she was inclined to swear like a sailor in an urge to keep sentimentality off both port and starboard.

Lucikles was more circumspect and more analytical, perhaps because Rain refused to entertain hypotheses about what had actually happened on Ithira Strand. The Captain, catching Lucikles on his own one afternoon, made her opinion about his dalliance with Rain quite clear. "*I'm* not married to your wife, you are. And I realize I'm not running a choir group to the Island of the Saints for a festival picnic and tableau vivant. On the other hand, we have four young men with no female outlet for their appetites, not to mention I live with my own dubious impulses, such as they are. So be a decent passenger and keep your hands to yourself at least during the daytime."

"I shouldn't have thought anything I did would bother you," he said, "and anyway, I wouldn't be so crude."

"Still, you don't want to be thrown overboard by jealous crew members."

"Jealous? I thought they were *scared* of Rain."

She threw a handful of pistachio shells in his direction. "Oh, release me from the simplicity of men. Especially civil servants. I'd wager that the twin sentiments of fear and jealousy are not exclusive."

Well, he took her point. In the evenings he'd been lying with Rain for half the night, not in a hammock in the dark—nice to imagine but rather too awkward—but beneath mothy blankets. The salt air had a stimulating effect. They bedded down behind the raised hatch where the night shift couldn't see them. The noise of the open sea even on a still night muffled their bitten cries of pleasure or alarm, or once in a while, laughter. Or so they hoped.

Neither Rain nor Lucikles were afflicted with a sense of wrong-doing, and what Stalta Hipp truly thought about it was unclear. She was being paid to carry them the same way she was reimbursed to haul sacks of beans or a flock of sheep from one island or another. What the beans or the sheep got up to in the privacy of the night wasn't hers to legislate.

Still, her caution to Lucikles was sound. The sailors had been spooked by the approach to Ithira Strand, with its famous complaint of plague. They hadn't been privy to Rain's mission, carrying out the will of the Caryatid chieftain by seeding a generation of trees on that benighted island. The sailors didn't know why Rain had flown there, but when she hadn't come back and Lucikles had followed, they feared the worst. As soon as the witch and the overseer appeared next morning, disheveled and ragged, all but varnished with a newfound affection for each other, the sailors muttered about hexes. Possession by evil spirits.

Yet the passengers brought no evidence of sickness back with them, so the *Ocean Heron* had pulled up anchor and left Ithira Strand east by northeast. The crew members, each in his own fashion, and Stalta in hers, were aware of the way the high seas are never either here or there. What happens between fixed points seems not to happen at all, sometimes—neither love nor death. A corpse wrapped in bunting and dropped from the side of a ship rarely raises a tear in a seasoned sailor.

Rain and Lucikles conducted a love affair on a wooden floor that refused to level. To both of them this seemed somehow appropriate.

But Stalta Hipp wanted to know about Ithira Strand, and about that strange crane who had brought Rain's seashell to the deck of the *Ocean Heron*. Lucikles and Rain were too involved or oblivious to her pointed questions. But Iskinaary was willing to tell what he knew.

From the makeshift nest they'd arranged, a bundle of packing straw in an empty orange crate, Iskinaary sat upon the pair of eggs that Silverbeak had surrendered to the foragers. "Perhaps she figured it was the price of insemination," said the Goose. "She seemed more than happy to yield them to us. Perhaps she saw a better life for some of her offspring if they were born off-island. At any rate, she didn't put up the ruckus my wife would have done at such license." Eskadonna; what was she up to these days? He'd been gone a while.

"The witch and the overseer aren't talking much, except to each other," said Stalta Hipp. "What do *you* know about what happened? I find it hard to believe there are any circumstances, except in children's stories, in which a seed can root overnight and flower in the morning."

"Then you've never seen how fast mold can grow on a cluster of grapes that fell behind the sideboard at yesterday's lunch," said the Goose complacently. "Life is avaricious, Captain. It wants to live. It wants to devour everything."

"Life also wants to rot, and rust, and falter. Teeth to decay and eyesight to weaken. Did she hex the seed, our resident witchy mascot?"

"Who knows," replied Iskinaary, not mentioning the page from the Grimmerie. "You see, I myself was pinned between two extremes of ailment—some version of the island sickness, and a sweet return of the fatherly instinct I hadn't felt in a while. I suppose I could have given up the Goose ghost had Rain not ventured to magick a suggestion to the neighborhood to pull itself together and shake off its lethargy. She herself might have died, but she'd spoken the spell first. She seemed ready to succumb to mortality—taking her clothes off and lying in a graveyard—yet she woke up in a carpet of blue blossoms beside our resident Minor Adjutant. Not dying does a power of good for the instinct to carry on a little."

"She succumbed to a fainting spell of sorts. So did Lucikles. And so did you. But how did you get Silverbeak to bring the seashell to the *Ocean Heron*?"

"A word in her earless ear? Who knows. The instincts of the mute animal are no less refined than those of the garrulous. Maybe Silverbeak possesses some sense of communication, like a dog laying a stick at the toes of its companion human and begging for it to be tossed again. Or even compassion? Anyway, it's clear she was returning the shell to its source of origin."

"Why did the crane stay behind when all her flock abandoned the island?"

"Why do you leave to ply the high seas when all your sisters stay home and become farmwives or dutiful daughters?"

Stalta Hipp laughed at that and tossed the Goose a heel of a rye loaf, which he caught in midair before settling back down on the eggs. He said, "I don't know what the gestation period of a crane's eggs are, but my wife's clutch used to take a month or more. I would help out from time to time, by sitting upon them or at least by hovering nearby if she needed to feed or to stir her limbs. Yes, we've lost our share of offspring to predators and to disease. These two exported goslings—or colts, it's hard to know what they will turn out to be like—will endure their own good fortune and relish their bad luck, in that contrary way life requires of all of us."

They had come too close to the question about how fertilization had been achieved, and while Stalta Hipp was no stranger to the mechanics of sex, she was wary enough of magic not to want to pull aside the gossamer curtain in the interests of clinical scrutiny. But sex was all around them on the high seas this season. "I hope they're taking precautions," she said as she noted Rain doing some leaping about for exercise, and Lucikles sitting aside, laughing fondly at her.

2

A fair wind kept them company across this next and longest stretch of their journey. North Orgole was a protectorate of Great Northern Isle, not far west of that outlier island. But when the *Ocean Heron* was still two or three days from port, after a series of sunny mornings and blustery afternoons that had powered the sails to peak performance, the seas becalmed. The waters went glassy and thick, like melting gelatin; the waves low and the current sluggish. At deck level the air turned stale. There was little to do but sing chanteys and wait it out.

The lads—three young buckoes, seasoned enough to have a few inches of beard per chin, and a junior one with a face only slightly more befurred than Lucikles's son's—relished one number in particular. The youngest lad couldn't say much but *gagu, gagur, gagu,* but he laughed when the others laughed.

> Sing ho! for the life of a seafaring man.
> A seaman is seaman whenever he can.
> Live wild, my boys, live free.
> He lives for the waves and he strives for the wives
> And he dives for the door if the husband arrives.
> Sing ho! For the life of a seafaring man.
> Live wild, my boys, live free.

This was followed by a set of infinitely variable and randy quatrains, some clearly canonical and others improvised. They gave Lucikles a headache and did nothing to improve the mood on board. The more limp the sails, the lustier the rondos.

But what kind of mood was it, really? The Minor Adjutant from the House of Balances in Maracoor Crown wasn't inept in bed. Still, outside of it he sometimes felt that he flailed in the wallows of emotional ambiguity. The women he'd encountered on his administrative meanderings had treated him like something between a client and a congenial cousin one might as well make at home. He'd given these women comfort and cash and that little thrill of a pretend romantic interlude—the dinners, wine, the little gifts at parting—but he hadn't sought them out the next time, nor recorded their names in his log. Pay up and move on.

But Rain, such an anomaly. Perhaps even more now than in the moment when he first laid eyes on her and thought, foolishly, she might be a demiurge or dryad whipped to life for the arcane plan of some backstage deity. That instant seemed a hundred years ago, though it was only months. In the orchard above the temple on the island of Maracoor Spot. She'd been running from him, hiding her presence. The dog, loyal Cur, had sniffed her out. Her or the Goose. She'd spun around in the circle of trees, her face like someone who'd been wakened while sleepwalking. Unknowing and—he could look back on it now with more understanding—also unable to fathom the depths of her loss. Her memory had been whacked out of her and her recovery was slow. The youngest bride of Maracoor, that little girl Cossy, had admired Rain back into some sense of self. Still, the green visitor had seemed as if she'd just hatched from a peapod. More innocent than the dog, the child, or the mountain air that swept through the limbs of the tree they called Mother of Olive.

Now, with the power of her broomstick recovered and her mission discharged, she seemed to Lucikles almost like a different person. As if this was the second night of a cycle of mystery dramas, and tonight the heroine was being portrayed by an older actress with a sharper sense of presence and gravitas. It took a few moments upon the torchlit stage of the amphitheater before the new performer could command belief. Once she did, last night's portrayal of the younger heroine seemed premature.

Rain was modest in her demeanor on ship. Lucikles had the good sense not to ask her to define the nature of what she was feeling for him. Her eyes occasionally glowed upon him with a welcome, cherry-brown glint. The witch and the overseer spent a good deal of time loitering at the rail together, dancing when someone brought out a lute or a concertina or a reed pipe. And under blankets at night of course. But when her face was turned away from him to examine the horizon, or talk to someone else, Lucikles felt that he vanished from her mind. He felt he'd become invisible even to himself. Sometimes he tried to drag up the simulacrum of Oena, his steady wife, and of his son and daughters, Leorix, Poena, and Star. Everything he had done in his adult life had been for them. But they wouldn't stay put. Mere outlines sketched in soluble ink on pages hanging in the rain. They were disappearing.

He ought to be panicked about this, but he could afford to delay panic, he thought, until Rain and the Goose said goodbye in Great Northern Isle and headed back to that country of the mind, Oz. If there was such a place. If the uncommon visitors hadn't actually been spirits from the empyrean all along.

He consigned his moral vexations to tomorrow's chores, abandoned there beside other matters that it would be premature to fret over. Matters like the filing of a travel log with Borr Apoxiades, his superior in the courts of the House of Balances. Hiring a roofer to redo the back section of the home in Piney Quarter. And seeing about an apprenticeship for Leorix. Assuming that the trouble over the invaders had died down by the time Lucikles returned to the capital.

Instead, he allowed himself to sway in the moment, listless and inert, like the tunics strung up on a ratline getting some sun. With no wind to unsettle them. He liked feeling hung out like a piece of worn clothing, pinned to the moment, useless to effect any change. This moment like all others would pass, but since he was unable to do anything but wait, he waited with pleasure, sometimes basking in Rain's attention and other times fading out, even to himself.

Iskinaary and Stalta Hipp were playing some sort of game with the set of cards that Rain had filched from the Oracle of Maracoor. She didn't seem to mind. The lads were squatting on the deck doing some repair work on tired lines. They leaned against the rails on the port side, catching what shade there was. "You're bored," Lucikles said to Rain, sidling over to her.

"This reminds me of the work the brides did every morning of their lives," she said. She flicked a hand—two of the crew members whipping areas of damaged rope, the other two plaiting strands from a bundle of coir to one side. Their movements were deft and sure and their conversation uninterrupted. "At least this rope will be useful, assuming the wind ever picks up. Hello, company's coming?"

He looked to where her eye had swiveled. On the horizon, a pretty slip moving at a clip; its beige sails billowed. "You'll want to run up a tray of meringues or something," Rain called to Stalta Hipp. "Folks may be stopping by unexpectedly."

The Captain lumbered to her feet and availed herself of her spyglass. "A very peculiar operation that can harvest a wind when there is no wind," she said. "I'd like to know how they manage."

"Couldn't there be a pulse out there we aren't near enough to catch?" Rain asked.

The Captain didn't bother to answer such ignorance. "If she's bent on stopping by, we can't outrun her, neither can we do the polite thing and come about to meet her halfway. Still, men, tidy up the lines now. And bring in the laundry. I may not be pinning on my tiara but no need to publish my undergarments." The men hopped to obedience, as they all found rope-wrangling tedious. The Goose returned to the box where his eggs sat, those two smooth items, one ivory mottled with umber, the other a pale porcelain blue.

"You've spent your professional life going to sea once a year. What are the protocols of ships passing this close?" asked Rain. "Need they salute and visit?"

"There are no rules," said Lucikles. "It's neither encouraged nor prohibited. What with that ship of corpses that washed ashore on Ithira Strand, though, visiting among ships has fallen off quite a bit. In this case, since the *Ocean Heron* is stationary, it's up to the captain of that vessel, who is bearing in rather swiftly, no?"

"Someone in distress, perhaps," said Stalta Hipp. "Menexis, go collect the sawbones kit in case there's emergency assistance needed at once." The youngest of the seamen issued his standard *garu, agu, gagur* and hopped to obey.

The Captain's pose became more rigid the closer the ship came. It was a honey of a vessel, longer but, it seemed, narrower than the ships Lucikles boarded for his annual tour of island outreaches. A certain robustness of the angle of central mast, the way it sat so confidently, even smugly, lower in the water than most vessels on the high seas would dare to do—it made the Minor Adjutant wonder if this might be a ship from a port outside his usual round. "Does it appear at all familiar?" he asked the Captain. "Could it be a stray Skedelander scout?"

"This far north, I doubt it," said the Captain. "You saw their vessels in the harbor when we left. They were readying to head south, back to home port. Anyway, Skedish sloops are taller and broader of beam than this one."

"There might be more than one design favored. This honey seems built for speed—look at her come." He waited for the Captain to cry out that they ought to brace for impact, as there was no maneuver they could take to divert. Impossible to awaken the agency of the drifting *Ocean Heron.* But Stalta Hipp kept her tongue.

When there were only moments before an encounter, the Captain barked out, "Should these prove to be pirates, prepare to surrender your valuables. If you have any." She glanced at Lucikles and Rain only; she knew her crew didn't carry valuables. Iskinaary, who had vaulted to the roof of the pilot's cabin, flopped back down again in an ungainly mess of feathers and settled upon his nest.

"Hide the soothsaying cards somewhere," said Lucikles.

"They can have those cards," replied Rain. "I don't care about them." She slipped the box in her apron pocket, but hurried to lean her broom up among a cluster of fishing rods and a marlin spike stored behind a hinged bracket. Far the most valuable thing she possessed, her lover realized. Without it her passage home would be, perhaps, impossible. The broom had the weather-worn look of a household item ready for replacement. So that was lucky. Least likely thing to be appropriated by robbers on the high seas.

At almost the last moment the approaching vessel came about and, scraping, slid alongside the *Ocean Heron.* "Of the winds and waters, identify yourself," called the Captain, neither belligerently nor with particular warmth. "I catch sight of no name on your prow."

The men on board—they seemed all men, though some clean-shaven—were busy managing the sails. The ship was a bronco under them; it needed taming. Finally a boss officer separated himself from the others and strode the center of their deck, lower in the water than the *Ocean Heron*'s, and looked up at Captain Stalta Hipp. He was swarthy and thrust-hipped, hardly Skedelandish such as Lucikles had recently come to identify the type. A beard of copper coils so waxed into place they could have been cut off and used to decorate the edges of a picture frame. "Prepare to be boarded," he said. The accent was guttural, perforated with aspirations.

"Not without identification," replied the Captain, as if she had a narwhal lance at the ready, though all she could muster was a steely expression.

"Axen Axeli," he replied, "skipper of the *Great Unknown*." His men were tossing ropes affixed to grappling hooks, marrying the boats. With a low hand gesture, Stalta Hipp stilled her men from throwing them back. The crew of the *Ocean Heron* was outnumbered by double.

"Approach, then," she said to Axen Axeli, who was already halfway up the attached ratline. "And your business with us?"

"Call it animal attraction," he said, stomping his sandals on their deck as he vaulted over the rail. "We haven't seen a mating ship in some time. We get lonely."

"We have nothing for you," she said. "There are no Maracoor maidens on board except me, and I'm not your type." Lucikles began to step forward but the Captain said, as much to him as to the visitor, "I'm in need of no defense and I offer no further argument on the matter. Is there anything else we can do for you before you take your leave?"

"Where are you headed?" said the impertinent captain, perhaps to buy time as several of his crewmates swarmed up ropes behind him, to his left and right.

"North Orgole, for provisions; then on to Great Northern Isle. We carry no cargo worth plundering if that is why you're boarding uninvited. Now I've answered your query. Do me the same courtesy. Where are you from and where are you headed? And what is it you really need?"

Lucikles noticed that Rain had sunk into the overhanging roof of the pilot's cabin. She wasn't hiding, exactly, but in the purple shadow her peculiar aspect wasn't as evident as in bright light. So far Axen Axeli seemed not to have taken the measure of the six other humans traveling northeast on the *Ocean Heron;* his eyes were riveted upon Stalta Hipp. "We come from here and there, penal colonies on the northern slopes of Lesser Torn Isle, mostly. We don't keep résumés on file. As for what we need—well, something drew us to you, some cast of luck. Honor the appetite, I always say." A dagger flashed from his belt to his hand, as if it had suddenly grown there from the sweat on his palm. "I wouldn't deprive a ship of her captain unless I had no choice. Is that a young miss keeping shyly out of the sun? Come here, my dear, and let my lads survey the goods."

Rain stepped out of the shadow with her chin high and no apparent caution, though she couldn't, thought Lucikles, be oblivious of this danger? Or maybe she was more certain of her effect on people than he had dared to hope. Axen Axeli didn't quite blanch, but he squinted his eyes, as if suspecting a bout of sunstroke. "You ate something that didn't agree with you," he said. Beside him his companions spit on the deck, warding off infection.

"You should know we have just come from Ithira Strand," said Rain. "You see what the virus can do to you if you happen to survive it. This is the last stage of putrescence, we witnessed it. If you stick around—or if you'll have me—you'll find an anomaly you didn't expect to meet in this life. My body will stay animate after my flesh finishes decaying, and I'll keep your hold haunted for some time to come. Too bony for agreeable companionship. To judge by the skeletal ghosts we met on Ithira Strand." Lucikles admired her gambit but the only way to corroborate it would be to encourage the pirates to take her, and he couldn't risk that.

"Unholy terror," said Axen Axeli. Lucikles had to admire the man's composure. "Why did the wind bring us straight to you, then?"

"I wondered about that myself," said Rain. "We saw you coursing merrily along while we sit here becalmed as a potato in a tureen of stew."

"She's a witch," said the right-hand man of Captain Axen Axeli. "Back to the *Great Unknown*, then, sir?"

"Not so fast," said Axen Axeli. He was looking over the crew of the *Ocean Heron*, whose men stood back but tensed for combat. "Take a peek in the sleeping quarters, men, and see if they've hidden someone more comely and less off-putting than this old ewe and her off-color daughter. If not—" He didn't finish the sentence, but nodded at the boy, Menexis. "He may have to do."

"Not likely, no," said Lucikles, "not happening." He limped forward, realizing himself to be the portrait of incompetence.

"Kerr Lucikles," said Stalta Hipp, "this is my operation."

"I represent the Bvasilate of Maracoor Abiding," Lucikles continued.

"I'm supposed to fall down in rapture?" Axen Axeli laughed. "The Bvasilate put most of us in prison for simple infractions like failing to tithe or talking dirty in the presence of a priest. Or murder; all right; it happens. No, that authority doesn't hold much sway over us. Mind your tongue if you want to keep it in your head."

"*Gaga garoo, garoo, garoo,*" said Menexis. It had never been easy to guess what he might be meaning, but his crew members closed shoulders in front of him.

"He's young so he'll be docile, and easily brought around to new ways, if there's no young bride to be found. A cunning enough morsel. Meaning no respect to you," Axen Axeli added, theatrically hypocritical, as he nodded in Rain's direction, "and begging your pardon *of course*. You've made a potent point and we're inclined to respect your sovereignty."

"I tell you, we're all infected," said Rain, "I'm just more advanced. I wouldn't stay here a moment longer than you need lest you carry the germ away with you. Then you'll see what I'm talking about even if you leave empty-handed from us."

"She's a witch, I tell you," said the first lieutenant. Several of their band were returning from the hold, which was small enough to be examined with a single sweep of the head. A returning investigator shrugged: nothing of value down there, female or otherwise. "They're as out of stores as we are," someone hollered. "A second-weight of hardtack, that's it."

Stalta Hipp played for time. "You haven't answered our question about the secret agency of your ship's speed," she said. "In this doldrum, you enjoy a private zephyr of some power. If we let you take anyone at all—and I'm not inclined, to be frank—at least tell us how you're assured you can outrun us."

"Perhaps you lot can be possessed of a virus, or maybe you've only got a good storyteller in your midst, who knows," said Axen Axeli. "Likely we won't hang around long enough to be sure. But we have a haunting, too. Our ship has become possessed. We're powerless to control when it wants to move and when it wants to loiter, not to mention in which direction it cares to drive us. We haven't made landfall for months. We've been dragged here to commandeer what we need."

"How did a power of intention come upon your ship?" asked Stalta Hipp.

"No need for you to know," said Axen Axeli. "If there's no interesting food and no plunder to intrigue us, we'll take the boy and call off the massacre. Wouldn't want to alarm that pesky virus you're suffering any more than we have to," he added to Rain with a smirk.

"Captain," said the second crew member, now appearing from belowdecks. He was holding Rain's leathern satchel, the one that had come with her all the way from Oz to Maracoor Spot, across the great nation and back again. "I've found what we must be looking for."

The only things in the satchel were the seashell that had carried the pollen of the Caryatids and the page discovered from the Grimmerie, fished out whole from the padding of the nest of Silverbeak. "It's another of those papers. We've been dragged here to collect it, no doubt. We're to assemble that volume sheet by sheet, it seems."

The great Axen Axeli looked ashen, a puff of coal dust in the air. Lucikles barked, "You're hunting for leaves from a wretched book of spells?"

"Is that what it is? We have a binding and eight other pages. This is the third one our ship has honed in on. I might have known," said the pirate captain. To Stalta Hipp he said, "You've found the secret of our individual weather, Captain Lardass. I'm afraid we're in thrall to a cargo we can't unload. But it gives us advantage, oh it does—" He raised a palm up as if testifying, and he paused to groan and to pick out of the fleshy base of his thumb the paring knife that Captain Stalta Hipp had just landed there.

"It's time to go," she said. "You'll take no document and you'll take no prisoner. The boy stays with us. I'll make a bargain with you, Captain Axen Axeli. I won't hunt you down for crimes on the high seas if you release to us the bits of codex you say you've picked up on your wanderings. You may find that you're liberated back to the normal behavior of the weather once you deliver your cargo to us. You weren't brought here to steal from us but to pay us fealty. I'll give you a count of fifty to produce the items you mention, and then—"

"The witch," said one of the *Ocean Heron*'s crew members. "You don't want to get on her wrong side."

"She's a ripe rank one, and don't we know it," said another.

"Fellows, please," said Rain. "This is embarrassing."

Captain Axen Axeli's hand was dripping blood; Lucikles offered his own neck scarf for binding. The game was balanced; the pirate ship had superior numbers but had admitted to weakness. A story about plague to frighten ignorant sailors was a transparent story despite Rain's unusual coloring—her fellow travelers on board the *Ocean Heron* looked hale as summer heather.

Behind them, Menexis seemed perhaps to have finally cottoned on to his plight as a possible pawn in this negotiation, and he was weeping softly, his muffled *gara garoo* in a boy's soprano that wasn't doing his cause any good.

"I don't believe she's a witch," said Captain Axen Axeli at last. "She'd commandeer that broke-backed book if she had magic in her to do it."

"How do you know she hasn't brought you here?" said Lucikles.

"Cast a spell and make me see your strength," commanded Axen Axeli.

Rain lifted her head and smiled. "All right," she said, pivoting on her heel a quarter-turn.

> *Goose, oh goose,*
> *Loosen your throat,*
> *Speak to these louts*

She couldn't think of a rhyme for "throat" quickly enough, but it didn't matter. Iskinaary threw himself into the role of a lifetime with a mighty quawk that ushered out of his lengthened neck. "Quawk, qua-raaawk," he trumpeted, clearing his throat. "The stone from my throat is rolled away, the queen of witches has had her say. If I were you I'd go away." He bowed as if accepting applause before a set of stage torches. "Far away," he added. A bit over the top, but it did the trick. Talking Animals were unknown in Maracoor, and the pirates on this rogue ship had been out of touch with current events for months. They hadn't heard all that had happened on the mainland.

"You can keep the kerchief, I have others," Lucikles called after the departing men.

"I still want what you have found," declared Stalta in triumph. "You'll realize the book has delivered you from your penitential servitude, and you'll come to thank the witch who drew you here with her magic winds."

"Don't overdo it," muttered Lucikles.

"We don't want that thing, any of it," said Rain in a desperation that turned her nearly white.

"I am the captain of this ship," Stalta reminded them, and picked up the paring knife from where Axen Axeli had dropped it on the deck.

"*Gara garoo, garoo,*" wept Menexis, this time in the shock of relief.

THE CAPTAIN OF *THE OCEAN HERON* had improvised out of panic but her inventions were pretty much on the mark. Once Axen Axeli had delivered a parcel snugged up in a goatskin tied with leather cord, and Stalta Hipp had confirmed it was a segment of a severed volume of unknown origins and writ in a secret language, the *Ocean Heron* and the *Great Unknown* were loosened one from the other. The winds began to freshen nearly at once, for Stalta's ship, and the *Great Unknown* could take some benefit by a revived wind, though the vessel set sail in the other direction.

When enough distance had been put between them, and North Orgole began to hint of itself on the horizon, Stalta said, "This thing that brought us into danger and maybe rescued us too, who knows. Show it to us." Rain found it impossible to refuse the Captain's order. She untied the strings and unwrapped the book, and saw its water-spotted binding again. She'd drowned this book months ago but it didn't seem to want to stay drowned. The damage was minimal, though there were only eleven leaves—six secured still to the spine of the codex, several loose sheets inserted for safekeeping between. To these Rain added the page Iskinaary had found wadded up in Silverbeak's nest. The pages were rippled but not smeared; the ink had not run. If anything, the colors looked somewhat revived after their saltbath treatment.

She wasn't quite sure about all this. To what end this heartache, if the Grimmerie were incapable of dissolution. All these months of travel, worry, of effort, of lives put in danger and perhaps even lost because of her campaign to thrust away from her the immortal power of magic. She ought to feel crushed, her life made a mockery. And yet, her hand on the cover of the book as she closed it for rewrapping, she thought: Something in a book cries out to be read. Just as for the *Great Unknown,* it makes its own weather, it drives its own life. I am not a character in the Grimmerie but I am in the life it is having in this world. I am altered for having read from it once or twice. I can't help it. No reader throws off a book's influence by mere intention.

With this twist of logic she made some peace for herself. A witch in apprenticeship, still, learning that the limits of her power were as important to register as the reaches.

GREAT NORTHERN ISLE

1

Captain Stalta Hipp would never admit by which force the wind had been seized in order to drive the pirate ship hither and yon. Still, once the scraps of the Grimmerie had been delivered to the *Ocean Heron,* outsize influence evaporated. The winds stirred to life with ordinary vigor. The Captain approached Rain to demand a disquisition on the Grimmerie, but Rain's dark expression brooked no approach. Leave unread books unread, decided Stalta Hipp.

The ship made the approach to North Orgole in ordinary time. The residents there, a small hardy band of mussel-eaters, regarded the glamorous Rain with indifference. Stocks were purchased, a little fern alcohol consumed. Basic pleasantries shared with efficiency, in words of one syllable.

The chieftains handed over a slab of hard cheese as a goodbye present. A local delicacy, aromatic as wet wool, sweating a little in its paper wrapping, which proved to be another page from the Grimmerie. Apparently the remains of the amputated book of spells had kept themselves busy circulating around the northern ocean. No worse for the excursion, either. Rain glanced at the ornamental heading. *The Rendering of Milk into Silk or Sow's Ears . . .* it said on the recto, and continued on the verso *. . . or Cheese.* The Grimmerie had a wicked sense of humor, apparently. Once the travelers had gotten out of sight of the island, the nasty tile of cheese went overboard to startle the marine life below, while Rain slotted the next recovered page of the Grimmerie in with the previous ones.

From North Orgole, a brisk two-day sail to the chief port of Great Northern Isle. The strappy little city was situated at the far inside edge of a water so capacious it might better be called a bay, though its name was Skeleton Harbor. The conifers that lined the steep bluffs, having dropped their needles for good, looked dead. Taken together in forest density, the harbor seemed fenced in by laddered light or, yes, Lucikles found it easy to see, skeletons linking arms. The aroma, oh, balsam on seawater—another kind of enchantment.

The North Orgole harbormaster knew Lucikles from his annual tours of inspection. Functionaries turned out in ranks to extend their greetings to the overseer and his attendants. Neither Stalta Hipp nor Rain liked being seen as subsidiary, but once on land Captain Hipp's authority didn't cut much sway. Whatever. The better grade and variety of cuisine wasn't unwelcome. Only so much hoopla you can get from a pickled herring.

The crew members remained behind, uninvited into salons and reception halls. Took turns guarding the *Ocean Heron* and spinning a few coins in the wharfside pubs and game alleys. Rain, however, went along with Stalta Hipp and Lucikles. She wasn't precisely Lucikles's escort or consort but as she was so clearly younger, his shepherding her through a doorway or to a seat next to him at table could be read as avuncular. She thought this, perhaps she hoped it, but it didn't register with her as important to worry about.

In any case, Captain Stalta Hipp didn't want to be paired with the Minor Adjutant of the House of Balances, and entered any room on her own, single file and unaccompanied. A female ship captain wasn't unheard of in these northern lands, but nor was it commonplace. She tended to shut down idle chatter with a particular brusqueness of manner she must have refined for occasions such as this. In only a few days she developed a great fan club among the locals. They were largely terrified of her, but oh, intrigued.

For Rain, the reception was convivial enough. Outlying settlements in this barren if civilized province could be home to clans who grew green moss in their armpits, for all she knew. The island seemed dense with the types of growth Rain had seen on the highest slopes of the Great Kells. Lichens, tree fungus, hardscrabble knitted furze clinging to rockface and the north edges of trees. The dominant color scheme was a muted, stubborn verdure. Rain might as well have arrived green as a token of respect for local customs.

2

They would stay two nights in a small hotel before Lucikles and his other companions departed aboard the *Ocean Heron*, heading back to Maracoor Abiding. Rain and Iskinaary would then fly around the southern edge of the great island, taking it easy at first, short hops for practice, keeping the coast in view, building up their stamina before sheering east across the ocean.

After a banquet featuring a mode of traditional choral singing inspired, it seemed, by the sounds of strangulation, Lucikles and Rain escaped to their chambers. The windows looked out over a laundry courtyard where ladders were stored for the repair of shutters. The shutters clacked in the wind anyway. Sleep would be interrupted by the conversation of windows. But the witch and the Minor Adjutant both felt sleep was something of a waste of time, now that their separation was imminent.

Their states of mind were imprecise even to themselves. They didn't talk about it much. An abiding sense of tentativeness obtained, even as their final hours of intimacy became the warmest they'd known. Privacy, they were finding, allowed for privileges as yet unexplored. The clattering shutters stood in for the missing yawns and midnight sneezes of the *Ocean Heron*'s crew on night watch. But that the floor didn't rock and pivot underneath the lovers rooted them both to an uneasy precision they hadn't known before.

Well, Rain hadn't known it. She was nearly a novice at sex. Her earlier experiences with Tip had been what eroticism first provides when it is not forced upon one. Tip had been as startled by the robust insistencies of the human body as she had been, so their tiptoeing across that margin from ignorance to exploration had been done with mutual wonder and even disbelief. On the other hand, Lucikles, a man of the world, a father of three, a husband for a decade and a half maybe, was practiced in the art of arousal. What he lacked in astonishment he made up for in expertise.

Lovemaking with Tip, such as it might be called, had been less aggressive than the same with Lucikles, though for all that, thought Rain, the former had seemed more thrilling.

About Tip, Rain did not speak—not to Lucikles, not to anyone.

The shutters clacked. The wind off Skeleton Harbor played castanets with the roof tiles above their heads. With a provincial rectitude, a wind-up clock in the stair hall alerted lodgers that it wasn't yet the hour to wake up.

"I'll miss you," said Lucikles at last. "You've come to mean something to me."

"Have I come to that?" she said. "I thought I'd come to a parting of the ways."

"I'm not canny with repartee on matters of the heart. Take it easy on me. Accept what I'm trying to say, even if I don't quite know what it is."

"You'll go back to your family," she said. "You ought to and you will. If I've learned anything in my tenure as a bruised soul abroad, I've learned that home has an unnamable . . . essential . . . without which it's nearly impossible to thrive."

Making this statement out loud, she realized that her first destination back in Oz, should she reach Oz, would be to visit her father. To let him know she was still alive. To let him know she'd somehow moved beyond the paralysis of grief.

They drank a little port from a single glass and could not get comfortable. A candle guttered before the mirror. In the reflection, the shadows wavered across their faces. It was hard to tell green from anything else in such low light. Whether this made Rain feel more beautiful or more ordinary, she didn't know, but she was on the verge of suggesting they snuff the candle in the interest of canceling their doubles when the shutters clacked again with a more decisive thump. "Voyeurs?" said Lucikles laconically, favoring his wounded foot as he got up to try again to secure the shutters. But he saw a head in a sort of woolen turban rising between the uprights of one of those ladders. "Company? At this hour? We're not suitably attired to entertain," he said, hoping that Rain wouldn't be alarmed, though he was ready to raise a ruckus at the first sign of threat. Rain swore softly and drew the blanket to her clavicle.

"She here, she here, they say so," said a gruff voice. A woman's voice. "No? The green witch?"

"Who wants her?" said Lucikles, reaching for his tunic and the small dagger he kept scabbarded in an inside sleeve.

"Nobody wants her, is my guess, but here, these is hers." The dim candlelight made of the woman's cowled face a wax effigy—she was likely keeping her eyes down so as not to be recognized. "I been chosen to do the deed, let me do it and scarper, Kerr Lucikles." She looped one arm around the top rung and with her other hand rummaged in a cloth sack. "Don't even like to touch them but somebody got to." She thrust a cylinder tied with string over the windowsill and onto the floor. "Nobody aims to see these ever again, mind. Should we do, next time you come to make your annual inspection you'll be inspecting the muddy floor of Skeleton Harbor."

"Why didn't you just come up the stairs?" he called after her descending form.

"Too many people know about this, too much trouble. Mark my words."

"But who are you?"

"The one who drew the unlucky straw. Good night to you and better night to us." She disappeared in the gloom of an overhang, letting the ladder fall noisily against some empty ale kegs.

They didn't need to open the cord to know what they would find. Another remnant of the Grimmerie, this signature complete with stitching still hinging the pages. When Rain scurried to join the prodigal pages to their kin, she thought they fairly leapt to the spine. The earlier pages shuffled to make room for them. They seemed to have grown in number, like a salamander regenerating its tail.

"If the Grimmerie has that capacity, better it be kept together," she murmured, "than that two dozen baby Grimmeries go floating about the northern Nonestic Ocean, making trouble."

"The Sea of Maracoor," said Lucikles. "Different names for the same immensity?"

"Nothing remains stable, especially water," she said. As she closed the book, her eye fell on that first page—*On Vagaries and Variations.*

"I could absolve us of some of the misery of parting," she said, questioningly. "Maybe?"

Lucikles didn't want to fall sucker to a love potion; he wanted the genuine article with its drawbacks and thorns and tender emergency miracles. "What we have left to us has its own nature, it needs no improvement," he declared, and drew her to him. He blew the candle out. She muttered something that he couldn't hear. They fell back onto the bed, knowing one of these times would be the last. The down coverlet, worked over in native patterns derived from reindeer rack and pinecone and upland iris, lifted its four corners, and lifted the lovers too, several feet into the air, buoying them the way the rocking of the sea had done when they had comforted each other on board the *Ocean Heron.* Being suspended is all that love is, really—but it's enough.

AT THE SIGHT of the blood on the floor, congealing in the dawn light that bloomed periodically through the clapping shutters, Rain felt for Lucikles's pulse to make sure he was still alive. Yes, no doubt of that. But the danger was real. His bad foot cantilevering off the bed was red at the wound, brown and plum from ankle to midcalf. His face receded into the shadows of the pillow because it was more blue than ruddy or even sallow. "You're in a bad way, jolt up," she said, a cross tone to mask her worry.

He had a hard time coming around, so she dressed quickly and covered his nakedness and went for help. The chatelaine, a sour-sweet auntie type with a prominent gold-lacquered overbite, hoisted herself to the room to look in on her guest. She made an obscure gesture to ward off evil and tried to turn Rain out of the house, but Rain wouldn't go. A physician was sent for and arrived in due course, panic distorting his professional mien. "You were in Ithira Strand; this is their curse, then?" he said, diagnostically, not wanting to enter the room but standing on tiptoe with his chin thrust forward, trying to see over the threshold and the mounded blankets.

"This is not plague," snapped Rain. "He cut his foot on a journey in the wilds out to the west of Maracoor Abiding. A scarab embedded itself, maybe. It's been getting worse and he was going to see to it when he got home to his family."

"I'm told you're a great sorceress even though you're an idiotic young woman."

"Someone is telling you partial lies. I can't heal him, if that's what you want to know."

He rummaged in his valise and pulled out a few more pages. "Anything useful in these rare items that have come my way?" He handed them to her, and then slapped his hands together as if to vanquish the dust of menace from his palms.

She didn't even look at them. "No, I don't do trickery. Haven't you something to stanch the bleeding?"

"An unguent and a stretch of sun-bleached linen. You'll have to do the application yourself." He handed her a clay tub of some streaky ointment smelling of celery. "Start at the discoloration below the knee and work down. Rinse your hands thoroughly before you get to the open wound, wherever on the foot it is."

She had no time to argue with him. Lucikles was beginning to moan, and that was good; maybe he could hear that help was near. "And you'll do what," she said, "stand in the doorway sending up whispery incantations for your own continued health?"

"I'll try to be quiet about it. And I won't leave you till you're done."

She did as she had been bade, trying to turn her mind away from anxious spells that were suggesting themselves to her. Is this what it is like to be a poet, she wondered, you can't get away from your own voice. Fragments of possibility—

> *Tourniquet, varnish, vanish and banish*
> Biin tonna paralex paraliin shyne

She didn't want it; it didn't come through fully.

But also, while she was trying to still the commotion in her head—

> *Biin tonna paralex*
> *Curses and alter-hex*
> *Faucet of blood*
> *Biin tonna, biin tonna*

The runes were fighting for purchase; she was pushing them back. She didn't know why except for fear of their unbridled strength. She was too inexperienced to judge potency or anticipate downstream complications, and she didn't want to take the risk. Yet, however unwelcome, the words insisted themselves.

Blood of the scarab, blood of the crown
Biin tonna paralex, *pale of the moon*

Why were the words coming intelligible and also not, why in known language or secret, this twinned stream of garbage.

She clawed a great gloop of the salve and began to massage Lucikles's left calf. Like basting a leg of lamb with oil and herbs before roasting it. He moaned and made as if to pull away, but his speech was still too muddled to pose a reason why she should stop. When she reached the foot, she did as the physician had recommended. In the porcelain basin, she washed her hands with a gritty knot of soap the establishment had provided. Then she went back to him and coated his bad instep and heel. The wound now unregenerately flapping like the mouth of a fish; she could have slipped a finger inside. Not being the praying sort, she had no prayers with which to work, but she found herself repeating—

Blood of the scarab, blood of the crown
Biin tonna paralex, *pale of the moon*

as her fingers worked the skin over. Trying to keep her stomach from flipping, she bent back the flap of flesh, like the overlap of a pocket or a purse. Rubbed some salve into the underside. Then wrapped the white linen around the foot, as if the binding could force the skin to grow back together.

She looked up to the physician for approval, but he had disappeared, sacrificing his unguent.

THE MINOR ADJUTANT emerged from his threshold of fog and impermanence, and language keyed up. "I see my foot is swaddled like a newborn."

"Or a corpse," she had to admit.

"I hope it's not dead." He had meant this as a joke but her expression, always inscrutable to him, conveyed something that he didn't like to witness. He added, "You're no doctor."

"That's for certain. But living in the mountains with my father and his herd of sheep, I've seen the way sepsis can hide deceptively while it gains strength, and suddenly break out in a full-blown systemic threat. The foot will have to come off if you're going to live. Nobody wants to go lame into the afterlife, but better a strapped-on stump and a cane than a rot that causes you to limp throughout eternity."

"Who tells you this nonsense? You are a child."

"If so, I am a witch-child. Don't trust me if you don't like. But I'd hate to say goodbye to you and think you were lurching out of this life as swiftly as I hope to get off this island and on my way."

"I've told my wife that I would take myself to the Groves of Salanx upon my return to the mainland. The holy physicians there will heal me if I can be healed."

"You take a risk to wait that long. Won't it take you a week or ten days to get back to the mainland? Or more? You may not have the luxury of waiting."

"Are you actually saying some sawbones should take off my foot?" He felt himself blanch.

"After I leave and I'm no longer a liability to you, get yourself an opinion or two. Your calf is rotting from the wound in your heel. It may still be salvageable if you take off the foot."

"Where did you get the body of knowledge to make such a summary?"

She shrugged. Then she took out the cards she'd stolen from the Oracle of Maracoor. Out of their little furred box they slid, seventy or so palm-size rectangles of glossy paper printed with the same design on the nil side. She shuffled them—she was getting better at this—and then went through the pack again, selecting three cards at random, or not random, who could tell. She laid them on the side of the bed where he still languished, and changed their positions several times. He watched with an anguish like that with which he'd brought Oena to the birthing pavilion for the delivery of each of their three living children, and the dead one, too.

Before she turned the cards over, she looked at him again, studying him. "I've never known whether I liked you or not," she said, "but I have loved you. Can you explain that?"

That he understood what she meant and that he couldn't explain it either made his eyes blur. "Read the cards, get this charade over with," he grumbled.

With the same iconography the whole set used, the first card, on the left of the three, showed clots of celestial weather from which a godly hand was emerging. The hand held an implement not unlike a scythe but angled in the wrong direction. Something like a skiving knife for leather, a slanted blade. A surgical tool. "Does this mean you would like me to spread some butter on your breakfast bread?" he said.

The second card, on the right, revealed the ubiquitous and busybody hand, this time proffering a demure maiden, very pale indeed, nearly white, with her eyes down modestly and a veil of some fancy design covering half her face. Her dress was white and her clasped hands held a small bouquet of golden snapdragons. "Is this a wife of some sort? Are you going to marry me?" he asked.

"You're already married."

"Well, turn the last one over and let's finish this up."

The final card, the central one, was unmistakably a figure of grim mortality. Clad all in black with a high pointy hood, he sat in the godly palm with insouciance, dangling his legs in the air. He held a farm implement. This secret character was an impartial and untroubled harvester of life. The clouds from which the great hand appeared were darker here, and there was a hint of lightning in the background. The ground far below was some sort of grave-yard, with stones and obelisks and statues of fantastical angels and griffons.

Lucikles snorted. "He'd be fun at a party."

"I don't have a skill of interpretation," she said, "not yet or maybe not ever. But these cards were the ones that insisted being cho-sen. I could feel that instinctively. It's like iron filings to a magnet stone. Read them as you like. It's your life, after all."

"I think these are only suggestions of what could be. Maybe only suggestions of what you yourself are worrying about. I'm a rationalist, Rain. The arcane art of choosing cards at random—I can't argue with you about what you feel, though I don't feel it myself. But anyone can make a story about three images. Indeed, probably any good story needs only three images to get up a re-verberation of association. But I could tell this like so: an innocent maiden needing to cut the cords with her family and get married or risk death by paralysis of the heart. No? That's not valid?"

She didn't demur, but she tapped a finger upon the picture of the maiden. "You spent your life supervising the brides of Mar-acoor. By bringing infant girls there, you consigned them to a sev-ered life. And—maybe you knew this or not—their daily routine involved scarring themselves in the feet, bleeding their feet every morning and salting them in the sea. Now it's your blooded foot that threatens your life. I see that bride more menacing than the doom man with his razored axe. You might do best to sidestep a death sentence and accept the penalty life is offering you by way of substitution. Your foot is not going to get better. Either you kill it or it kills you."

"I had lots of other jobs all year long," he sputtered. "Overseeing the brides of Maracoor was only one of my obligations."

She put the cards away. "I'm going to find Iskinaary and see if he is ready. The longer I stay here with you the more you're tempted to avoid the moment. You don't have too many moments left to squander before the decision is taken out of your hands."

"Don't leave without saying goodbye," he said, his face lowered into his palms. She said no goodbye. Goodbyes were nonsense sentiment. But she left behind for him the bit of pounded metal that had fallen into her hand from the wall of the surgery or morgue on Ithira Strand. Unthinkingly she'd carried it in her pocket. Only after the adventure with the pirates off North Orgole had she even looked at it. A tin foot.

3

Rain did make it her business to run into Captain Stalta Hipp. "You could have left us for dead, there on Ithira Strand," said Rain. "You didn't. So I have to express my grudging thanks to you for that. Will you see that Lucikles or his body gets safely home to his family?"

Stalta Hipp raised her eyebrow. "Just how wild a night did you have?"

"I'm not joking, I don't know how to joke like that. He's in serious trouble. I don't believe he's facing the truth of it. By delivering me this far you've fulfilled your obligation to me. Whether your charge is also to get the Minor Adjutant back to the mainland—that's not my business. But if it's yours, good luck to you."

"Will you come this way again?" asked Stalta Hipp.

"I've learned only this much: that my life has been too poor, too ragged, for me to make any predictions about what next. I didn't plan to come this way in the first place. Would you like me to read your cards for you before I go?"

"I place no trust in the trickery of accident."

"A turn of the cards might accidentally be telling the truth."

"Let it tell the truth to the tabletop then, and reveal nothing to me. I already have reasons to worry. I don't need to multiply my aggravations."

Stalta and Rain embraced with uneasy formality. Iskinaary stood to one side looking as if he'd bought a ticket to a show he didn't care to see. He quawked a farewell, though, as he and Rain made an about-face and launched upslope from the quayside. Rain carried her satchel and those parts of the Grimmerie that had come back to her, and bundles of provision, beside. On top of these, wrapped in green felt, were the two eggs of the border crane. And, resting upon the eggs, tied with cord, a handful of blue blossoms from the graveyard at Ithira Strand. They were proving reluctant to wither.

Below them in the square: the old woman who had climbed the ladder in the middle of the night to deliver pages of the Grimmerie to Rain. The physician who had given Rain the salve for Lucikles's foot. Neither knew the other had had a secret mission with the green witch. But something in the sky turned their heads away from the plashing water. Not much higher than the tops of the trees, that young woman on a broom. The Goose who was her familiar. They scratched the horizon with possibilities both horrible and merciful. "Strange weather we're having," said the physician at last. The old woman grunted and made the local gesture to ward off evil.

PART TWO

THE HIGH ROAD
ABOVE THE SEA

1

They battered against gusty air round the southern coast of Great Northern Isle. Lucikles had told them, and Captain Stalta Hipp confirmed, that shipping preferred the longer northern route. Fairer winds, you see, and the possibility of calmer seas. But Rain wanted to work herself against tougher weather while there was still land close by, if needed, and Iskinaary was game.

Left unsaid, at least for now, was the problem of endurance. They both believed that their initial flight from Oz, and that of the monkeys who had been sent by Rain's father to find her, would likely have ended by drowning in an eternity of ocean but for the unnatural storms called up by Rain's jettisoning the Grimmerie somewhere midway. Rain knew she didn't have the wherewithal to puzzle it out. How far apart were the continents. Without benefit of hurricane energy could they make it. When they made the final launch from some bluff at the southeast tip of Great Northern, would that be their last footstep ever on soil. Was Oz now a dream only, as unreachable as the cruel innocence of childhood.

The first day or two allowed for moments of equanimity Rain hadn't known for some time. She came to realize that this had something to do with the height at which they were flying and the particular path they were sticking to, while they could. Great Northern Isle was a massive pile of rock and forest and ice, a small continent, if you will. Flying as high as she dared—for practice, and to see if the higher winds would increase her speed—she reached an altitude at which the surface of the world below her was evenly divided—land on her left shoulder, water at her right. Eventually they would leave Great Northern Isle behind and the world would be only water. This duality of effects, a balancing of sorts, gave Rain a sense of steadiness she hadn't expected. Something she cherished.

Landing—for they weren't quite ready to strike out across open water yet—she tried to express this arresting sense of calm to Iskinaary, but he would have none of it.

"You're always finding something to go on about," he complained. "If it isn't horror or outrage, it's beauty. So predictable. Can you just pretend I already know all about it, as your wobbly commentary doesn't interest me much?" He poked his head in Rain's satchel to investigate the crane eggs. "I'd hate the change in barometric pressure to crack the membranes of these sketchy coots before they're ready for the world."

"You should know all about that; your membrane has been cracked for quite a while now."

They were preparing some supper on what was their penultimate evening in Maracoor—or perhaps final, no one can be sure in advance of the date of any separate death. Their badinage was partly theater and partly a rash of mounting irritability. For the Goose, Rain arranged some broken crusts of rye on a bed of browning lettuces. For herself, she crumbled some cheese on bread and crushed some walnut meats between two stones. They had half a bottle of wine to drink between them, which meant that Rain drank it all, as Iskinaary preferred water. They ate in silence, facing out to sea. Rain felt hateful but forgave herself some of that; she guessed that she was probably just anxious about the great trip ahead.

Iskinaary did have his mind on the eggs under his care, but he was also bothered by Rain's dalliance with Lucikles. It wasn't the man's being married that worried the Goose. Iskinaary himself had been the most steady of spouses, even if he often couldn't remember his wife's name—still, the dalliance with Silverbeak had happened. The human players in this world put more stake upon the statement of commitments than he ever had. No, it wasn't the morality of the correct and proper that bothered him. It was Rain's apparent breeziness, dismissing the man with his poisoned appendage as if she had no feelings anymore at all.

More than one way to pick up an infection, he knew. He hoped her insouciance was a kind of aberration and not a Portrait of Lady Indifferent. What a way to grow up. He'd hoped, first, that she would survive, but he'd also hoped she'd have merited the care he'd expended on her. The risks he'd taken.

The Goose was still trying to think of a way to broach the subject without sounding the genuine prude when Rain spoke. "The waves are breaking green, not white," she said. Pointing. "Something rotting in the water."

"In the vegetable kingdom," pointed out the Goose blandly, "the colors of regeneration and of corruption are virtually indistinguishable."

"Are you making a personal comment?" That was almost a joke from Rain; the Goose was relieved. She continued. "It stinks, too."

They both watched. About twenty-five yards out of the small promontory on which they'd perched, a disturbance fomented in the surface of the sea. Behind it the waves rolled in white, and they were white again when they crashed against the indifferent boulders at the shore.

"We have company, I wonder?" asked Iskinaary. "Some sea monster, some behemoth of the deep—a kraken with a vendetta, a scourge of disgruntled algae?"

"Or an underwater spring—a hot fissure erupting in this cold sea," suggested Rain, for now the surface began to steam as if rolling to a boil.

They were neither of them right. What emerged after another few moments were five or six sleek grey heads of some unknown species. For a moment Rain was put in mind of the harpies she had met in High Chora, on the mainland, with their fussy peahen bodies and their human faces. But these faces were not humanoid—merely intelligent. Like pounded grey leather. Large dark lashless eyes, pursed mouths, attentive noses that twitched, and twitching whiskers besides.

"A committee come to investigate us," said Iskinaary. "How de do and all that, you lot."

The most forward of the brigade opened its jaws to reveal a set of interior white lips and sharp greasy teeth that looked as if they'd fed only on sea lilies. The leader barked in a language unfamiliar to the travelers. *Aa-rraan-ah me-roh-na pon-een-a-rah-na.*

"Come again?" said the Goose. The leader tried with a set of syllables more noticeably human but not in a language that Iskinaary or Rain could understand. As the spokes-figure puzzled out yet a third system of communication, others of its type were venturing closer to the rocks. Rain didn't know if she and Iskinaary should feel menaced. If the undersea bodies were commensurate with the size of the heads, the creatures were like large otters, perhaps. But who knew if they each didn't trail long coils of sea-serpent carcass underneath their shoulders and submerged torsos?

"We arrive," said the leader at last, finding the right dialect for the moment.

"Evidently," said Iskinaary. "To what do we owe this pleasure?"

The three leading swimmers had now reached a gravelly verge and were working with their upper limbs to bring forward a scrap of detritus secured in a luscious emerald wrap. They swarmed out of the water with some effort. Rain had to work not to gag at the smell. The physical appeal, to one of Rain's makeup, wasn't all that obvious, either. They seemed to have a seahorse spine, flippers from the shoulder that resolved into paws or three-thumbed hands of some sort, and they all trailed elegant tails of shimmering viridescence. "Mermaids?" muttered Rain to the Goose.

"Anomalies of the deep, and if I were you I'd ask no further questions," quawked the Goose back. "After all, you're not one to talk."

"Be I Mee-rahn-nah," said the leader. The gender was indeterminate. "We not surface often, but we come honor you effort and ask you blessing."

"No blessing we can give that you would need," replied Rain.

As their leader squinted at the green witch and shook its puzzled head, the merfolk were busy on the shore. With movements both grave and clumsy they began to pull away the green sheathing of their parcel. Oh, hence the smell, and mercy upon us all, thought Rain. It took everything she had not to vomit. Inside their package was the decomposing body of a merchild.

"This a present of some sort?" asked Iskinaary, for whom the odor was more curious than offensive.

Mee-rahn-nah bowed its head and scratched its chin against its clavicle. "We need you help. Need you bury soft quiet child in you soil."

"Not such an outrageous request," said Iskinaary.

"The sooner the better," said Rain.

"But why?" the Goose asked the leader of the merfolk.

Mee-rahn-nah came forward as the three bearers retreated into the water up to their hips. The companions formed an honor guard of sorts around their leader. "We lay soft quiet ones in elbow of certain cave, hidden far below in sea-soil. Not this one. This one unhappy. Disturb memories of soft quiet ones already resting under sea-soil. This one need private grave, separation. So other soft quiet ones sleep through ocean autumn."

"What about this soft quiet one, all alone, sleeping without other soft quiet ones?" asked the Goose. "You would leave one of your own abandoned, banished on dry land?"

"This soft quiet one before go so soft, so quiet, say us: please. Let not the sweet peace of soft quiet ones disturb. Me move away so no alarm pulls them from their rest."

"It looks quite young," said the Goose. "I mean, compared to you."

"Tadpole," came the blunt reply, with something of a shrug.

Rain had conquered her rising gorge and had fortified herself with some force of anger. She'd moved a few feet and squatted down next to the corpse. "And you came to us because you thought us ignorant enough to help you," she murmured.

"We come to deliver soft quiet one, but you here. In our way," said Mee-rahn-nah. "Still, you move on parchment soil more good than we move. Your tools serve you. So asking."

"All right. We can see to this, Rain," said the Goose.

"I don't know why we should." Rain brushed away a little of the furred green from the shroud. "How did this soft quiet one die?"

"Anger," said Mee-rahn-nah.

"Oh, please. Is the universe delivering me object-lessons? The Improving Story of the Little Angry Mermaid?"

"This soft quiet one found bed to sleep upon," said Mee-rahn-nah, indicating the wallety mass on the pebbles. "This soft quiet one not the same afterward and knows it. Wants none of other soft quiet ones to suffer nor soft swimming ones to suffer. Take it. We leave you now."

"No, wait," said Rain, choking. "All right, we'll do what you ask. I mean, why not. I see we have to. But give us a name. We can't bury a soft quiet one all alone on—parchment ground—without saying its name before we fly away."

"You can," said Mee-rahn-nah. "When soft quiet one dies its name goes back to the ocean current."

"That's the bargain," said Rain. "The name, or we'll toss it back in the sea."

"You are beside yourself," said the Goose to Rain. "Get a grip, Sergeant."

"The name. It's the least you owe us for our work."

Mee-rahn-nah bobbed for a moment in the current. The eye was keen, adjudicating. Perhaps canny. What it came out with might have been compromise or fraud; Rain had no way of knowing. It did speak, though. "The name of Mercy."

"Gotcha there," hissed the Goose to Rain. "Come on. Let's do an errand for Mercy and let that be the capstone of our sojourn in Maracoor."

Mee-rahn-nah turned and swam from the promontory, followed by a fanning contingent of its kind. It did not call any gratitude over its shoulder nor even say goodbye, but eventually dipped below the water. The green steam dissipated over the water, and the merfolk were gone in a froth of ill-scented bubbles.

Rain and the Goose hauled the small body of Mercy high enough up the slope that no ocean tide, even a storm surge, could ever reach to wash this soft quiet one back out to sea. They found a cranny between two high boulders, and rolled the corpse off its winding sheets into the dark grave. Soil and stone went on top— more than they guessed they'd need. It took several hours. The pit was deeper than they'd reckoned. By the time they were done, the shroud had finished drying in the sun and the algae had begun to fleck away. Rain brushed the dusty residue off these final prodigal pages of the Grimmerie. She tucked them beside their companions in the reconstituted spine.

2

The next morning, under a sky so severe as to seem clinical, they didn't look behind them to watch the last shoulder of Maracoor subside into a brow, then a mere shadow in a glassy green waterworld. They had buried Mercy, or what was left of it. Headed home to Oz, if they could make it that far. If not, they would become the next soft quiet ones to seek their own place in the bed of the ocean soil.

3

The Goose and the green girl had made their landfall in Maracoor—what was it, three months ago now? four?—thanks to the perilous windstorm. Without that force of nature blowing them at speeds, they'd never have been able to make the unmeasurable journey on their own. They would have disappeared into the sea before sighting land.

Returning, now, west to east, they found themselves benefiting from natural trade winds. The travelers were scooped up by the zephyrs and bowled along with steady unflagging force as if on invisible rail lines in the clouds. Later, much later, Rain would wonder if having the reconstituted Grimmerie in her pouch was also a motivator of the air currents. Nothing in Maracoor wanted the Grimmerie anywhere near its shores.

She'd never be able to say how many days or nights they flew. There was something about the steadiness of the wind that allowed Rain to sleep—the wind maintained a regular force at her spine. After much practice she could relax against it as she might against the loving body of someone sitting behind her, holding her up reliably. The skies went white and sometimes blue and then black. The stars swam above and the sun glinted on waves below, and sometimes stars seemed below them and waves above. She scarcely glanced at the Goose. Certainly there was no talking, no waving or winking. They would fly until and unless they died.

PART THREE

NETHER HOW

1

Having wandered the western verges of Oz's Thousand Year Grasslands for some months or even a year, was it, before she'd stumbled upon the Nonestic Sea, Rain had lost all sense of native geography. The maps she'd examined as a child suggested that the country trailed off into unchartered desert regions both west and east. Only a little more was known of provinces and fiefdoms to the north—Ix, Fliaan, the Constabulary of Lake Port Anfílle. The marches of the Nome King. Uncertain coordinates. Unstable compass roses.

Mapmakers dismiss life found at the margins. Even if edge communities are the richest, adjacent ecosystems borrowing one from the other out of necessity and curiosity. But Oz was large enough to be self-centered; it looked up no one's skirts but its own. Oz's farther provinces were too far from the center—the Emerald City—for them to register as worthy of attention. Here there be dragons; there there be bees. Buzz off.

So, after numberless hours and days and nights of flying, when a smear of low-lying clouds emerged on the eastern horizon, hinting at a possible landmass below, Rain had no idea where in Oz, or out of it, they might be approaching.

She was able to rouse herself from her stupor. The Goose was ahead of her, from time to time giving his wings the merest flicker.

He'd mentioned before they launched that if he'd been flying in a flock, his ability to sleep while aloft would have been limited to brief naps seized a few seconds at a time—out of fear of collision. But as a soloist with a single companion, his system could relax a little more. Whether he slept with his whole brain or only parts of it at a time, he neither knew nor cared about. "Seems to me you're getting personal," he had snapped at her. "I'll be awake enough to know if you tilt sideways and drop either of those eggs out of your satchel, believe you me."

Now she watched him flicker to attention. Perhaps cloud-shapes on the inside of his eyelids had varied the light pattern enough for him to come around. He angled his head to make sure she was where she should be. Gave a jolly extra wobble of his scapular zones, like jiggling his epaulets. How high in the air were they, who knew. The sea the color of pencil lead, looking from this height like a slow moving landslide of lentils trying to swamp the earth. Little by way of whitecap or blue-green translucence. A trick of the placement of the sun.

Time to descend a little. Rain pulled up on the haft, slowing the forward rush through increased resistance, allowing her broom to drop softly.

The continent surged forward as the sea yielded. Came the marriage of sand and sea, the water shading to more vivid color, aqueous rust-brown with hints of turquoise. Ruffles of spindrift above the white fringe where sea encounters stone. The sun behind them, sinking faster, going fibrous melon in Rain's peripheral vision, throwing their shadows in advance of them. First upon bowling water, then upon beach threaded with grass and lousy with tidewrack. The travelers caught up to their shadows, and stood upon them at last, on a sandheap of no renown that, for lack of other landmark, had to stand in for home.

2

But they couldn't sleep on the sands; the wind blew too strongly. They'd be covered by dunes come morning. And now that they'd emerged from the somnolence of automatic flying, as they might have named it, hunger and thirst took possession of them.

"Look," said the Goose, lifting his beak as Rain might a forefinger. A tenebrous veil of low-lying smoke, inland. "A cooking fire, perhaps."

"Let's walk. My rear end is more grooved than nature intended."

"You walk if you like. I'm too hungry." Iskinaary was way past negotiations. He made a stumbling launch due to the unstable sands, but gained some height and began to circle away.

"I am *so* ready to say goodbye to you," called Rain, but she remounted her broom and followed him.

She'd walked sands like these. She'd trudged the grasslands with several native populations whose language she could not speak. Back before she left Oz, she hadn't even flown the broom until reaching the ocean and deciding on a quest to drown the Grimmerie for once and for all. Now, with the spellbinding pages dragging on the satchel strap across her shoulder blade, she gained a new sense of this desolate and affecting scrapland. The badlands of Oz. The wind sculpted bevels into the desert the way a fork leaves parallel trails through milled flour. The grasses all curtsied in the same direction. Scorpions so newly born as still to be translucent, scurrying.

A hump of outthrust clamshell rock provided a break in whose lee camped a clan of native humans. Six or seven tents, and several unfamiliar ungulates closer to the ground—like camels without the high neck. A scrappy dog or two. On strings hanging from stakes, bells shook and clanged. Perhaps to guide back anyone who had decamped to find a private place to relieve the pressure. Rain and the Goose came about, descending. With no discussion or gesture between them, the voyagers alighted at a distance comfortably out of reach of a javelin. But making no effort to conceal the fact that they arrived by air. They didn't have the wherewithal for a nuanced strategy.

They smelled pottage of onion and something arresting if dodgy—maybe seagull. Despite an instinct of revulsion they both felt, their hunger insisted on being slaked. Iskinaary quawked in an anonymous voice, and Rain called out, "Hail, and friendship." She dropped the broom and raised her hands, opened them to show that she carried no weapon. The clan, a family of ruddy skin and coarse, cornsilk hair, seemed apprehensive. The apparent chieftain drew a dirk from below the belt of her leggings.

"We have nothing to offer them as tribute," she said to the Goose. "Unless you want to surrender one of your eggs."

Iskinaary adjusted the pitch of his neck and spoke in a language Rain didn't know. The nomads weren't surprised at a talking Goose—yes, this was Oz all right, then, and not some distant desert island under the rule of Maracoor Abiding. The chieftain lowered her knife but didn't put it back in its scabbard. "What did you say to them," Rain demanded of the Goose.

"That they can kill you if they want to but I'm off-limits. I have offspring to hatch."

She didn't know if she believed him. "They'd like my old sea-shell, which is now the best-traveled seashell in the history of the sea?" She pulled it out and showed it to them. They had seen better and rolled their eyes.

"When you have nothing else to offer but company, that has to do," said Iskinaary. "Stop weaseling about with the notion of bar-ter. It's cheap. No, they don't want to see the Grimmerie. They're going to give us something to eat. Don't fuss with your satchel, you're making them nervous. You're making the eggs nervous."

"I'm making you nervous."

"Just for a change."

The chieftain spoke some more. Iskinaary answered at some length. At a pause, Rain murmured, "What are you on about?"

"She's an alarmist. Wants to know where we've come from. She says they met a green woman hereabouts some months ago, but they're uneasy about your flying. So I said you're not that girl. We're from Maracoor, and you're a witch. End of story."

"But I'm from Oz."

"Just now, you're from Maracoor. It's easier for them—a witch of Maracoor Abiding. That's a different variety of green woman in their minds. Not that they ever heard of Maracoor, but it isn't around here."

"Nice to feel welcomed."

"You *are* welcomed. Look." A little man, older and certainly smaller than the chieftain, was tottering forward with something wrapped in a woven cloth. How rewarding, thought Rain, that it was real goat-hair cloth and not more pages of the Grimmerie sneaking home. He lifted open the top panel and revealed four or five pieces of gluey sweet, scented with mint and rosewater and ornamented with ground pistachios. The Goose grunted. "Great. Now we have to eat that tripe."

They spent the evening devouring and regretting the foodstuffs that the clan offered, but when they slept at last, they might as well have been murdered in their beds, so black and dreamless the midnight hours.

After a breakfast of warm milk of the what-is-it, Rain and Iskinaary prepared to make their departure. They had little idea where in the great western deadlands of Oz they might be, and whether to proceed due east, or on a northerly or southerly slant. But their energy was revived. Restaurant fare or not, the tribe's menu had done the trick. As the clan began to roll up its carpets and break down its boxy tents, the chieftain squatted upon a small leather stool and lit a pipe with three stems and three bowls. She indicated to the Goose and the green girl that they should join her.

"I'm *not* going to take up smoking at this late moment in my life," said Iskinaary. "No thanks."

"Well, join us anyway; you may need to translate something."

Rain had her own misgivings about this tribe. Could it be true that these were the people with whom she had harbored a year ago when wandering disconsolate with the Grimmerie in her sack, trying to figure out what to do with it—how to avoid the tragedy of the disappearance of her Tip—how either to live or to perfect the art of dying. This clan seemed to take it on faith that, because she'd arrived from the air, she wasn't the same green woman they'd met a year ago. But she didn't recognize *them*. Had she been so beyond caring that she hadn't noticed the nuances of a family group, of a single face. Or—and this worried her more—had she not fully recovered from her amnesia, after all. Was she going to wander vaguely homeward and fail to see the signals of posterns in her personal life. She didn't want to say this aloud to the Goose. Nor to herself, in fact. But the itch of worry wormed under her scalp and wouldn't scrape itself out and crawl away.

She accepted the pipe and took in the faintest of drafts—enough to roast the top pocket of her lungs—before immediately exhaling it. She tried to put on an expression of comfort and pleasure, but the old woman took her own long drag and held it in for nigh onto a minute. Risking social offense, Rain passed up a second go at the mouthpiece.

Because the Goose and the girl had no sweet candies or astringent smokes to offer in return, Rain rooted around in her satchel and came up with the befurred carton of cards she'd stolen from the Oracle of Maracoor. The chieftain, whose name was something like Xzulda, lowered her eyelids suspiciously at these brightly colored items. She reached out her hand to review the whole pack. Rain made a gesture—not yet—and said to the Goose, "Tell her I'll read her future if she likes."

"This could go very wrong," said the Goose complacently. "On the other hand, we haven't had enough adventure yet today, and it's already past breakfast." He quawked the offer in those chopped-salad syllables used by the tribe. That Xzulda person made an indefinite gesture, partly a shrug and partly a pout of disdain. "That's a definite yes," said Iskinaary.

Rain shuffled the pack and laid out three cards. "Why don't you ever use four?" asked the Goose. "A four-legged stool is more stable than a three."

"Not if one of the legs is a different length than the others," said Rain. "Shut up and let me do my work." But suddenly she felt uncertain whether she should be turning the cards over at her own instinct or at Xzulda's. They were sitting equally distant from the row of three. "Ask her to point to one of the end cards so I know where to start."

When Xzulda had obliged—identifying the same card that Rain had yearned toward—it turned over to reveal a godly hand from a cloud, near which was suspended a hot-air balloon like the one the Oracle of Maracoor had bequeathed to the Bvasil. "I don't see this leading anywhere," said Rain. "What can Xzulda know or care about such an item?"

"It's a big blasted red-in-the-face metaphor, isn't it?" said

Iskinaary. "Isn't it saying 'Get me outta here' or something? Exit strategy? Any means necessary?"

Rain flicked over the card on the other end, hoping for some narrative line she could intuit, or pretend to. As she'd never examined the entire deck, the few times she'd tried to gamble with intuition revealed to her things she had never seen before. That, or this magic deck had the power to swap out old images for more useful ones as the situation required. Now, the second card she turned over was that great descending hand cradling, this time, an egg. Relative to the hot-air balloon this egg would be the height of a mature oak tree, but Rain took scale to be immaterial: it was the item that meant something on its own. Presumably.

Xzulda leaned over and rubbed her right eye with her gnarled root of a fist. She made to touch the rendering of the egg in its subtle, glowing colors, as if to see if it was hot, or at least edible, but Rain pulled the card back. Preserve the mystery even if she didn't know whether any mystery was worth preserving. Or was it a waste of time.

"Three's the charm," droned Iskinaary, like some sort of junior officer without enough work to do at his desk.

Rain hovered her hand over the central, unturned card. She wondered if, now that she was back on home soil, she might have a new instinct for arcane knowledge. She was ready to be startled by the world. That, perhaps, would be a sign of her having healed, at least a little—a capacity for surprise. But her hand picked up nothing.

"I'm a fraud," she said to the Goose. "Don't tell anyone." She turned over the final card, the one that was supposed to pull the other two images together into some sort of narrative. A proposal for the future, or at least a reading of the present in a novel and revelatory manner.

It was her turn now to lean forward and peer. The card was

blank—blank of everything, even of the hieratic palm from the clouds that brandished images of significance on all the other cards. She studied it to see if there was an image that had worn off, or faded into near oblivion, but she saw no evidence of ink ever having stained the cool white nothingness of that oblong. "Look, Iskinaary. The wicked pack of cards has a bout of amnesia, just like me."

"I don't pretend to care about any of this," said the Goose, "but: weird. Just weird."

Xzulda grunted, as if with understanding. Well, this is Xzulda's future, isn't it, thought Rain. Who cares if I can interpret it for her. That's hardly the point. Though it makes me redundant, and that's putting it as politely as I can.

Behind Xzulda, the wizened shaman or berdache leaned forward. He muttered and inched away to manage some business behind them. Rain made to sweep the cards back into the pack, but Xzulda lowered a vise grip upon her green wrist: *Wait*. The rank old coot came forward with something in his fingers. He set down upon the blank white card a piece of that gluey sweet—the green one, dried mint and pistachio perhaps—cut neatly in half. Two pieces on a white backboard.

Now Xzulda grunted with satisfaction and nodded. She growled something that Iskinaary leaned forward to pick up. "I think," said the Goose, "she is saying, In the absence of any other stance to take, try welcome—hospitality—what have you."

"This seems to be our fortune, not hers," complained Rain. "Flying, and with a pair of eggs, and an unknown future ahead?"

"Filled with sweetness. Half portions. Or double portions," said the Goose. "How am I doing as a Goose Witch? Do I have the goods? I think we're supposed to eat this."

"I don't like sweets in the morning. Or at all, really."

"Refuse their gesture and provoke their ire just as we're about to leave. Sure. Why not."

She forced down her half of the delicacy. Xzulda and her companion smiled broadly for the first time. "You know," said Rain, "I think maybe I sorted the cards but it was Xzulda who read them."

"Now you're getting someplace," said Iskinaary. "The first rule of witchery is to acknowledge your deficits."

"How would you know?"

"That's the first rule of everything, really."

3

The clan could offer little in the way of navigational advice, but they gave blessings and small presents to the Goose and the green girl. Rain intended to lose them in the sands as soon as they were safely out of sight. Twisted bits of creature carved from driftwood, totems of some sort. Rain bowed from the waist like a hinged doll, stiffly, and they beat as dignified a departure as they could, given how much sand the Goose disturbed in achieving liftoff.

It was a decent day for flying. Thanks to the sun, easy enough to orient themselves. Oz was a great oblong sheet of a nation. Rain pictured it like a poorly rolled-out crust for a pastry. Heaps of mountains—higher in the west, the Vinkus; lower ranges in the south and east. The country's edges, tattered and fringy, its borders mostly badlands petering out through lack of attention.

After spending a night in a cave, which come morning turned out to have been the home of a sand bear who had been out carousing all night, and wasn't happy to find unannounced company awaiting her at home, they made another good day of it. The weather held. At the height they could fly, with the gift of wind, they could bear the heat of desert and pampas. The sun was punishing, though. Rain realized that her skin had begun peeling from exposure. Her face ached down to the level of fiber and matting. "We're going to need a day of rest in some shaded location," she told the Goose when they'd made a descent for relief of the kidneys. "I don't want to finish this quest by burning to a crisp just as I'm about to run into someone I knew in my previous life."

"We're in luck," said the Goose. "Just before we came down, I saw a horse-beaten road a bit to the north. Must lead to a settlement of some sort. You do need a rest. You look like an overcooked sausage."

"Nice."

"An overcooked green sausage, at that. You want to try rubbing your face with blue pollen from your bizarre bouquet. Could serve as a kind of applied shadow, and screen the sun on your grimace."

Rain did just that. "Tones down the green, too," said Iskinaary. "Not that traveling with a flying heap of lettuce has ever bothered me."

They launched once more and Iskinaary followed his beak, veering a bit northeast. A low smudge of mist suggested a change in the climate—more available water, which meant more arable land, habitable environs. Sure enough, they glimpsed something approximating a real road, and they followed it in a northerly direction. The afternoon moon rose upon a wind-worn farmstead or a small village of sorts, a cluster of higglety-patchwork sheds with sloping single-angle rooflines, no spires or monuments of self-regard. "Just because Oz is home we shouldn't expect hospitality," said the Goose as they came about to land.

"*Especially* because it's home," replied Rain. "But let's hope."

"One of the gifts Xzulda left us was a parcel of those treats. We could share."

"Do let's share, generously. I hate that stuff."

To try a different strategy this time, the Goose and the blue-smudged girl came to ground some short distance from the establishment, intending to approach by foot and raise as little expectation of sorcery as possible.

The old place was certainly downbeat. Eaves in poor repair, shutters banging. But with an air of life, and a smell of life—in fact, a farm smell. Sheep. They could be heard, now, making comment from the largest building, apparently a barn. The voices were animal, at least so far as Iskinaary and Rain could make out. The person coming around the barn door with an armload of moldering hay was a child in a rough-weave tunic. A boy, about ten, perhaps.

"Hail, hello there," cried Rain. The boy dropped his hay and stared but didn't run. Then he answered. At first Rain thought it was another unknown tongue, but her ear untwisted the sounds. She'd become accustomed to how the people from Maracoor had accented their strain of the nearly common language. This boy's cautious greeting was more normal to her ear, and felt like balm once she recognized it.

"What the shit are you doing here?" he said, or something like that.

"Travelers passing by. Lost our way, gone off course," said Rain. She motioned to Iskinaary to keep mum, saving the revelation of his Animal nature for an emergency if needed, but he also was pleased to hear the tones of his homeland, and cried out his own hello.

The boy let them approach him. "You need help with that lot?" asked Rain. "It's a great haul for someone your size to manage."

"I manage," he said, proudly and sullenly. "I suppose you'll want some of our food."

"I suppose so," said Rain, "if there is any to spare." They'd reached the kid and she helped him pick up the fodder. "Dinner for your herd?" He nodded.

There were fifty or sixty head of sheep and half as many lambs penned into a space too small for them. In the gloom, some other children were hauling buckets of water to troughs and a couple more were mucking out the revolting mess of manure and hay that congealed upon the earthen floor. "Company," called the boy who had seen them. His name, he said, was Aubiano.

The children kept at their chores though their pace slowed. They stared with unsmiling but keen faces. "I suppose we should meet your people," said Rain.

"We are our people," he replied.

"I mean your parents."

Aubiano shrugged at that. "We're our own parents by now."

"But who's in charge?"

"Help me in with the last of this hay and we'll find some grub for you."

She did as she was told. Iskinaary was no help at hauling hay. He trained a keen eye on the flock and spoke to them in a pulpit voice, hoping to raise an intelligible response. The bleats that came back at him were cheery enough but not exactly informative.

When the flock's supper was portioned out, Aubiano clapped his hands of dust and doused them in the sheep's drinking sink. He gestured Rain to do the same. She noticed his eyes trained on her movements. He was wondering if she was leery of water. Smart kid. He must know that old folk story about green witches and water. If it was a folk story—it didn't apply to her. She washed her hands vigorously and dried them on what was left of her apron, which had become beribboned with stress rips during the ocean flight. Then she washed the blue off her face.

In a kitchen, a few children were boiling potatoes in a cauldron. Others were scraping the papery husks off onions and the dirt from root vegetables. They all fell silent when Aubiano entered. It was hard for Rain to tell if the boy was in charge or if he took seniority at the moment because he'd been the one to see them first.

"We have company," he said. So grave, so reserved for his age, he might as well have had a small pipe and a tankard of ale.

"Why she so green?" asked a girl of about four. "More too much green." She was roundly shushed and began to cry gluey tears, and went immediately to Rain to be picked up.

They ate in silence and in haste. Night was falling and it was clear this was a household that ran by the sun. When Rain had brought out the sweets that Xzulda and her tribespeople had supplied, the mood lifted a little. A taller, officious girl lit an oil lamp carefully and set it in a wall niche behind an iron gate that kept it from being knocked over.

While Rain patted the soft dirty hair of the tiny one who had fallen asleep in her lap, Aubiano answered Iskinaary's questions. The children were members of a group of families whose parents had, almost to the one, set out some months ago to try and put an end to a rogue rock griffon preying upon their sheep. Two mothers had been left behind to tend the flock and the children until the others returned, but one mother had fallen gravely ill and the second mother had tumbled into a beseeching fire she'd built up to summon help. Both women were dead within a few weeks, and the other adults had never returned. This was a year ago, or some.

"But someone knows you're here, someone will come to find you?" asked Rain. "The village you started out from, the cousins and friends of your parents?"

"We're a separate sect," said Aubiano, sadly and perhaps proudly. "Our families wanted to live apart from the sin and bad living they used to see, in the back-of-times. So no one knows we are here or cares if we are alive except our other parents. Wherever they are. Is there another square of that sweet goop?"

"Are we the first visitors to come along since all this happened?"

"First and last, who knows. We're still here, though. The ewes keep having lambs. We separate the rams most of the year. We've

lost half the flock so far, but they know how to replace themselves."
Only now did Rain notice that the material on every surface, including on most of the children, was wool.

"Why would you trust us?" asked Rain. "If you're wary of human
danger."

Aubiano shrugged and pointed at Iskinaary. "Animals don't
scheme the way people do."

"If you only knew," said the Goose, primping. Then he turned
to Rain. "Why don't you sing to them?"

"Why don't you." But she knew what he was getting at. She
rooted about in her satchel and pulled out the pack of illustrated
cards. Something to amuse them, a gift of some sort, in their hard
lives. She shuffled it and put the stack on the table and turned over
the top card. The image showed the usual hand of fate slipping
out through coils of storm cloud. This time in its palm sat a box
lined in fur with the pack of fortune-telling cards. "Okay, that's as
far as I can go," she said. She let the kids look through the cards at
random, smudge them, giggle, puzzle, share them as they might
the pages from a picture book. She followed Aubiano to a room
up a few steps and put herself down on a cold mat. She drew over
herself a cold blanket. She thought she'd be sleepless but she fell
into a velvety void at once.

SHE AWOKE TO THE SOUNDS of children being children, for
all that. Teasing each other in their bedclothes, stumping to some
sort of common bucket in the back hall, thumping down steps and
clattering a pot in the kitchen. Standing on tiptoe, Rain looked out
the window and saw several small boys and Iskinaary leading the
flock out into some kind of a paddock. Whatever was going wrong,
these farm kids had been workers before their adults disappeared.
They were getting on with it.

She grabbed a hank of bread and grimaced at the sourness of it but stepped out the kitchen doorsill to sample the morning air. The clouds that had pulled and twisted across the landscape as she and the Goose arrived last night were this morning cleared away, at least for now. Across the road lifted the palest of translucent screens that she took at first to be further weather, and then realized with a sense of both dread and relief were, most likely, the west-facing front of the Great Kells. Oz's largest mountain range, running north and south. On the other side of the Kells stood her father's homestead, from which she'd set out more than a year ago. If it was still there. If he was still there.

She was eager to get going. "There's nothing we can do for these children," she said to the Goose. "We can't stuff them in my satchel and rescue them all. They're self-sufficient. We can let some authority know that they need help. Perhaps their parents have been abducted, or even slain by that griffon creature. But others of their tribe should take care of them."

Iskinaary turned the beadiest eye upon Rain with which he had ever favored her. After a long winter of silence, he said, "Well, I'll leave it to you to arrange all that. While I stay here with them till someone arrives to organize a better rescue than I can."

"You can't be serious. What can you do for them?"

"Well," he said, "frankly I can be as good a sheepdog as a sheepdog. I mean of these sheep anyway, who aren't the brightest. And I can be a sheepdog to these orphans. I can offer a little parental wisdom even if I am of a different order of creature. I can tell stories at night. You could do all of that too, but I know you have a mission to complete. So let me merely ask that when you see Liir, tell him that I did what I was bade. I found you and I followed you, and the flying monkeys and I more or less rescued you. And I brought you home, for as long as you needed me. You're proving yourself quite capable of continuing on alone."

"You bet I am," she snapped. "And anyway, I rescued myself."

"That's what we all say about ourselves," he replied. "And, to give you credit, in a way it's true. We can't rescue one another. We can only stand by while others do their best for themselves. Anyway, leave the border crane eggs with me. It'll lighten your load as you press on. Give you one less thing to worry about."

"What do you want those eggs for?"

"Better sociability than I ever had from you. If the eggs hatch, they might begin to lay eggs themselves. A nice variety of diet for this cohort of underfed farmerlings. At any rate, *you're* not going to sit on them. You've made that very clear in so many ways. Let the eggs rescue themselves."

She could hardly look at him, and barely stopped herself from rolling the eggs out on the ground so hard that they shattered prematurely. It couldn't be long now in any case. She offered the Goose the old seashell, too. It had done its job. "A souvenir of our happy days at the shore. Put it on a shelf somewhere."

"I don't want it," said the Goose. "Rather have the magic gossip cards. The kiddos can make stories out of them."

She reserved for herself the top three cards, which were probably the last ones she'd turned over, so no surprises there. She threw the rest of the pack at the Goose. The rage and loss, the holding back worse. "Let these children tell their own futures. They don't need guidance. They're doing better than I ever did." She mounted on her broom and left without thanking Aubiano and his siblings and cousins for their hospitality. The Great Kells loomed, a henge; a challenge; her own sorry future; icy resistance.

GEESE AREN'T PRONE to prevarication, and the Goose was nothing if not honest. After Rain left, he conceded that he missed her. But what a selfish maenad. Green as turnip shoots, sure of herself as salt. And a royal pain in the nether feathers. He hoped he'd live to see her again if only to give her what-for. Abandoning these kids. And after she'd been such a decent custodian to that wretched Cossy! Though he supposed Rain had felt responsible for Cossy's misadventures, whereas here she'd walked in on this forsaken lot, so found it easy enough to walk out again. Cool, detached from feeling. A right witch, if truth be told.

Not deeply reflective by nature, in his new loneliness Iskinaary found the time to consider that rather human designation: the witch's familiar. Was he one, or was the notion a joke? He wasn't sure that the job description had ever suited him. He was a companion more than an aide. A chaperone, a ringside pundit, a sideways opinion delivered on the slant, either to correct the trajectory of a campaign or to confirm it. He'd been that to Rain, for sure. How would she get on without him? Was that all there was to being a familiar? That, and sheer stubborn adherence?

If so, he'd been a familiar to her father before Rain, too, for Iskinaary had flown with Liir in the Great Conference of the Birds, during the first stirrings of rebellion against the then Throne Minister, Liir's uncle Shell. How well Iskinaary remembered the chorus of birdcall coursing around the Emerald City: "Elphaba lives! Elphaba lives!" Of course, probably nothing could be heard intelligibly at ground level, just a lot of avian ruckus. But the birds having stirred themselves into unity, the moment had been noted and remembered. In the harshest of times, unfriendly populations can sometimes unite despite their instincts to clan it up. Iskinaary had loved Liir back then, more than he'd ever come to love Rain. But Liir had seasoned into a wise and cautious fellow, a hermit before his time. Once he'd learned to keep his own counsel, Iskinaary had preferred to tag along after Rain as she figured out the ways of this wicked world.

Aubiano caught the Goose staring at the eastern sky. "You miss her," he said.

"I do not. Who? What affair is it of yours? She means nothing to me," said Iskinaary. "Look, it's none of my business, but I am afraid a few of your cousins have gnits. Shall I get to work eating them out of their scalps, do you think? It would be my pleasure."

"I'm just a kid," said Aubiano. "You're supposed to be with her, I think. I don't deserve a familiar, and I don't need one."

"You certainly don't," said the Goose in as polite a voice as he could muster. "You could do with a barber, though, and a hygienist. And an adult opinion to wreck your complacency."

"I don't know what *complacency* means," said the boy. "You mind your eggs, and I'll mind mine."

"We'll mind all of them together, how about that," said the Goose. "And while we're at it, let's think about how to get the rats out of the hay barn."

"There's nothing wrong with rats."

"Except that they eat eggs, and, remember, we're helping each other out here."

"All right." Aubiano walked off, whistling. Was Iskinaary fooling himself to think that the boy looked just a tad more relaxed at the notion of a seasoned parent on staff, even if it was a Goose? If only Rain had been more of a team player. But that's a witch for you, going her own way come hell or high water. Or both.

4

It was the first time she'd been truly alone since, after leaving her father's hermitage near Nether How, Iskinaary had caught up with her. Just before she'd stumbled upon the Nonestic Sea. During the months of this failed campaign—for here she was returning with the reconstituted Grimmerie, after all—the Goose had stuck by her side. Stubborn, argumentative, disapproving, but loyal. His abandonment of her now, at the end of her quest, might be a credit to his superior moral sense—but she hated him for it.

She tried to ignore her angry conclusions and couldn't; tried to solve for x, if x was her unknowable self, and failed. The higher math of ethical justification exceeded her grasp. He was an Animal and she, she was—well, even to call herself an animal was, perhaps, an insult to blameless creatures of the wild. She was a mere human. She thought, Why isn't there an uppercase Human to distinguish from a human. Maybe we just haven't gotten there yet. Maybe we can't.

Because the wind was going that way, she headed north-northeast. She'd crossed these mountains on foot a year earlier; presumably she'd make better time now. Her eyes teared up as she saw the rumpled brown burlap of sullen land begin to support cliff oak. Mountain thorn tortured into ghoul shape by relentless wind. Then the smack of aroma, the pines that made their home by the billions up and down the thousand-mile brace of ice-topped mountains. It was a jolt of childhood this high in the atmosphere.

Attempting to fly over the high peaks on her own would be courting suicide. She couldn't guess how the mighty winds met and battered each other at such points. She'd have to cross through hanging valleys, searching out portage on foot until it seemed safe to launch again. Without the Goose to give her the benefit of his long life of navigation, she was, she saw, inept at this.

But the slopes of the Great Kells gave more succor than the swells of the sea or the scrub growth of the Thousand Year Grasslands. There would be forage. Canyons, caves, even the odd hunter's lean-to in which to seek shelter. This much she did remember from her outgoing trip. Wild blueberries on exposed escarpments; fresh water in mountain rills. Fish if she could manage it; the edible vine, the beaded purse of mountain grape. Nuts, maybe. Depending. Yes, and here was a trapper's lodge, ready to borrow for the night.

She returned with supplies to make an almost decent meal for herself, gobbled it down in ten minutes while the sky stayed stubbornly daylight. Not having Iskinaary with whom to kick things around was proving a trial. She found herself fingering the cover of the Grimmerie—out of boredom if nothing else.

What she would do with it now that it had homed to her— she hadn't gotten there yet. But she turned some pages. They all seemed to have restitched themselves somehow—nothing loose fluttered out. For the lack of evidence of the soaking it had taken, she might never have drowned it. I wonder what it wants, she thought. Could a book want anything. Only to be read, maybe. What book prefers to go uninspected.

The drawings. Some were diagrams in a pale purple ink, marked out with cryptic notations. (*A. B. inv-machis. No. 4. No. 6. X. Y.* Arrows pointing to the right hand of the page. *Presto, anti-presto.*

Nul. Anti-nul. Nos. 9–13 inclusive.) Others were more representative. Cartouches in full color showing scenes from some arcane history or practice. Humans, she guessed. Here a unicorn, looking disaffected and a little wormy; there a demon with his face in his belly and what appeared to be a crown of male members sprouting out of his neck where his head should be. Also several pages of something like musical notation. *Sforzando,* what did that mean.

She ran her hands over the pages to feel the lift and settle of ink and paint upon vellum. It made a pretty pattern upon her fingertips but it didn't sing to her.

Most of the words seemed not to want to be identified, like mid-level government apparatchiks seeking anonymity during a raid on a brothel. Her eyes could nearly make out any number of headings, but they went misty on her. Perhaps, she thought wryly, this wasn't the book's fault. She was remembering how Lady Glinda Chuffrey had opened this book and asked Rain to read it for her, back when Rain hadn't yet had her first adolescent pimple. Oh, amnesia was so damned selective, allowing her to remember things that would sting and, perhaps, to forget memories that might console.

But it came to her that she had once read a charm—*To Call Winter upon Water,* that was it! She turned a few leaves over and, as if in apology, a yellow-green page ornamented with vine leaves in the margins contorted its oblong shape in a kind of curtsey to her. Its tricksy display caption unscrambled itself into legibility. *To Hear the Sound of Past and Future,* announced the heading, a little portentously, thought Rain. What good is that? Amnesia has confounded some of my past, and I've already given up on reading the future. Knowing what's going on at the moment would be more than enough.

Still, if this was what the Grimmerie was electing to reveal, she decided to look closer. Perhaps it would come in handy. The ivy scrim pulled back like curtains of a puppet theater. There was no written instruction for Rain to decode, only a picture of someone quite like herself—a younger self—with a seashell to her ear, and a look of concentration upon a face still annealed with innocence.

She turned the cover so softly she didn't hear it pat itself closed. Till the dark fell, she sat staring at the horizon, which had so much to say, but nothing in a language she could read.

IN THE MORNING, she reconsidered. *To Hear the Sound of Past and Future* required, she supposed, to stay alive in the present.

She felt she could remember being more stone sober and iron-willed, back in the months that followed the evaporation of solid Tip into the ethereal and costive Ozma. Rain could have led armies that year, had she found a lost contingent begging for a sergeant. Now she was a vagabond on the run. Returning to her father with little wisdom, without even the benefit of having achieved what she set out to do—to run out of town that great book that had tempted so many toward menace. Starting with the original Wizard of Oz, now posing as an Oracle of Maracoor—hardly a job promotion—and continuing on, as far as she knew, with her own grandmother, Elphaba Thropp.

But what other direction did she have. Precious little. She had to move to keep from paralysis. And perhaps the home to which she would return was not, somehow, the same place it had been when she set out. How could it be. After all.

Who can know anything about anything.

THE DEEPER INTO the Great Kells she went, the closer to more populated regions upon the eastern descending slopes. The more often she could find some haven for rest. One night it was only a dusty sleeve of space beneath an overhanging berm of rock, the next evening a trapper's winter hut.

Little by little she was back in the world of seasonal change. Suddenly it was early autumn. Advance notes of goldenrod meadow by day and shooting star midnights. Coquettish blushes of red in the brow of the maple, yellow on the thrust hip of oak. Give over, who needs you to call attention to yourself, I'm already watching, she thought, but she was nonetheless grateful. Maracoor Abiding, she realized now, lived in a different clime. Though she'd been abroad a fairly short time, the buildings had shown little sign of needing to be readied for deep winter. Maybe from time to time snow fell on lemon trees there. But not much snow, and not often.

The afternoon arrived that she recognized something at last. It wasn't a landmark mountaintop, which she'd been waiting to see. Mountains looked different approaching from the other direction, anyway, and she kept her green chin facing forward. Toward the future (toward the past). No, what she recognized was a certain chummy scent, a recipe of sudden rain on local rock and balsam needles underfoot. The petrichor of nostalgia. As the sun cleared the tops of the peaks behind her, the shadows clicked upon the ground with a nearly audible certainty. She'd come upon home ground within the day, wouldn't she.

Next morning, she woke to a mist that had stolen across a reed-edged pond. It claimed the horizon and even sealed the location of the sun, so in order not to lose ground—or air—Rain decided to wait until it lifted. She took the Grimmerie out of her satchel, and her hands played with its cover as if she were tempted to read it, out of boredom if nothing else. She didn't lift the cover. She began to be sorry she'd thrown out most of the Oracle's soothsaying cards. She might have found a way to play solitaire of some sort. Not much game to be had with three spare cards, one of them blank.

When the day warmed up enough for the mist to rise, she packed up again and set out across the water. She'd launched over the Nonestic Sea to find Maracoor, and now, what a joke—in coming back, and crossing a domestic scoop of water the width of a palsyball pitch, she went from being lost to recognizing where she was. On the far side of the narrow channel, as she cleared a bank of larches and thornbrittle, she rose high enough to see how the land lay ahead of her. She thought she was mistaking the furled knob of mountain to the northeast as Knobblehead Pike, but it was no mistake. She'd cleared the Great Kells by broom, just about. She knew more or less where she was.

5

The rhythms of domesticity pleased Liir. Every morning, clear away the three tin breakfast plates and soak two of them in the stone sink. Hang up the three mugs on their hooks. Trim the wick of the lamp used the night before; sweep the flagstones, turn out the bedding to air if the day isn't too damp or cold. The parchment, the ink, the fighting his own resistance to putting thought into words; his work could wait until householderie was finished. Last night's pages to number and stack; the dregs in last night's wine goblet to finish off before rinsing it. Flowers to freshen sometimes if he was feeling in a silly mood, as if the world need be any more ornamented than light and nature had already arranged. All the while, reflecting on the evening before, to see if he'd said or done anything to regret, to make amends for.

From where this mid-life caution had come, he didn't quite know and the question wasn't worth pursuing. He lived with himself and his own crabbed ways, up the dawn and down the dusk, to the garden and back, with his lovers and without. Silent as this backwoods cottage at Nether How would allow. He was precisely middle-aged now, he guessed—forty springtimes gone. Soon enough he'd begin to count how many autumns left, one by one. Hardly a grey hair at his temple—he was no sage yet, and probably never would be so. He had, perhaps, learned one thing in his halfway life, though—given luck, at only a halfway point—which is that he wasn't destined ever to gain a comprehensive understanding of anything. No epiphany awaited out there on tomorrow's horizon to set him straight. He'd learned instead to make do with instinct, blindness, with suffering, and then with setting aside regret or curiosity, setting aside ambition. To inch quietly without disturbing much in the world—perhaps not a noble calling, but a sound one. He hoped.

Headed to the garden to see what could be gleaned for lunch and supper. His basket on his arm, a set of shears. Took his cape because the vagabond wind could come off the brow of the ridge at a moment's notice, drop the day from sunburn to near frost in twenty minutes. He could hear the dwarf dragon in his stall, snuffing up the chestnuts, apples, and sheaves of highslope hay tossed his way. Could hear the jaunty farmer whistle, nearly a gigue. The melody would be calming to young Druwigardius, and helped him control his bouts of involuntary arson. (Too long a name for too short a dragon, Druwigardius; Liir preferred simply Gardius, because that's more or less what he was there to do.)

The garden had enjoyed a good season. The cucumbers were sharp and a little sour, if small this year; the staked tomatoes fairly rolled off their redolent stalks into his hands. The gooseberries ample enough for birds and humans alike, the stemfruit a little deliquescent, but it stewed up just fine. And the onions! Going mad. There'd be onion soup, onion tart, onion oatmeal, onion cheesecake by the look of it. All winter long. Only the melons had failed to thrive this year. Always something new taking its turn to be difficult.

Fall was on its way, or perhaps it had arrived. A flock of geese overhead, quawking their redundant directions to one another as they left the northern Kells and headed south—to Ev, maybe to Quadling Country, or someplace else he didn't know about. In itself, the sound of migrating geese didn't bring up nostalgia for the passing of summer—if geese were keeping to their schedule, the world was functioning as it ought. But the way they drowned out the whistled tune issuing from the small stone barn gave Liir a moment of apprehension. He finished harvesting what was needed for the day and turned back.

Out of the silence of whistle and the noise of geese, another instrument. That voice from his dreams and nightmares. It made him drop the basket. He fell to his knees beside it, pretending to the universe he only wanted to reclaim spilled produce. But really it was that his limbs had gone to water.

She appeared in a stand of birches and browning ferns. Thirty feet up the path. She had called him from that far so as not to startle him, but she had startled him just fine. She'd said "Papa," a word she'd so rarely used that at first he took her for a vengeful spirit playing menace against him. But that was because he couldn't see her in the green shadows. She came forward, realizing herself in the light on the path. "Liir." Her more usual term of address, to steady him. "Get a grip. It's just me."

And that's all it was, just her, just his daughter and only child, back from wherever she'd gone more than a year ago. He allowed her to pull him to a standing position. Decent tomatoes that the summer had spent weeks growing were crushed underfoot as they took each other in their arms.

When they could speak, he brought her into the house. Much the same as when she'd left, though—quick as ever, he noticed— she said, "Three cups in the sink?"

"I set for three most mornings," he said to her, and before he could clarify, the door opened and some guy was there, darkening the rectangle with his blond fullness, surprise and apprehension at seeing her. "This is Trism," said Liir.

"Oh, is it," said his daughter. Wary, taking a step back.

"You don't need to tell me who you are," said Trism. He glanced at Liir. "So now this seems the perfect morning to rebuild the broken sheepfold gate? Yes." He walked up to Liir and put his arm on Liir's shoulder and spoke to Rain. "I always believed this day would come, maybe more than your father did." The taking of liberty dried the still dewy sheen in Liir's eyes. He shook off Trism's arm. Trism clopped away, whistling again, a jauntier melody. A triumphal march of sorts.

"Three place settings?" said Rain. Liir could tell she was trying to keep her face from setting like plaster. "The third one for my mother, after all this time?"

"The third one is for you. I've kept your chair for you, your plate and your pillow and your spoon and your coverlet, since that spring day when you left. A year and a half ago, was it? More or less. Every day."

She looked about the room, he thought, as if remembering it from her cold and dangerous childhood, remembering it from when she'd dug up the Grimmerie and harvested a broom from the broom tree and stolen away in the middle of the night. She'd be noticing some differences. The two end walls, formerly of rough-hewn log construction, replaced with solider stone. The ornamentations added—a carved mantel, and rose blossoms in beet-juice that Trism had block-stamped across the lintels. The ladder to the loft where Rain had slept was pinned to the wall now, but could be put back in place in a moment. The bed Liir shared with Trism was a tumult of sheets. He went to pull them straight and flop a blanket upon them. "I can send Trism away if it's easier. For the day, the night, for a week. We're almost in need of a trek to the post for provisions. He won't mind."

"Don't do anything on my account," she said. "I'm not staying."

"Nonsense." Fussing. Building up the fire and throwing tea leaves in a pot.

Rain leaned down and looked out one of the low windows toward the lower lake. "You've put a table and two chairs out there. An intimate setting."

"Room for one more if it's needed. We can take our tea there."

They left the cottage and took the path down the egg-shaped dome of Nether How, through the spindly trees and across grass that the sheep kept cropped like the lawn of a cloistered college in Shiz. Liir preferred Fifth Lake on the other side of Nether How—a long expanse with a duller sheen that took its color from granite bluffs at the far end—but Fourth Lake had a more domestic aspect, what with its fringe of willows, its low waterfalls emptying with endless plather. Two twisted-root chairs of comfortable proportion, a table. Rain seemed, frankly, disgusted at the effort at ambiance. She shook her superior head. Liir caught that and said, "I'm afraid we let the violinist have the week off since we didn't know you were coming."

She didn't want any part of this private outpost of conviviality, but Liir sat and patted the seat of the chair opposite him anyway. She came to lean on the chair's back, looking down at him like judgment itself. Umbrage in a skirt and apron. "I can see your grandmother in you more than I once did," he said in an even tone, not quite knowing himself if he meant it as a compliment. "Are you going to tell me anything about where you went? I know you snatched the Grimmerie and by the look on your face I'm guessing you brought it back. We have milk for the tea here if you take it."

"You don't seem so surprised to see me."

"It would be a greater surprise if you'd come back as a ghost." He grinned. She'd become more formal, a little less supple. But perhaps she was in some kind of shock. "I don't know where you went or if Iskinaary ever found you. When a year had passed I made the trek to Kiamo Ko and engaged some winged monkeys to follow the trail before it went cold."

"It's hard for a person to disappear into her own life, isn't it." She nearly smiled; that was an improvement. "You've almost managed, but you're a one-off. Yeah, they found me, the Goose and the monkeys. They all went farther afield than any of us expected."

He waited, hoping she would read his patience the right way. He didn't want to push her. The tea was strong, and a few loons warbled from one of the hidden coves.

"Oh, Iskinaary," she said, stretching out her legs in the chair and flexing her ankles, then massaging her calves. "He made it overseas and he made it back again. He remained behind at a farmstead full of abandoned children somewhere west of here, on the other side of the mountains. The Thousand Year Grasslands. If he can see the orphans to some situation of safety, he'll be back. I think. The monkeys, though, they stayed put where they'd landed."

"Overseas?" he said. A word that came from storytelling, like starry fields of heaven or the garden at the back of the moon.

"I don't have any standing to disapprove of Trism," she said. "Truth is, I slept with a married man. Those village rules of chapel, they can't always apply. Not that I'm proud of it, though."

"Overseas is the more curious word in this fond hello. What do you mean?"

So she told him the story of a wild ride, of an ocean beyond imagining, and an unknown nation beyond that. He had to wonder, to use a phrase he had come across in the army barracks when he was younger than she was now, if she had fired her brains out of her ass instead of the cannon as instructed. A whole second impossible world on the other side of a first impossible sea? And—he had to ask, "For what?"

"For what what?"

"Supposing a sea like that—why would you risk your life launching a flight across it?"

"*Supposing* a sea? Do you suppose I am only supposing?"

"Supposing is only a strategy of thinking that rules nothing out," he said. "It's not questioning your credentials. I merely don't get it. I know you were unhappy when you left in the middle of the night. With the Grimmerie—of course I saw you'd dug it up. You refilled the hole and even replaced the sod but the seams showed. You've brought it back home, I'll wager. Did that book tell you such a place existed? Is that why you risked your life to get there?"

"Not in so many words," she said at last, as if musing over the possibilities. She was going to say no more, or not yet.

"And Iskinaary at your side?"

"With a rolled-up umbrella in his beak, though he must have dropped it fairly early on."

"And you say you washed ashore on an island, and some child was accused of murder. And with the help of the flying monkeys you escaped from prison, and slipped out of town under disguise as one of those maunts—?"

She corrected him. No, as a pregnant wife. Yes, with the supreme figurehead of the nation who was in disguise, too. And yes, there were harpies and a dirt giant, and people made of living bark, and an Oracle who pretended to tell the future . . . And wait till you hear who *that* turned out to be.

"I think," said Liir, "you need a very long rest, my dear dear child. I can't keep this all in my head. You are home, you're home; we will pull a bottle of sparkling yellowgrape from where we keep it in an iron bucket in the lake, to be cold at a moment's notice. I only wish Iskinaary were here to—"

After a moment she completed his sentence for him. "—to corroborate your story."

"Listen to us," he said. "All the adventure in the world can't account for the magic that you are back home. That's all that matters. I had nightmares that you had died, waking Trism, who would hold me and say 'Aren't we lucky that dreams don't mean anything?'" Liir sipped his tea and watched the stone stiffness of her face. "I don't think you can be all that surprised about Trism or, really, in any serious way, alarmed? Or what is it—offended? Hurt?"

"Well, *he's* not my mother, that's for sure. But she'd left a year before I did."

"I'd not have taken you for such a stickler over an issue of propriety like this."

"It's not that he's male. But didn't Trism help train the dragons that attacked the Emerald City?"

"Yes. Which ended the war. And removed from the throne my despotic uncle Shell. An unsavory business, that's not in doubt. Trism has his own nightmares to wake up from, and at those times it's my turn to try to comfort *him*."

"He waited until I left the premises to show up. A bit of a sneak?"

"Mere coincidence. He didn't know where I'd gone except somewhere in the eastern Great Kells. It took him some time to find me. Rain—he's my man. Or I'm his. I guess both."

"So my mother doesn't come by anymore."

He raised an eyebrow. "What makes you conclude that? No, she doesn't, not often. But it isn't because of Trism, or not largely. She and I had our differences over the ways in which we tried to raise you and keep you safe. Putting you in a disguise to conceal your green skin. Lodging you as a young child in Lady Glinda's household, where we thought it unlikely anyone would look for you. Then sending you to boarding school at St. Prowd's. In the end, Candle came to think that we'd stolen your childhood not only from you, but also from ourselves. And she might be right, you know. But she couldn't forgive me for my part in it. As I think she couldn't forgive herself. We make do, you know—we try. We wince in regret. Trism goes off to the market crossing for a couple of days when she visits. I'm sure he'll be willing to do that today if it would make you comfortable, as you recover from your—ordeals."

"The market is two weeks by foot, what are you talking about?"

"Ah, there's a new little settlement downslope from Second Lake. I suppose in another couple of years it'll become a village. Right now it's a mill with a counter over which one can buy flour, other staples. And deposit letters for collection when the next carriage happens by. A kind of hotel or inn, and even a stableyard. We're not as alone here as we once were, I fear."

He could see her face trying to contort toward normalcy. He guessed it wasn't the maleness of Trism that was the problem, but that, in Rain's absence, Liir had recovered some portion of affection and love for life itself that, so far, had been denied her. Perhaps her affair with some married man—assuming an improbable overseas lover!—had supplied her with too little satisfaction, and she was more unmoored than when she'd set out.

He put his teacup on the table. The loons were looping the far woods with their freaky ululations. "Don't be a stranger," he said gently.

Rain got up and walked to him and put her old reliable satchel with its dangerous cargo down on the ground next to his chair. Then she sat upon his lap and put her arms around his neck. Now that they didn't need to look each other in the eyes anymore, he found that his collar ran with her tears.

6

She'd known about Trism already, if only theoretically. Her reaction of, oh, shock was it, didn't derive from the substitution of this beloved man for her mother. Any equation of simple replacement would be mere math—the situation called for melody. No, her being appalled wasn't as obvious as that. Nor was it squeamishness about the maleness of their mating. Or not much. It was rather that she'd left her father a single man, serene in his independence, building himself a solitary hideout and losing himself in his quiet work, and she'd returned to find he'd gone—common. Seeking common satisfactions. Or common enough. Companionship. Attention. Yeah, love too, in all its mess and cost. So what am I left with, she wondered. What is it. Simply more aloneness, is that it. I felt less isolated flying alone on my broom than I do coming home to a cottage with dishes drying on a towel and farm animals braying and snorting in the barn. Where everything is a matching pair. Except me, who matches no one and nothing.

She snorted. Self-pity, what a curse. She'd just get on with this as she had everything else so far. She rearranged her limbs in her own chair. Drank a few sips of tea and tossed the rest on the ground. "I won't stay for long," she said. "A few nights. To get my bearings. It would be too awkward to sleep in the loft above your occupied bed. Maybe I can rig up a hammock in the barn?"

"I'll ask Trism to give us some space," said her father. "He's eager to get to know you but he's no fool; he realizes that now isn't the time. Rain. You don't need to move on. You've been gone so long, and this is your home. We can make adjustments. Temporary for now. In the spring we'll slap on another room or even, if you prefer, raise a private cottage of your own. Calm your nerves. You're traveled out."

"I'm not ready to settle down, I have no nerves to calm, just snakes under my skin. I can't sit still in this watercolor landscape. Show me around. It sounds as if you've gone whole hog into animal husbandry."

"No hogs. But sheep, and donkeys for the plow, some ducks and drakes. Also Gardius, a dwarf dragon who, I fear, has a bit of a princess attitude in him."

"I knew there was something different besides a boyfriend in your bed."

"Give that one a bit of a rest? I know you need time but there's no call to be snarky. Here we are." The barn door hung from a set of rollers that slid along an iron track. Liir pushed the door aside and they entered the familiar space. The smell of fewmets overpowered more traditional barn aromas.

Rain didn't know sheep well enough to recognize individuals. "Why are they inside on a bright day?"

"Trism is working on repairing a fence. They'll be released once the paddock is secure. I apologize for the noise. They have a lot of breath but nothing much to say." Around the corner where the horse stalls were—never a horse installed here as far as Rain knew—two of the partitions had been knocked together to form a square space for the bigger creature. "Hey, Druwigardius, you have company." Liir reached a hand palm down for the bizarre creature to examine. The dragon allowed the hand to creep scratching fingers along his forehead and ears. Just where a dog likes to be scratched.

Rain's eyes adjusted. "A dwarf dragon, never heard of such a critter," she said. Not much bigger than a pony, the hairless, imbricating scales grey and mottled with moldy spots—or perhaps that was just protective coloring. "You sure it's not going to grow? It's not just a baby? Hello there, you." She put her hand out as Liir had done. "How do you come to be housing settled in this outpost?"

"Trism is by training and by instinct a dragon-whisperer. He came across this creature in a covered cage in a market, a quick glimpse permitted for a fee. Trism paid and peeked. Gardius recognized a fellow-spirit. That night he bit his trainer's hand and escaped, and followed the scent of Trism. He's been a sort of pet-companion ever since. I don't think we could lose him if we tried."

"A bit weird."

"For someone who relied on a talking Goose for a spiritual confessor, I have no standing to be sniffy about a stumpy dragon. I like him, actually. Don't I? Yes I do yes I *do*. I like you." Gardius was downright craven, primping for ever more lively demonstrations of appreciation. Just like a lapdog, though by the look of several scorch marks on the stone walls Gardius might burn your face off.

"Surely he's not kept here in the dark all the time?"

"No, of course not. But he's recovering from a head cold. Believe me, a dragon with nasal congestion who spits fire when he's irritable can sneeze up a hot mess of yuck. We're providing him mustard plasters, which he eats, and some herbal remedies. He's on the mend but it's another day or two, we think, before he can go afield."

"Does he help with the farm chores?"

"Shhh," said Liir, grinning. "He thinks he's the farmer and we're his staff. It works okay that way. Don't give him notions of subservience or we'll never hear the end of it. All his sulking and airs." Gardius was recovering from the ecstasy of a morning scratch. He opened his eyelids more widely as he took in Rain. His eyes protruded. The pupils were chocolate. His long and irregular nose twitched; an old shoe of a nose. He looked back and forth between Liir and Rain as if assessing. She could have sworn he raised an eyebrow in mock disbelief, but he had no eyebrows to speak of. Still, his manner spoke of skepticism.

She felt skeptical herself, but this wasn't the day to sow any more discord at home than she could help. "Catch up with you later, Gardius," she said. "You look as if you have a high opinion of yourself but I'm good at knocking that kind of thing down. We'll schedule a couple of sessions when I get my ducks in a row." Some ducks in a row, standing at the door, quacked, as if at Rain's taking liberties with their good names.

In the sunlight again. The cottage was now old enough to look shabby—an improvement on her childhood, back when she'd watched and sometimes helped her mother and her father slap it together. After they'd been reunited and before they were again separated. That brief window of traditional childhood that, come to think of it, had offered Rain nothing more consoling than ordinariness.

And ordinariness is unquantifiable until it has evaporated. The unperceived paradise of childhood. Only recognized by the forever exiled.

She saw Trism off in a field, working with a plane, sizing the end of a beam to fit in the hole of a post. She thought about the old-timey expression for sex—dragon-snaking—but resisted making a joke about having a boyfriend who was a dragon-whisperer. Well, if she could think up a joke, she must be accommodating herself to this already. She was glad but weary, weary to the very salt on her skin.

"Does he fly?" she asked.

"You mean Trism?"

"I mean the *dragon.*"

"Well. Of course most dragons do. And Gardius has wings. But we think he hasn't cottoned on to their usefulness yet. He swishes them about like they're his personal set of boudoir draperies. We're not eager for him to launch until he has better control of his combustible breath. He hasn't mastered that sort of continence yet."

Rain wasn't sure what came next. The weariness that had swamped her wasn't physical, and she didn't know if she wanted to lie down. She said, "When Trism is busy with the heavy labor, what do you do?"

"I help sometimes. Lots of work needs four hands. But I'm still writing." They had reentered the cottage. Liir made a gesture toward his pages on a side table. "Some days I've said everything there is to say, other days I've said nothing. It's a struggle and it hurts my head and sometimes my digestion."

"You were a cavalier when you were my age," she said, without scorn. "You traveled the tumbrel-track of those times. Which were, um, prickly. All that unrest, the civil war. The abdication of Shell Thropp from the Throne Ministership." She didn't want to mention Mombey yet, or Tip. Yet, or maybe ever. But still. "You flew with the birds. You were magicked into the form of an elephant. Do you even remember anything about that?"

"An elephant never forgets." He winked at her and went to pass his papers by, but she lingered.

"I'm being serious. After you've had the life of firebrand, however mild-mannered, I don't know how you satisfy yourself with this punishment post."

"*You* forget I've chosen it. I like it here. There's something—" He paused. "Well. A word I rarely use, but I'll risk it. Something sacred about this mounded hill between two lakes. I had a vision here once, when I was your age, or younger? Don't remember. Maybe I was just drunk. Or malnourished. But I've always believed that the Grimmerie was brought into our world right here. Its bearer just sort of appeared between the trees, out of nothing. In my dream anyway. I hardly trust that places are sacred—either every place is, or no place is. But perhaps places are like people. Maybe they can be seared by their history somehow. I feel it here. A wound. Another world broke through here. I like to get a seat by the door at the theater in case of fire. I like being here."

"Have you ever been to a theater?"

"Figure of speech. Yes, I'm still working on a treatise about the types of justice government ought to be capable of. If only to put my own thinking in order. But when it's finished I'll send it to the Emerald City in case it's of use."

He saw that she was hesitating. "Ozma hasn't yet advanced to take the throne," he told her. "The Cowardly Lion has agreed to stay on as her regent while she undertakes a course of private studies. Or that's what's said. History, I guess; maybe the rubrics of Palace protocol. No, I haven't been back to the Emerald City. Neither have I left this homestead except to the market village, not once since you left."

"Whyever not?"

He slanted her a look as if surprised she had to ask. "Ninny. What do you think? So I would be here to greet you when you got home."

SHE HAD GONE to the loft to find some old clothes, see if they would still fit. Dust hung in the angled heat. Immortal spores. Mouse droppings dotted the bedcovers, and the pillow reeked of mildew. She stretched out on the bed to catch a moment alone, and slept there unmoving till dawn. Almost a full cycle of a day and night. By the time she creaked down the steep ladder-steps, the breakfast table was laid for two. One set of dishes had already been used and was set aside in a drying rack.

"Trism has gone to market," said Liir, coming inside with a bucket of well-water. "He'll be gone two nights, maybe more. Wanted to give us time to catch up. Boy, that was an enchanted sleep. We could hear you snoring like a sawmill."

Rain didn't want to know if they had slept side by side, or closer, while she was passed out upstairs. Anyway, it seemed to matter less this morning. Accommodation. The natural erosion of expectation. She turned her back on the double bed in the corner and attended to a cup of coffee and a bowl of oats with late berries of some sort.

She and her father spent a half day orbiting around each other, speaking incidentally, scarcely troubling to rush and fill in the gaps. Rain was desperate to hear everything she could about Tip—about Ozma—but she didn't want to grasp at her father with questions clinching like pincers. For his part, Liir mostly tamped the curiosity he surely had about her adventures. Maybe he didn't want to encourage her memories of her travels. Maybe he didn't believe she'd gone out of this world and into another. Almost as far as that Dorothy and her much ballyhooed Kanzizz.

Desultory, that was the word. Rain took a long walk around Fourth Lake, looking for yesterday's loons, but they'd removed themselves this morning. She was pleased to see that she recognized quite a few specific trees. Whether her eye had been improved by meeting the Caryatids on the other side of the River Seethe, or whether she'd always clocked to the individuality of trees, she didn't know. Amnesia may have wiped that sense of herself away, and now it was coming back. What else might still be inside her, waiting to return if it had half a chance.

Liir met her as she rounded the verge of the farther cove. He'd taken the path on the other side. They sat on a log for a while and watched autumn gnits spangle the air above the water. So she told him about the Caryatids, about Tesasi, their uncrowned queen. About Rain's own promise to spread the tree pollen in a place that needed it. "Ithira Strand," she said, as if he would know what she meant by that. He nodded gravely and asked her if she had any other obligations to these creatures of another soil.

"I suppose you mean that in a contractual sense," she said.

"I mean it in any sense that it makes sense to you."

She shrugged and acceded. The willowy affability of her father; it made him hard to pin down. "I only owe them my life, I guess. In a way. They introduced me to the Oracle of Maracoor and he revived the broom on which I returned to Oz. So without Tesasi, who knows where I'd be."

"Oh, yeah, well. We're all in debt to coincidence, if it comes to that. But you're no longer carrying out a campaign for this tree chieftain."

"No. Just need to live. Nothing more than that."

He tried to skim a rock on the water; it plunked and sank without a single repeat. "One of the milestones of growing up is when we realize we can be done with living for others. Early on, we pay respect to the parents who gave us life by staying alive and living fully for them. Making their sacrifices worth it. I certainly labored under that belief for decades. But eventually we come round: we owe it to ourselves to live just as much as we owe it to anyone else."

"I didn't stay alive the last eighteen months to validate your fatherhood," she said, only a little disingenuously. So what was his point.

"During my firebrand years, as you call them, I thought I had to rouse the rabble because it's what Elphaba would have done had she been around to do it. I thought it was the least I owed her. In fact, the best I owed her was to live my life as genuinely as possible, not on her terms but on my own."

"Is this a Life Lesson for me?"

"I wouldn't dare try to give you a Life Lesson. I'm no fool."

As they walked back to the cottage, Liir told her about the signs of encroachment of farmers and hunters from the Disappointments and other points near the eastern Great Kells. "This isn't as much of an outback as it was a decade ago. Trism and I are even thinking of building a mill on the waterfall that comes into Fifth Lake. Not sure we could pull it off on our own, but we could get a team of fellows up from elsewhere to help us raise it."

Affecting a stagey nonchalance that made her own skin crawl, Rain told Liir about how she'd met his putative grandfather—the Oracle of Maracoor. Formerly known as the Wizard of Oz. Liir stopped in the path. His head cocked to one side like a dog's. It was, perhaps, rank disbelief. Did he think she was mad.

A long silence as he took it in and calibrated his response. "I'm only surprised to imagine that someone so old and so—um— fiercely traveled—could have absconded from the Palace—was that about twenty-five years ago?—and be holed up in yet another position of eminence in yet another nation."

"More like imprisoned, due to his age and infirmity. But why should you be surprised? I bet he isn't yet ninety. That's not unfathomably old."

"Did you catch any family resemblance?"

"With you? Hardly. But then, how many people that old have I ever met at all? The whole package was—" She made a gesture. "Something of a stretch to accept. Improbable."

"I'll bet. No, I mean, did you see any resemblance to yourself?"

"Ah. How could I do that? I hardly know myself. I can't even recognize myself in my own dreams."

"Travel is so broadening, don't you think?" He was ribbing her on several levels at once. Could he *really* think maybe she was making this all up.

"Tell me about the Grimmerie, though," he continued. "I'm as interested in the voyage that *it* took as I am in the one you took.

Did you practice trying to read it while you were away? You have some small talent at that, as I recall."

"Oh yes, I'm the Witch of Maracoor, now, didn't I tell you? Iskinaary said so."

"The Grimmerie," he reminded her.

She told him the what's-what of it as they went to the garden to find something for lunch. Some tomatoes with black spots that could be cut out, some robust broccoli, and a few fibrous whorls of asparagus that could be boiled into submission and served with salt. She told him about trying to drown the great book, and how her campaign had unleashed a storm that threw the world on the far side of the ocean out of whack. "And yet you have it still in your satchel," he said. "Or is that a portfolio of sketches you made of your grand holiday?" Adding, "Stop, I'm only trying to be droll. I'm sorry. Don't mind me—I've gotten out of the habit of kindness, maybe. Tell me what you want to tell me, and I promise not to interrupt with a slant remark."

Rain controlled her temper as best she could. "The book came back to me. Apparently it had no intention of remaining drowned. I've returned it as intact as possible. It was a fool's errand to think I could lose it." She wiped her eyes, casting about for a diversion. On the wall above the desk, suspended on a loop of rawhide cord, hung her mother's domingon. The shiny hairs of the bow were slack— maybe that was how it was properly stored—but the strings on the transept and on the fingerboard looked taut and ready for sound. "In tune?" she asked Liir, as much to change the subject as anything ese.

"I'm not the musical one," he told her, but took it down. She could nearly remember her mother playing the old folk instrument. It involved dragging long drones out of the tightened bow, or bouncing percussive repeats—while the other hand pressed a fretted note with the thumb, and clawhammering it with one or more fingers on the same hand, sometimes on two or three strings at once, as the modet required. Melody and mood, figure and surround, from the same player. Probably no harder than managing a piano keyboard—and certainly more portable. "Do you want to try it?" asked Liir.

"I'm a lot of strange things," said Rain, "but lyrical isn't one of them." She put her hand onto the strings and felt them vibrate, and imagined she could coax melody forward. "Is there any such thing as written music for this weird item?"

"There were one or two scraps of paper on which Candle had written some notations." He rummaged through a drawer. "Do you read music?"

"I hardly read, period."

"Ah, here we are." A browning length of paper that had once wrapped a poundweight of milled sugar. Candle's hand had drawn racks of notes in ascending slopes, but the lines—the actual music staff—were missing. So who could play them? "She knew the arrangement of strings and frets," Liir said, anticipating Rain's questions. "Those little bars and dots below are positional references. She told me about them. These are arpeggios—she described them as chords broken free of their pack, moving in the same direction either up or down the scale. Something like that."

"Music without ruled lines seems anarchic if not an invitation to migraine."

"She has a natural talent, that one," said Liir obscurely. "I won't give you the instrument, as it belongs to her. Once in a while when she does come along to make sure I'm still alive, she plays for me. Or for herself—who can ever know which of us deserves the suspended continuo or the broken chord? The domingon does both at once."

"One for each of you," she said, not certain if she was being ferocious or consoling. But that was music for you.

"About music, I only know this trick." He plucked a tenor string. A single note vibrated with confidence and perfect violence; you could almost see it. Before it faded, Liir hovered the pad of his forefinger in the air just above the string, offshore, not touching it. A second tone emerged, in keen pitch, a kind of response, softer than the first, following and amplifying the earlier testimony, riding a half-scale above the earlier tone. A steel pearl in the air like a tiny gazing globe, all the world reflected in it. "That's all the magic I know how to do," said Liir. "It's called a harmonic. Don't ask me how it works. It's a ghost note emerging from the world of the original. It doesn't really exist on its own, it only comes out as a response to the first. I suppose the way a shadow doesn't exist unless cast by an object. But the conditions have to be right."

"Is that a metaphor for my life?" she asked.

"I know you're still young," he replied, "but not everything is about you. If this is going to do heavy work in the Metaphor Brigade, it might as well be about me, don't you think? Don't I get a metaphor?"

They ate their lunch in silence. Then she took the Grimmerie out at last and plopped it upon her father's papers, where it pressed them flat, like a judge and jury. She turned her back on it, cutting it dead, socially speaking.

After lunch Liir lit a small pipe. They went to examine what was left of the fence repair that Trism had abandoned to give them their privacy. There wasn't much. With four hands at the job, they easily installed the replacement slats and then walked the fence, stringing cord across wider slots through which a baby lamb might conceivably bound by accident. Returning to the barn, they released the flock into its pasture. Gardius made moan to join them but Liir didn't think he was quite ready.

The next morning, a warm and inoffensive rain. More leaves had changed overnight. Yellow-gold, and red so red it was purple.

Chores were done swiftly, and a second pot of tea brewed, and a fire built up in the chimney. "Where are you going to lodge this book now?" asked her father. "If you tried to sink it and it wouldn't stay sunk, what's next? You want to toss it in the fire?"

She couldn't tell if he was joking again. "I don't think it would burn, or that it would stay burnt. The ashes might go up the chimney and then rain down upon the roof in specks of paper one letter at a time." She was being nonsensical and speculative at the same time, trying a hypothesis. "Anyway, maybe after all that, I was wrong to take it. The book is yours, isn't it? Not mine."

"Not mine either. But maybe it belongs here. If that little dizzy memory of mine has any validity, the old man who carried the Grimmerie materialized on Nether How. I heard that he walked north to Kiamo Ko and deposited it there for safekeeping. Maybe best it be kept safe here. If he ever again manifests out of nothing and comes back for it, he'll have to come across us first. We'll give him some tea and return him his book."

"Where *really* do you think it came from?" asked Rain. "The Oracle told me it came from his original world, which is someplace other than Peare."

Liir didn't know the expression Peare. Rain explained: "The whole world. The us-and-them of it. Not just Oz, not just 'here.' But all of it. All of us bound up. A planet, if we're a planet; a plate, if we're a plate. The word that means 'Oz and Maracoor and any place else not discovered yet.'"

"And where the Grimmerie comes from? Then—out of Peare, you mean."

"That's what the Oracle said. From his world. The world of Dorothy, too. It's a—a sideshow world to ours. A glimpse, I guess. A nextdoor world. I don't really understand it."

"Dreams always seemed to me a nextdoor world." He continued, "I used to think they were a rescue, and then sometimes I thought a curse. I would dream of Trism quite often, and I'd be both glad and also in mourning when I woke up. I knew him only well enough to know I loved him."

Is he changing the subject to dreams because he thinks my talk of Peare is madness.

"I wonder if you dream of Tip," he said cautiously.

"Oh, all the time," she just about shouted. "Once I recovered my memory, I recovered my sorrow. That's how it works. Every night he is there with me, in the nextdoor world as you call it. I wake up and I spit. It's a good thing dreams don't mean anything, isn't it. As you said."

He waited a half a day more before saying anything else. It was raining, but it was warmer. They lit no fire, just pulled chairs up to the open door and listened and watched. Browning ferns and the exquisite bouquet of mud. Once he reached out for her hand. She made to scratch her nose and then repositioned her arm out of his reach—behind her head.

He sighed. "It seems to me you left here to flee your sorrow, and maybe by dint of all your escapades—"

"'Escapades.' Flattering. Nice. Go on."

"I mean you put life and distance between yourself and your sorrow. Maybe that smash-up with amnesia helped some, or maybe it slowed down your recovery. Can't guess at that. But you're still yoked with a ton of anger on your back."

She flexed her green toes out into the water that dripped off the eaves, wishing the rain would melt her away like a sugar turtle left out in a cloudburst. A different kind of drowning. She stayed solid. The only way to get out of here was to get out of here. With what she hoped was an adult breeziness she said, "I think I'll be moving on tomorrow. If you have a way of signaling Trism that the coast is clear—put a white stone on the windowsill or whatever you do—go ahead."

"This is his home now, too; he doesn't need permission to enter under its lintel." For the first time Liir sounded irritated at her. "Are you going to take yourself off in a snit because I told you what I think?"

"One snit is as good as another, so who cares what the reason is? I'll leave the Grimmerie here, though. I've carried it about for too long. If you think I have to drop my anger, maybe dropping the Grimmerie where I found it is a start."

"I hope you're going back to the Emerald City. To see Ozma. To put this to rest. Lest you suffer your whole life."

"Suffering a whole life is one way to know you're having a life."

"I feel as if I'm arguing with your grandmother."

"Elphaba? Should I take that as a compliment?"

"I'll have you do one thing first, though," he said. "Before you leave the Great Kells. Make your way to Kiamo Ko. They've improved the upper road by putting in a rude suspension bridge. Dizzying. Still, it cuts out days of descending into steep valleys and climbing out of them. Oh, but you can fly, too; I forgot that."

"Maybe I'll leave the broom here too. Confront whatever life affords me on my own native strength. Or weakness. But why do you want me to go to Kiamo Ko?"

"Four winged monkeys left there to hunt for you and Iskinaary. By the tale you tell, they were sped over the ocean behind you and now are moored in this Maracoor. I think you have an obligation to report that they're safe even if they're never coming back."

"I didn't dispatch them." At his expression, she said, "Oh, all right. But if you refer to my life as 'the tale you tell' one more time I will wrench open the Grimmerie and turn you into some stunted dragon and your dragon-whisperer can have all the fun he wants whispering into—" Then she said, "I'm sorry. I'm sorry. I'm going to bed."

In the celibate's loft, the daughter; in the unmoored raft of the double bed below, the father. They tossed at a distance greater than the breadth of any hypothetical or actual ocean. An ancient tragedy: filial attachment compromised by parental caution.

SHE WAITED TILL Liir had gone to do morning chores with the sheep and Gardius before saying goodbye to the Grimmerie. Goodbye for now, maybe for good. She put the book in the middle of the table and leaned over it, studying the object as if to memorize it. The binding, a bluish purple-brown. Stout, dry, strong. Dots of gold leaf in the creases where the leather buckled into raised bands that fortified the spine. The deckled edges of the pages showed no evidence of their saltbath. If anything the book seemed thicker, healthier, than it had been when she'd dug it up to export it more than a year ago.

Well, it was a little thicker—she'd put the last three cards of cartomancie in it, for safekeeping.

Though she was abandoning the book of magicks, maybe she'd keep those cards with her. She flipped through the volume, trying to hold back from reading alluring headings or glancing at images, diagrams, portraits, and recipes. The script fairly cavorted beneath her, attractively, taunting her, but she found one card, then the next. The last one, the blank-faced card, was hiding, and she had to leaf through the tome several times. Old spells from her past waved at her. *To Call Winter upon Water. On Vagueness and Variation.* Oh, there was the card, sticking stubbornly on a diagonal below the display script that jauntily asked *Where Are They Now?*

Where Are They Now?

To hide the spell, to keep from reading it inadvertently as she tried to work the blank card free, Rain took the two other cards, the broom and the book, and she laid them vertically beneath the blank card. But one line of script remained visible at the bottom of the page, in words she couldn't help but understand.

No answer arrives until the question is posed. Otherwise it is no answer.

There was no way around it. Despite herself, she put her right hand on the image of the book and her left hand on the image of the broom.

Akemmish alekko, minzumah ckiiri.
What's become of the one that I most want to see?

Tip, Tip, she said, though she knew she was playing with poison. Tip, are you gone for good. Where did you go. Where does anyone go.

"Where did you go?" she said. "Did you survive? No one knows."

She leaned forward and focused her eyes upon the blank card under the script Where Are They Now?

The dull gloss white of the card stock took on a different sort of sheen, as if a bright light over Rain's head were falling upon it from the ceiling. She looked up, wondering if a bit of thatch had suddenly come loose and daylight was lancing in precisely upon the page. No, it was the card itself that shone, somehow. So the old huckster's shabby card deck, designed to bamboozle blistering fools, could be cozened into performing a magick after all. That's the Grimmerie for you. Adjacency.

"Where did you go," she said for the third time. Third time's the charm.

The white card seemed to spread suddenly like spilled milk all over the page. She pulled her hands back so as not to be stained, or burnt, or turned to marble. The whiteness ran over the images of broom and book, covering the text of the spell and the spell's title, too. It was a blank page, drenched with nothing but possibility. Oh, come back, she said inside herself, come back.

Then—and later she couldn't say in what dimension this occurred, whether she was looking at a flat image like an illustration in a book, or if somehow a form grew like a writhing weed out of the white surround and raised its head upright—she came face-to-face not with her Tip, her lover, her lost heart, but merely with herself.

She didn't know where she herself had gone, and she didn't care. That wasn't the question she'd posed. But there she was. It was like looking in a mirror—until it wasn't, suddenly. She was looking at herself as an older person, as a woman who had survived this unendurable heartache, after all. She was looking across time. At some older herself.

Or was this no mirror.

Her hands were not on the book or on the table but crossed upon her heart. "Elphaba?"

The green face turned this way and that, as if hearing the name spoken, but not certain if she were imagining it. Her eyebrows raised and her eyes narrowed.

"Elphaba?" said Rain.

"I never know when I'm having a seizure or just a mood," said the other green witch. "I talk to myself like any other crazy person, but I feel there is someone else listening. What do you want, and why are you bothering me?"

Rain sensed that she had no question but the one sanctioned by the Grimmerie. "Where did you go?" she asked.

"Who wants to know?" snapped the older witch.

"Nobody, really. Just me."

The witch—Elphaba, if it really was Elphaba—rotated her head upon her neck and lowered her pointy chin. Her penetrating eyes seemed to drill through the impossible miasma of magic. Rain felt . . . she felt anointed with notice.

"Another pesky vision," said the Elphaba thing. "Why do you care about me?"

"You disappeared," said Rain.

"Everybody does that. It doesn't take special talent."

"No one knows where you've gone, or if you're still alive."

"Not my business to clarify. Live with ambiguity or die from intolerance of it. Good luck to you."

Rain said, "Are you still here? Can I find you? You could help me—I'll come to you! Where are you now?"

"You've answered your question already. Where am I now? I am here, now. That's where I am. Now. If you don't understand, turn yourself around and *you* speak to the past and speak to the future. What you say matters. What you do matters. Love whom you will, cherish them while you have the time, don't give an inch when the bullies kick at your stilts. Kick back, and then give them a poultice if you've hurt them. The past and future are just window dressing. Where I am is here. I'm busy with a potion that seems to come with this distracting side effect and I better make some corrections before I start hearing violins in the water closet and seeing comets in the chowder. Do you have anything else, or is this just chatter? I hardly think my younger self worth the cost of conversation. Didn't have much to say then and have less to add now, after all this so-called living."

Rain wanted to ask about Tip, but she felt ashamed. "Can I just tell you what you've done for me?"

"I'm a busy woman. I don't take compliments. Write it in the guest book. If you're a ghost from the future"—just for a moment the older green witch looked clement and almost wistful—"if you're from the future, take better care of it than I've done of your past." She began to fade.

"Are you still alive?" cried Rain.

"You tell me," said Elphaba waspishly, and somehow, with some twist of her wicked wrists, she slammed the Grimmerie closed from the inside out. The three tarot cards escaped in the draft. Rain collected them from the floor, tucked them in a pocket, and backed away from the book.

HAVING SAID SHE WOULD GO, she had to go. Whether this demonstrated strength of will or a sad rigidity of character, she didn't bother to judge. She left the Grimmerie where it was, on the side table, quashing Liir's scribblings. She helped herself to some bread and cheese and a few eggs boiled in their shells, and a scrap of ham discolored with a glaze of onion pickle.

She could see Liir rescuing a duck who had wandered into some briarweed. The duck was snapping and drawing blood but Liir worked on. Rain boiled some coffee in a tin pot and decided not to disappear without notice as she'd done more than a year ago, beginning the adventures that cast her ashore in Maracoor Spot.

When he came in, and his eyes adjusted to cottage shadow, he saw the broom propped in a corner next to a mop and a butter churn. Rain waited in outline, her back to the window, her hands gripping the sill as if preparing to snap it off.

"Hope you slept well enough, then. You're not taking the broom?" When she didn't answer, he continued, "It's a steep climb."

"I'm on my way, after coffee." Too jittery to sit at the table. She hovered with her mug while he cut some bread and sat for breakfast.

He said, "I don't suppose—"

"No," she agreed, "don't suppose."

He sighed. "You've been gone a long time to come home for such a brief stay. You have business to finish, I can tell. But this is your home still, Rain, if you're ever ready to come back to it. I can't stop you leaving. It would make me feel less worried if I thought you understood what I am saying."

"I have to see—her. I have to put an end to what had no real end. Or else I'll be stalking the highlands of misery my whole life. I'm too young to settle for that yet."

"You might not need ever to settle for that. But I agree—I think you have to see her again. And who knows?"

"Who knows what."

"Who knows anything? Rain, I first met Trism when I was more or less your age. I would never have guessed that he would become the centerpiece of my life. No—not centerpiece—that's the wrong word. But the stabilizer. The buttress. I wasn't looking for him, I didn't know he was out there to be sought. I was about as inept as a human being can be, I mean when it came to affection. Think about it. My father—Fiyero Tigelaar—was assassinated before I was born. My mother was the so-called Wicked Witch of the West. How's that for parental blessings? It's a wonder I could apply butter to a slice of bread. But the world has tricks of revelation. Spring and autumn are just the showier moments. Something new is always turning itself over for your notice. Maybe your shock hardened into silent fury. Maybe you can let go of that. And see what happens."

"Do you mean you think I might learn to love Ozma instead of Tip?"

He shrugged. "I loved your mother, and in many ways I still do. Then I met Trism and my romance with Candle was changed. Oh, sweet Oz, it's such a temptation to think always of either/or. I'm not telling you what to think or do. I don't know. I'm only saying that to be burning awake instead of frozen asleep allows for more life to happen."

She was trying not to be argumentative. "Iskinaary had a romance with a border crane who wasn't even a sentient creature. He fertilized some eggs of hers, and I carried a couple of them with us across the ocean. Who will those poor creatures be, born abroad, a tossed salad of species?"

"Assuming they were actually fertilized, the eggs will hatch into something new. Only creatures can name themselves, really. And we're from a line not much different from that, if you accept your Oracle's"—he corrected swiftly—"the Oracle's declaration of being Elphaba's father. We have strange blood in our veins too. Not as strongly as Elphaba did. I'm a generation from that, and you're two down. But this is how the world revises and strengthens itself. Otherwise it might die of boredom, or complacency. Or self-adoration."

They tidied up the table and walked into the sunlight, which was thinned by a mist hanging over the bone-oaks and the barn. "Okay, tell Trism I don't hate him. Whatever, it's not his fault."

"I don't think fault enters into any of this."

She didn't reply to that. "How is Gardius's cold?"

"Improving too slowly. Nothing like flaming snot to make one regret having taken up animal husbandry. If he were in better nick I might have proposed he accompany you to Kiamo Ko at least, and maybe onward. I don't like the idea of you lighting out on your own."

"You sent Iskinaary after me once and then flying monkeys after both of us. You're entirely too involved. I can take care of myself."

"I'll watch that happen with great happiness." He sighed, as if he thought the likelihood slim. "Anyway, Gardius is beholden to Trism. Want to say goodbye?"

"Not really." But they ducked in the barn anyway. As the sheep and donkeys were now out to pasture, the dwarf dragon was hunched in a corner of his stall, eating stale hay with a pessimistic air. He looked up and sniffed as they approached, but when he saw they weren't Trism, he paid them no further attention. "What is the plan with this lump?" she asked. "He's just going to be a big house pet, once you have him trained?"

"He likes to play fetch but too often he burns the stick. I don't know. He's here for now. Just like the rest of us."

"Not me. I'm off then," she said. She gave her father an awkward embrace. Gardius raised his chin and snorted as if critical of in-authentic gesture. "I don't need your approval," she said over Liir's shoulder to the dragon.

"I know you don't," said Liir, misunderstanding. "But you have it anyway."

Outside the barn her father walked her down the slope of Nether How and pointed out the path along the left edge of Fifth Lake. "This will take you to the hanging valley between those two ridges. You're not looking where I'm pointing. Do you see that yellowing crabapple? There."

"Weird crabapple," she said. "It's mostly yellow, but those lower branches have blue specks."

"That's the one. The path starts beneath it." He added, "Trism grafted some sprigs of oldstyle blue grape onto the crabapple last spring. They took pretty well for a season but I don't think it's a permanent change. They seem to be reverting. The lower half of the tree was blue two months ago, and look at it now—it's aging into its old self."

She promised she understood how to find the route leading cross-slope to the new catwalk bridge, and on up into Arjiki territory. She left him without another goodbye—redundancy, who needs it—and without looking back. He watched her pace the path as it neared the edge of Fifth Lake. A witch of a girl, her reflection in the green water was almost unreadable. No broom, no book. Just a blank twist of possibility.

7

When Trism returned the next night, he wasn't surprised to see that Rain had lit out. "A girl on a mission," he said. "Still, I hope my being here didn't alarm her too much." He dropped the satchel of provisions on the table. Some salt spilled from a screw of paper, and a green pepper rolled into the fireplace.

"I don't think so," Liir replied, though he wasn't certain of that. "I suppose she was just following her own hunger. Not knowing what will slake it, if anything. The way you did. The way I did, too. All love is anomaly, don't you think?"

"Stop talking for once and come here right now," said Trism.

KIAMO KO

1

She followed her father's directions easily enough. At the end of Fifth Lake, the path petered out in the forest, but the opening made by slopes angling above her reappeared just as she worried she'd lost it.

Here, the inevitable streambed—nearly dry at the start of autumn. The stones, flattened over time into pavers and steps, proved more accommodating than gnarled roots and underbrush. Next she ought to come upon an old stone bridge. She did, but it had collapsed since last time Liir had been up this way. She skirted the rubble. Getting up the slope by the waterfall's drop—which allowed now only a mere thread of stream—was quite the job. Well after high noon by the time she reached the pond at the waterfall's head. Busy with upslope gnits and water-walkers. An odor of invisible roses and dried-out mud, but deep enough to sink into.

She removed her clothes and submerged herself. Wrung water from her long hair and looped it onto the back of her head with the aid of a walnut-wood skewer and a tortoiseshell comb she'd pinched from a drawer under the dish shelf. Perhaps it had been her mother's, and Liir had kept it for sentiment's sake. She was happy to have it, and happier to have stolen it. More portable than the domingon, anyway.

Emerging from the bath feeling about as dirty as when she'd

entered it, as if the soil had been just switched out. She remembered the pool at Toe Hold, when she'd seen the snake slip its skin. She'd come some ways since then. What had happened to the creature. Eluded hawk and raccoon, weasel and coyote still, maybe. What an unnatural creature to feel a kinship with. But Rain was unnatural herself, in harsh mood and in her plain old questionable glamour. Still wishing she could slip her own skin, except perhaps she'd find there was nothing much underneath it.

In days gone by, an overland trek between Nether How and Kiamo Ko, that outpost where Elphaba had once made herself a sanctuary, might have taken the better part of a week. Liir said the new suspension walkway would slice off half that time, and maybe even more if Rain, being young and strong, could keep up a pace. Not that there was a hurry. No one was expecting her in Kiamo Ko. She had a simple mission: to deliver word about the flying monkeys. Faro, Finistro. Thilma. And the other one—Tietro? Tiotro. They'd have family or friends who might be glad or angry at the news. Whatever. Rain could just spill the beans and get on her way.

When it was way too late, she thought to turn back and look at the distance she'd traveled. The hump of Nether How and those blue buttons, Fourth and Fifth Lakes, had long been swallowed up in the heaves of stone and forest. She didn't care one way or the other. The world tended to interrupt itself, didn't it. That was its job—

She slept earlier than intended. Her perch was high enough now that the shawl she'd lifted from a hook was welcome indeed. And the bugs were lulled into inactivity by the lowering temperature.

Come the morning, she began to feel a little ill. Perhaps a bout of mountain weakness—she'd forgotten about that. As she pulled herself together and continued her climb, she felt her limbs protest. But this was normal, surely. When you don't climb a real mountain for more than a year, your legs are going to tell on you. The approaches to High Chora and to the Tower in the Clouds had been a child's playground compared to the Great Kells. She was out of shape.

She became a little less despondent when she spotted the imprints of human boots. She'd met the Arjiki before. Were the stories true, her grandfather Fiyero had been an Arjiki prince, heir to the line that had skirmished over Kiamo Ko generations back and made it their stronghold. While she didn't have the language, she hoped she might trade on some clan semblance. Her dark hair, her high brow. Her green skin. Well, maybe not that.

The path turned another angle and the catwalk came into sight.

She couldn't imagine how anyone might have engineered this spider-strand slung from one high facade of rock to another. How had they even conceived it. Maybe flying monkeys had been called in to assist. A slap-up job, in any case: seven or eight parallel ropes lashed with planking. A solo traveler might be expected to hold on to rope rails on either side and tiptoe or run for her life. In the wind, the way the whole thing danced so, Rain was surprised it didn't loop itself like a child's jump rope. Parties traveling with pack animals would still be taking the valley route.

I've flown across an ocean on a kitchen broom, she thought, so how hard could this be. But the height of this charmless human structure!—more intimidating than she'd imagined. When she remembered that wind could pick up as well as slacken she knew she'd better not put it off. She began to regret having left the broom behind. Bravado, fool's courage, that. Here we go.

The wind shoved at her in irregular thumps. The walkway shivered and tensed, bowed and relaxed. She had to look down to find her footing. She tried to concentrate only on the ropes, not on the valley ten thousand miles below.

About a third of the way, the impulse overtook her and she threw up. She suspected this wasn't the first time the valley below had seen dinner catapulted upon it.

This high in the mountains, she thought, exactly the place to disappear. No wonder her father had made his home at Nether How. No wonder her grandmother had holed herself up at Kiamo Ko. No more plundering the past for sorrow. Just wind, and light; the heights and depths of any given day. No past and no future.

In the middle of the air, without magic of any sort. Still alive.

She was at the halfway point before she realized that the starting stage had been higher than the landing stage on the other side. The final stretch wasn't kitted out with flooring but became a kind of crocheted ladder, like the ratlines on the *Pious Enterprise*. She was a manatee on a spiderweb, oppressively heavy. With too little to shed. For the gesture if nothing else, she dug out of her satchel the voided seashell she'd been carrying for years, and she let it drop. It whistled a high-pitched alarm as it went. No sound of impact.

She was moving above an imaginary sea. As other things came to her, she pictured letting them drop away into the void. The steamy times with Lucikles. The snippiness of Iskinaary. The tender maternity of Tesasi, the reckless idiocy of the Oracle. Closer to home, if she still called it home—and she wasn't sure if it counted anymore—her cryptic, confused sense of her own father. The nerve of him, to have a life of some satisfaction when her own life had been shattered. She let her umbrage tumble. Uncoiling off her like—like stink. Washed in the tidal winds.

In the middle of the steps of air, she had nothing left to shuck off. No diversion of anger and resentment; she'd divested herself of that already. Inching down the slope of nothing, feeling with her naked feet—she'd discovered they were more attentive when unclad—she descended into the reality of what she'd lost.

Inch by inch, and by design, she admitted to Tip. Tip before he was Ozma.

If in the moment before death one's life flashes before one's eyes, she thought, this is taking its sweet time. I hope I'm not going to die a lingering death.

She had no choice. She couldn't climb back to where she had been. No going backwards up her life to when Tip had been her first love, and an innocent and inexperienced and most tender romancer. She didn't just remember it all—she felt it. How learning that you *can* love is a twin revelation to knowing you can *be* loved. How hard that is to believe, when you've spent your life turning away. Even as a child, on the run, in hiding, in disguise. Never yourself, because you don't even know yourself. You wouldn't recognize yourself in a mirror. Would you.

But you recognize yourself in your lover, because when he turns and looks at you, you see yourself refracted back in his eyes. A strengthening exchange of—of power. No. Of virtue, maybe. No, not virtue: of ripeness. Authenticity. The disguise drops. The hands touch. The bodies electrify. The brain melts and some new organ of apprehension takes its place. Perhaps it's the soul making a stab at gestation. You finish being born at last.

And yet—she was thinking all this, thready rung by rung— and yet the soul that emerges isn't your lover's soul. You aren't two-made-one. You are still one. There are other ways to get there, other ways to be born. Simply an accident that for Rain the key to gestation was love—a teenage romance. Not terribly novel. Hardly earth-shaking. Except to her. And, at the time it had seemed, to Tip too.

She let herself feel all this, and she began to tremble. A panic attack of mood while suspended between heaven and earth. But what could she do. This was the place to leave her paralysis behind. Either that, or leave her own self behind, at last. Her Auntie

Nor had done that. Throw herself into the void. Rain would whistle as she went, like the damn seashell. If she couldn't live with the
reality of loss, she had no business living. Her life had brought her
this golden opportunity for escape.

Still, however slowly she moved, her feet still descended and
swung to find each next strand. The thinnest of cords to bind her
to her life. Almost like an animal, she was still seeking them.

As her weight descended, the pitch of the walkway altered, and
some law of physics she hadn't anticipated caused the catwalk to
slam toward the cliff face on the opposite side. Maybe in the lee
of the mountain the pressure of the wind slackened. She became a
heavy stone sliding down the strand of a necklace, pulling it taut.

Manage this, there's a circus in my future.

She was too scared to look down at her feet, had to thrust them
to find the right place in the webbing. In mid-maneuver, as unen-
cumbered by mortal distress as it was possible for her to feel so
near a possible death, a small cloud passed over her. She didn't
risk looking up to identify it. If that's Iskinaary come to rescue me
again, she thought, I'll wring his neck. The past is in fragments;
let it go.

With feet so sore from trying to be prehensile that they were
nearly numb, she neared the cliff. It became more like climbing a
rope ladder, suddenly easier. She was however bewildered to smell
a torquing twist of smoke.

The cloud materialized into the lumpy indignity of that dwarf
dragon. On his wings he had humped himself across the great
height. He was waiting like a dog on a dock, his paws hanging
down right where she would have to climb up. He was panting
with exertion and happy expectation, and his breath had scorched
the stabilizing cords at the landing station. They were fritzing and
curling up in threads of red and white, ready to explode into flame.

"You bloody menace, get back," she shouted. What happened

next she didn't entirely comprehend. She was a yard from the docking station when one side of the walkway snapped and whipped her sideways against the stone. Gardius dug his claws into her shoulder and her head and kept her from dropping into the void. How she scrambled from there to safety, and whether it was genuine safety, she didn't know. The rope bridge wasn't entirely ruined. It hung by seven of its eight strands, out of commission but reparable.

2

Her first impulse, besides wondering if she wouldn't rather have plunged upon the rocks below than be holding parts of her scalp together with her hands, was to murder Gardius. Since she couldn't murder her father. The dwarf dragon seemed as little responsible as a big mutt, but she guessed her father had sent him after her. Always engaging a babysitter. First Iskinaary, then the flying monkeys, and now this inept thump of creature on his virgin flight.

When he went to lick her torn and bleeding hairline, she pushed him away for fear that in his enthusiasm he would burn her face off. There was a limit to indignity. Better an intact green face than a broiled one.

She couldn't send him away, though. He didn't respond either to instruction or to tone. He galumphed around her in circles, nudging her up the path and away from the drop the way a black-and-white collie will bully a laggardly sheep.

Before long they came across a mountain stream where Rain could rinse the blood and pus off her arm and head. A patch of skin the size of a farthing came away with the hairs attached. She was glad she had no mirror to examine the cut. She tore a strip off her underskirt to bind around her head the way she might do if addressing a serious toothache. Her tunic was shredded at one shoulder.

Once she'd stanched the bleeding she was able to look at Gardius again. He was dipping his jaw in the current of the stream and worrying at something in his mouth. He turned to her with a plaintive expression. While he growled low in his throat as she put out a hand, he allowed her to coax his mouth open.

She found lodged between several of the lower teeth a brace of sharp wooden splinters digging into his purple-grey gums. The wounds were recent and raw, some bleeding. One by one she worked the scraps of detritus out of their sockets. He'd broken through his stall, maybe. Maybe he'd come on his own instinct. Just possible that Liir hadn't sent him. Oh—she was being silly—maybe the whistling seashell had signaled him to her precise whereabouts. Who could tell, when so much else seemed unlikely.

Why, why now, she wondered. She hadn't made common cause with him at Nether How. He wasn't even Liir's great wild pet, he answered only to Trism. So why.

She had no answer for any of this, but he settled with his head in her lap when the last spear of wood was gone. She angled his head so if he coughed up flame while dozing in contentment he wouldn't endanger his human pillow.

Had he saved her or had his arrival imperiled her. It had happened too fast for her to take in, she couldn't deconstruct the sequence now. Did it even matter. What a complete fool she was. "I don't have the time to become a sentimental idiot. If I can't send you back, you'll have to come on with me, and keep up. I don't know how far you're coming, and you're as free an agent as I am, but I'm not hanging about for your leisure sleep. Move." She dumped his head unceremoniously on the ground and he rolled his eyes up at her with such slavish affection that she was revolted. Took everything she had not to bolt.

TWO HOURS LATER, Rain and Gardius came to a ridge where the trees opened up and the mountains disported themselves in a way she found familiar. Well, why not. She'd been here hardly two years ago, was it—another autumn. That time with Tip. As Arjiki tribes often married their young at an early age, Rain and Tip had been taken for a couple. They'd begun to play their roles, at first with self-mockery and then less so.

The Great Kells had imprinted themselves on Rain's sensibility more than she'd imagined. Sure—before amnesia they'd been here all along, describing the limits of her world up until then. Down this valley and across another tributary that fed into the Vinkus River, and she'd be on the apron of Knobblehead Pike. Before she could see them, she began to remember the settlements they'd encountered. Fanarra, Upper Fanarra, and the Windmill place. Red Windmill. It had once taken a week, but she was now only a few days from Kiamo Ko. The witch's castle.

Upland pastures got good sun and ample rain, and flocks fared well. Now, at the start of the autumn, Rain could see shepherds moving their flocks to lower pasture for the winter, which came earlier to the heights. She worried about Gardius and whether he'd continue to behave like an ill-raised farm dog, pestering anything that moved. She cut a switch to carry with her, not so much to hit him—she never did, and wouldn't—but to make a swift sound in the air. It arrested any impulse he had to gallop and carouse. He kept to her side, though not to heel.

The first villagers catching sight of her did her the honor of letting her pass unmolested. The last time she'd come this way she'd been younger, and hadn't looked green, except in the way that green can mean untried and ignorant. It was a quarter century, more probably, since Elphaba Thropp had stalked these slopes, if she ever came out of her witch's keep at all. Who did the citizens of Fanarra and Upper Fanarra think Rain was, some ghostly return of that green-skinned dominatrix. Did they think Rain was her own ancestor. (Aren't we all—in time.) Who cared as long as they let her pass.

She recognized the general layout of the small settlement but didn't remember which one it was. No one bothered to tell her. The Arjiki tongue was largely gibberish to her, but she picked up something through expressions and gestures. No truncated dragon with malevolent breath was coming into any stable or cellar, no ma'am, not in a thousand years. But outside, all right. She and her traveling companion could doss down in the courtyard of an inn and ale house. A pair of milk-tooth boys were told to sweep the ground of leaves and small stones, and to bring blankets. Their father or uncle built up a fire because the nights came brutal even at the turn from summer to fall. Rain and Gardius slept in proximity, Rain with a blanket and the dragon apparently oblivious to the plunging temperature. Well, if you carried your own furnace in your lungs, central heating was, perhaps, redundant.

A day later they arrived at Red Windmill, the last village before Kiamo Ko. She recognized it by the derelict structure that had given the settlement its name. The great pinwheel armature was denuded of sail, but traces of original color still outlined stonework on the lee side. Like the blood that dries under the fingernails. When she indicated that she was headed to Kiamo Ko, the town elders allowed her and Gardius to quarter themselves inside the mill. She supposed if a dragon torched it from the inside and it collapsed, the townspeople would consider it a benefit to the community. At any rate, nobody lived in its weird pillar-box of a structure. The only casualties would be the two strangers themselves.

She wanted to get this done, she wanted to dash in and out of Kiamo Ko and make no great party out of it. The obligation was simple: to confess to their heirs and assigns the whereabouts of the

four flying monkeys. If their family was of an exacting or vengeful sort, Rain might need to apologize. Though an apology could
only bend so far before it broke with illogic. She hadn't requested
their help. She was finishing up a story, that was all, or as far as
she could tell it. Living with their own reality, that was up to the
denizens of Kiamo Ko. She didn't care how they might manage it.
She'd leave them to their grief, bepuzzlement, or apathy. No concern of hers. She'd get on with her own mission.

Which still she couldn't name, but she could feel it coming
closer, unnamed.

3

The peak of Knobblehead Pike was northwest still, though not far. Aloof the year-round. A frozen whitecap rearing out of its sea of green and gold forest. Kiamo Ko, as if in emulation, presided over its own lower slag-heap of ridge. The castle rose as if it had been carved from a single stone outcropping. An air of molten menace, of inorganic and inert tumult. An ungainly human structure for all that.

"We're going to be swift, decisive, and not stay for tea," said Rain. Gardius couldn't understand her but she believed perhaps he liked the sound of her voice. Sometimes he whimpered as if in agreement or, more neutrally, offering a placeholder reaction, like *Oh* or *I see* or *Is that so.*

They traipsed across the wooden bridge that spanned a dry and wretched moat. The flooring probably had once been hinged, capable of lifting to slam closed against approaching armies. It had long since been pegged into permanent position with stone balustrades. Huge doors were shuttered against armies, beggars, and mountain cats, but a smaller door cut into the larger one wasn't even latched. Rain pushed it open and they ducked through.

When she and Tip had arrived here the first time, they'd interrupted a funeral service for her aunt Nor. The unexpected reunion with the Cowardly Lion, however rewarding, hadn't eclipsed that shock. Rain found that she couldn't really remember the layout of the establishment much beyond the color of the stone and the sense of structures struggling toward turrets and bulging with garderobes inside the demesne walls.

So she found the splash of gold and plum beyond the great doors bewildering, unnerving. It felt as if she'd wafted into a dream someone else was having—someone whose life had been less steeped with misery than her own.

Gardius ran ahead. His instinct for investigation, his sniffing and beating of wings in excitement, caused leaves to rattle and fall. It was an orchard of trees, that was it. Well, why not. The court-yard was open to the sun, and its walls protected the grove from the worst predations of wind and exposure. The trees grew out of the cobbles, bulging them irregular.

"Who planted a secret harbor of gold here," she said aloud, as if in this unexpected magnificence perhaps Gardius would be changed to a Dragon and answer her. But that would be mere fancy, storytelling of an irresponsible sort. Dreamwork. Gardius galumphed with animal joy at a new place to make home, perhaps to befoul with his fewmets and his raspberry-stink of urine.

"Who the trespasser to ask the question?" she heard back. She looked up for the source of the voice.

Nine feet up, a monkey was squatting in the crux of a branching limb. His wings drooped with a sort of limpness that made Rain think of aging celery. His look was cruel and keen. "Who gave you permission to come tromp around our orchard."

"No signs posted outside saying go away."

"No monkey here can write letters. Even so. You might have knocked."

She didn't feel as if she should need to introduce herself. If her green skin wasn't good for anything, it ought to be a calling card in this house of pesky magicks. Still, the sentry was making his way down the tree with arthritic gracelessness. The monkey said, "And this foul thing with a pair of tattered bellows for wings, I assume it's your chaperone. Call it off."

Rain called him to her, not expecting the dragon to obey, but he romped over and sat before her knees, panting. "Have you been taking lessons on how to be a dog?" she asked, and scratched his head. He began a sub-glottal growl of appreciation. She stopped before his breath got too warm and she suffered burns on her forearm. "I'm Rain, by the way. Rainary Ko Thropp. There are other names too but those are enough for now."

The creature now hopped to the ground. Trailing his wings, he came nearer to peer at her. "Some clever ruse, is it? Are you fashioning yourself as some flyaway sketch of the Queen of Menace?"

"Elphaba. Yeah, sure. I'm her granddaughter. Can't you guess by my skin color."

"Color-blind," said the creature, unconvincingly. He looked skeptical but his face relaxed a little. "What did you say your name was?"

"Rain. Who are you?"

"Agitor."

"I need to see your oligarch. Can you bring him out? Or her."

"Chistery? He's busy. Anyway, his wife makes the supper around here. She's high command. What do you want her for?"

"I have a message for her."

Agitor raised his head and let out a howl that sounded like a steel colander shaking stone arrowheads. Rain fell back at the horrible noise; Gardius let out a warning lick of flame. Suddenly the courtyard was alive with other voices—they were instant, and everywhere. Rain whirled about and gripped at the scruff of Gardius's neck for safety. The whole golden orchard was filled with monkeys. They'd been quiet, hidden stock-still in their trees. Two, three dozen of them. The holler leveled out as the voices converged on a set of three or four notes—not precisely harmonious, but on pitch. Like being inside of a great steam furnace whose rotors and valves perform at peak play. They kept it up, an organic klaxon, an alarm curling into the sky, rolling up the sides of the castle keep, the turrets and side houses.

The sound of shutters being thrown open and a human voice, aggrieved and anything but musical, sluicing down from above. "The racket, and at this hour! I ask you!"

"At what hour," yelled Rain. "It's nearly lunchtime!"

"I keep my own clock, as ever was the case. What stripe of hooligan is this who causes such barracking?"

Rain raised her head. She couldn't see through the dense golden foliage but she believed she knew the voice. She ran past Agitor, heading through the grove to where the steps lifted to a ceremonial doorway. She remembered the route now, it came flooding back like tidewater. How this castle was organized, its weird halls and sloping floors and bitten-off staircases, its industrial protrusions from some long-abandoned function of civil engineering.

"Hey," said Agitor, "not so fast." He'd have made better time but for his listless wings. He swung his body as his forearms knuckled the ground. The monkey chorus became a rabble of alarm, and a few monkey souls dropped from their trees, but they were curiously static, more keen on observing than in mixing themselves up in this morning's contretemps.

The castle keep was steeped in the gloom of an abandoned factory, one whose wheelworks and devices had been removed and melted down for other uses. A rich smell of stone-mold soured the air. Of the banner tapestries that hung from high pegs, several were greened over with lichen or a verdant mildew. Rain and Gardius barreled up the rail-less stairs that hugged first this wall and then, after a corner, that one. Rain was put in mind of climbing to meet the Oracle, back in the Tower of the Clouds, but this was different. She'd been here before. This had been Elphaba's final redoubt, her stay against the world until her invincibility had run out. This must be like putting on your mother's party shoes, if your mother had ever had party shoes. Rain was playing at being a witch. In play does instinct become talent; through practice, then, talent is refined into prowess.

At the head of the stairs, a landing. A table with wobbly legs. A bouquet of henbane littered petals upon its dusty surface. Another monkey was resting nearby with her chin on the head of a broom. She looked up from a morning snooze as the voice of Agitor climbed the air from below. "Jixiana, company! Look sharp!"

Jixiana, an older flying monkey, lifted her chins and surveyed Rain and Gardius, who had paused for breath. Rain doubled over, her hands on her knees. Gardius hissed out little stoppered flames in blue and copper. Jixiana's eyes were heavy-lidded and her wings looked plagued with muscle fatigue. She'd dropped a few feathers along the baseboard. "You people never give adequate notice," she said. "I don't know how we're expected to cope. I suppose you're here to chinwag with the old wag-chin herself?"

"And Chistery."

"They're together up there." She motioned with a crippled finger to a scrappy set of listing wooden steps that ended at a door. "Tell them I sent word ahead you were coming but it didn't arrive in time. No dogs allowed."

"That's okay, he's not a dog, he's a dragon."

"Sorry instance of one." She shrugged. "But I shouldn't talk, as I'd trade my wings for his in a heartbeat."

Rain and Gardius took the staircase indicated. It rose through an oblong shaft like a bell tower, braced with the unplaned trunks of broad-beamed trees that crossed the gloom at irregular angles. At the top they found a suite of rooms appointed for human habitation. Some threadbare carpets, some portraits on the walls, though

one was hung upside down. All the doors were open. A sound
of urgent discussion stopped mid-sentence as Rain and Gardius
arrived at a set of double doors suggesting a salon of some sort.

"I'm told to announce we've been announced but the announce-
ment is late to arrive," said Rain.

"The mails, who can trust them," said Nanny. "But I've been
expecting you."

She was sitting in a kind of bed-chair, an upholstered nest, like
a hip bath kitted out with down comforters and doilies. To one
side of her sloped dear old Chistery, with a wisp of white beard,
looking like the mottled King of Time himself. To the other side
was the chattiest of the flying monkeys to follow Rain to Maracoor
Abiding, the one called Thilma.

"Yes," said Nanny decisively, "this time I know you're not Elphaba. I'd probably have made that mistake, memory being what
it is, but Thilma has been catching us up with your adventures in
this dollopy dikkety backwater you skived off to. You nasty child.
You had us all worried silly. Well, I've only just heard about it, but
I'm worrying myself silly as fast as I can to catch up."

"Child," said Chistery, his eyes running. "The very fletch and
spark of Elphaba, that old bitch! Come to Chistery."

"I don't really do the huggy thing anymore," she said, but he
would have none of it. His wings seemed in better shape than those
of the other flying monkeys in residence, and he launched himself
into her with such force she'd have fallen over but for Gardius,
standing behind her, providing buttress service. The embrace was
rank but not unwelcome—somehow easier to accept than affection from her father.

"We'll need some tea and maybe some cheesy crackers," Chistery hollered down the stairs.

"I'll send a message to the kitchens," called back Jixiana, who
sounded as if she hadn't budged from her resting position on

the landing, and didn't plan to budge now. Below, the chorus of monkeys in the golden grove had hushed. Apparently the entire establishment was trying to eavesdrop on the reunion.

Nanny sat up a little straighter. "I can stand up if I start thinking about it a week ahead," she said, "but I haven't had adequate notice. This Thilma arrived just last night, too beat by her long journey to speak. She was just telling us about her jolly adventures. They found this huge water, you know about it, and against their will a great big fat wind blew them ashore to a distant wasteland."

"However did you get back?" Rain asked Thilma.

"*Thilma's* wings still work," said the flying monkey with, perhaps, a touch of condescension. "Once Lucikles returned from seeing you off, Thilma thinks Thilma's task in High Chora is done."

"So he got back safely." The thought of him. It wasn't all welcome, now. Still, Rain hadn't quite realized that she'd banked her apprehensions of Lucikles into a sealed vault submerged in a lightless sea. But Chistery didn't want Thilma to talk about foreigners.

"She's back, she's back," he crowed, pointing to Rain, "the savior of the winged monkey nation."

"Thilma?" asked Thilma, preening; her misunderstanding was willful.

"What about the others?" asked Rain. "Tiotro, those other two? Whosie and Whatsie? And I trekked all this way to deliver news of your whereabouts. You beat me to it."

"Only Thilma," said the intrepid monkey. "The others afraid to fly the ocean again. Thilma afraid too but more afraid of not ever being home again." She grinned bashfully at Chistery, who was probably her distant ancestor by generations.

"I for one don't believe it," said Rain. "I couldn't have made it without magic. Either direction."

"Rain not Thilma," said the returning hero, and that was true enough.

At this point Agitor arrived at the apartment and signaled his approach with a stagey clearing of his throat. "I'm asked to announce that there are visitors arriving," he said, and with a flourish of his hairy knuckles, "and here they are. I'm afraid they brooked our ample defenses with their cunning and oppressive force."

"Not cunning or oppressive force, we just came through the unlocked door," said Rain.

"Wicked ingenious scheming, that. I'm asked by Jixiana to say that a message will be sent to the kitchens for tea. Sadly there may be no tea leaves on the premises. If that's so, we will send out for it, though delivery could take half a year. Apologies for the delay. We can play cards while we wait." Having unburdened himself of all official duties, he went and squatted upon Nanny's humidor and began to groom his underarms, airing them in the breeze through the open window.

"You monkeys will talk in non sequiturs, it was always thus," said Nanny. "I suppose you got it from us. Rain, Rain. A sight for sore eyes. I remember about you. I remember you were here a few years ago. With that young fellow. But I don't understand why you went so far away that your father had to request the winged monkeys to pursue you over land and sea."

"Oh, Nanny," said Rain. "I thought your brain would be chopped cabbage by now."

"When one's brain has always been chopped cabbage," she replied, "there isn't much left for the vegetable hatchet. No, my dear, it defies my understanding. The older I get, the clearer I seem. It is the opposite of that thing—that forgetting disease they tell me you had. What is it called again?"

"Amnesia," said Rain, and laughed at the thought of being able to remember it.

"Indeed. It's true that there are lapses for someone in her ninth or tenth or maybe eleventh decade. I lose words. I suppose I become somehow—I don't know how to say it—"

"Inarticulate?"

"That'll do. But the long life I have lived seems to resolve into sharper focus. It's uncanny. Either I've become adept at persuading myself that everything I recall is actual fact, or some protocol against human decay has allowed me to strengthen my mind." Now she rotated her upper arms, and Chistery and Agitor came to each side of her. Perhaps she'd forgotten she said she couldn't stand up. They raised her to her feet, and bravely if unsteadily, she took a few steps forward. "You won't come embrace me, so I'll approach you to stare at you. My eyes have weakened, I'll admit to that. No, you do look like your grandmother, more than ever. I suppose you must carry something of your Quadling mother in you, but I don't see it myself. What is she known for?"

"I don't really remember. Candle played the domingon. Liir used to say she could read the present the way others could read the future. Then I'm not sure I believe in soothsaying, so maybe 'understanding the present' is another delusion. A trick we play on ourselves to keep from becoming unmoored by everything we don't know."

"Don't talk sly philosophy at me. Not before I've had my tea. May I reach out and feel your face?"

"I suppose so."

The ancient woman who had helped raise Rain's grandmother from infancy leaned forward and nearly toppled over. Her hand was a soft scented posset. Gardius gave a low-throated growl, emitting flame that licked at the quilted flowery comforter that Nanny had had sewn into a kind of dressing gown. It seared a seam but died out. "Wouldn't that be rich, if I went up in flames myself as some have done before me!" said Nanny. "They used to burn witches, did you know? Beware of fire yourself, my dear. A hot-tempered hound was an expression, it didn't used to mean a live flame. I'd get a different dog if I were you."

"This is a dwarf dragon."

"If you insist on keeping this mutt, I'll tell you what. Locate a tin loaf-pan and a pair of shears and cut out one end panel, and strap the hood over that snout. Your fellow there loses his train of thought and snorts a flame, it'll heat up the tin and make him sorry he was a bad boy. A bad bad boy. Aren't you the bad boy? You can't help it, but you must learn." She knuckled his forehead and he gave out a chuckle that was only a few glottal repetitions short of a purr.

"Come now," said Nanny. "Since Elphaba seems to be out for the day, let me be granny. Everyone needs a grandmother, and I'll do my part. Sit down next to me. Tell me why you left the country without as much as a note at Lurlinemas to say you were going."

Rain felt she'd lost something of herself being this high up in the castle, as if the air were thinner. Somehow she'd become a servant player in the grand interior life of Nanny. She didn't mind, at least for the while. It was in fact a bit of a break. She pulled up a cane chair and Gardius settled at her feet. Nanny allowed herself to be lowered back into her podium seat. Chistery and Agitor stopped rustling their wings, and Thilma went out to see what was holding up the delivery of something or other in the way of nourishment. Of course, thought Rain: this had been Thilma's home before she launched across the Nonestic Sea. She'd know the ropes.

The sun swung along its invisible track in a mountain sky so thin that, if you stared at it, first it paled to white, and then it thickened to black before reverting to blue. Until skeins of cloud inched along. Without cloud, thought Rain, how could we ever stop measuring infinity. We'd become deranged by the effort.

She told the old woman about how Tip had really been Ozma in disguise, without his knowledge and against his will. How the old sorceress Mombey had set about to remove the elephant aspect off Liir, but how the mighty spell had rolled round the room and removed other enchantments as well—the disguise of Tip upon Ozma, the camouflage placed upon Rain to conceal her green skin from public scrutiny. How the abrupt loss of her lover had caused Rain to retreat to her father's hermitage in the Great Kells. Then, because the rage and frustration wouldn't dissipate, how she'd decided to steal the great magic book called the Grimmerie and prevent it from any other possible interference in her life, or anyone else's. How, upon the discovery of the Nonestic Sea, she'd decided to fly out over it and pitch the book from a great height. How this created a great storm that catapulted her and Iskinaary to a foreign land. Where, after adventures too numerous to recount, she'd met up with a person who claimed to be her great-grandfather. The Oracle of Maracoor, as he called himself there. Or the wonderful Wizard of Oz, as he'd styled himself here.

"That old coot, he's still flapping about?" Nanny waved her hand as if she was being pestered by a no-see-um.

"Stuck up in a tower, just like you are. Can't move. *He* won't be bothering anyone again."

"I'm not stuck," she said. "True, the stairs are a bit much, but we've rigged up an aerial stagecoach. See that beam over the window? It has a winch on it. If I've had enough sherry and the cords are tight enough, I allow myself to be lowered to the courtyard so I can enjoy a picnic under the choke-chestnut trees. At lunchtime, when the air is warmest."

"Nanny," said Rain. "I only came here to tell Chistery or whoever might be in charge about what had happened to the quartet of monkeys who flew to rescue me. I realize that the news has already arrived."

"Jixiana keeps track of our comings and goings," said Nanny. "Chistery is gone to seed."

"If I've gone to seed, you've gone to ground," said the senior flying monkey, without rancor. They grinned at each other like an old married couple in dementia who weren't sure they recognized each other but remembered about politeness.

"Not that there's so much coming and going these days," said Nanny. "It was hard to come up with four creatures both able and willing to fly west to see if they could find you and Iskinaary. Your father came here himself to ask them, to pester them about it and to select the team."

"There seem to be a lot of drooping wings, I've noticed."

"Do you know," said Nanny, "this is a problem."

"Among some," said Chistery. He flexed his upper back muscles, and his own wings raised with crisp lines on either side, impressively. Though there were patches of moult or mange.

"What is it? A blight?"

"No one is sure, really," replied the old winged creature. "We aren't the scientific hotshots that Elphaba was. The whole breed was her doing, did you know that? But after all these years, something strange is going on. Quite a few monkeys are losing the capacity of their wings, which are appendages. Annoying, to hear them tell about it. I once walked in from the rain wearing a cloak I wanted to shuck off but the clasp had gotten bent somehow and I couldn't unfasten it. Wings can feel like that. A heaviness, an inconvenience."

"But then you can't fly anymore."

"Not everyone who can fly wants to. Ask your garden-variety duck which she prefers, the river or the sky. Still, you're right. For some of the monkeys, the wings are a redundancy—once liberating and now, alas, a punishment. Chains and weights even for walking around. Not only no lift, but added drag, if you get my drift."

"But it isn't consistent throughout the population?"

Chistery cleared his throat and mumbled, "Some of the newer generations are being born without wings at all. And some others are born without language. We treat everyone the same but it's less clear to know who we are."

"Recidivism," declared Nanny, stabbing the arm of her chair. "Is that it? Regression? Some word starting with *re*. Repulsion, regret. Rejection? Repossession. Religion. No, I've lost the thread."

"Reversion," said Rain. "Like when a tree with a graft on it decides to go back to its former self. The graft fails and the original takes over. We were just talking about that. Liir and me. But Chistery—is it worrying to you? Have you made an effort to arrest the condition? Without working wings you'll be stuck here."

"We rarely make vacation plans as it is," said Chistery, but he took Rain's hand in his own. She saw that he didn't want to complain about his lot in front of Nanny, who for all her alertness was someone who needed constant tending. "We get along all right."

"Perhaps you need a booster spell to correct the condition."

"You're a witch. You volunteering?"

She shook her head, not only to say Not on your life, but as if to clear away the notion of being a sorceress. "Whatever I am, I'm not competent. Really, at anything."

"You take after your grandmother," said Nanny fondly. "She had such ambitions but she couldn't lace up both boots on the same afternoon. She'd get distracted."

"I tried to get rid of the Grimmerie, and I failed. I tried to drown it."

"Oh, please," said Nanny. "No wonder you failed. You tried to drown the Grimmerie when you really ought to have been trying to drown your anger at the world. You have to hold it under the water till it stops breathing, like kittens. No wonder the Grimmerie didn't stay put."

"If the Grimmerie is still circulating out there," said Chistery, "perhaps you might consult it on our behalf and prove yourself a witch at last by doing something useful?"

"I'm not a traveling showgirl." But she felt guilty as she spoke. What was so wrong with being a traveling showgirl, anyway? It's not as if she'd ever accomplished anything else in life besides mere survival. "What do you mean, Nanny, drowning my own rage? I'm guessing you didn't mean drowning it in lager or spirits."

"Once a Nanny, always a Nanny," said Nanny, sighing, enjoying the eternal regret of the overly responsible. "Listen, child. There are times in your life you have to walk out the door and close it behind you. There are other times when you have to stand in the doorway and count to ten. Or a hundred. You're too young to know the difference. You aren't done with Ozma and Tip because you both—you all?—dropped the cards in mid-play. Whatever happens next can't happen until you pick them up and read them honestly. Maybe *then* you'll walk away and close the door. But if you do, you'll leave your paralyzing anger behind. You'll be free to grow up. Don't you think it's about time? Darling, this is becoming tedious even to me and I've only met you twice. How it must grate on you to be you. Beyond my power to imagine."

"If there were an invisibility spell, I would cast it upon myself. I don't want to cause any more mayhem."

Nanny said, "Nonsense. Either you're collateral damage or you cause it. Probably both. There are no other choices. Regardless of what your father thinks, sitting it out there in his tidy hideout. There's no tidiness in this life, dearie, until they fold your hands upon your breast in your coffin, and sometimes not even then. You might get out of the mess by dying, but you leave it behind for others to inherit. Just ask Elphaba. Invisibility schmissasomething, I can't say it."

"Nanny, you have some nerve."

"I know, don't I? I scarcely know where I get it." She hummed a little to herself and patted her lap as if there were an undrowned kitten drowsing there. "I think back on my life, Rain, and I remember your grandmother as an infant, and *her* mother. Melena. What a piece of work *she* was! It was she who slept with the rascal who would become the Wizard of Oz. You never knew her. She had no interest in her children, really, especially in Elphaba with that horrid green skin. Mean no offense, darling; sorry; yours isn't horrid, it's just the perfect shade. Yummy. No, I tried to take care of Elphaba as best I could, to give the child some guidance. I suppose I failed and all of human history since is my fault. It's hard to be a Nanny." Destroyer of nations, she sighed contentedly. Chistery rolled his eyes.

Sitting on the floor, Rain hugged her knees. Tight as a furled morning glory. Gardius came up and banked himself against her. Nanny was talking to herself now. "I'll tell you, I don't even know why I'm still alive, or why I'm so wonderful. The notorious nanny of Oz. I ought to be dead. I sometimes think I can remember stealing a sip of some weird potion she kept among her jewels and lotions. It did me a power of good. But age has unmoored me—I'm not sure if I'm only imagining that. Sometimes I dream of being at Elphaba's birth, and I was a creature of some sort, a Badger nurse, or a Raccoon midwife. But I wasn't there; I didn't arrive for several months. So who knows what all that is about. Tipple never took with me, if that's what you're thinking. It was only a taste. A sort of chartreuse, a licorice elixir of sorts. Good for what ails you."

"She needs to rest," murmured Chistery. "Frankly, we all do, unless the tea ever gets here."

"We could have beer?" Agitor sounded hopeful.

"I'll stay the night," said Rain, "but tomorrow I'm headed to central Oz. To see if I can meet up again with Ozma and find out—whatever there is to find out."

"I'm old enough to remember when Ozma first disappeared. I was a young maiden of clean reputation and she was scarcely a toddler. We used to bake apples back then, not stew them. Also music seemed louder, and more—more confident. But dental care? The coal pits of hell. Don't ask."

"Nanny," said Rain, "isn't that a kind of regression, too? The slipping back to memories of your youth. Even ones that aren't your own? Is that what we have ahead of us—that systems fail, that grafts give out, that wings wither and language stutters, that charms erode?"

"*My* charms are intact," said Nanny, lifting her forearm to amplify her bosom. "No, you're just talking about natural corruption. It's necessary for regeneration. Where will the new world arise from if there is no mulch from the old? All processes fumble eventually, my dear. Even I, despite my apparent immortality, will give way at last. I'll send out a notice when it happens and say 'No presents.' Everything turns about." She gestured. "The ice griffon wheel in the sky, the summer collapses into autumn. There are only two things that always move forward, as far as I know."

"What are they?"

She pressed the edge of her pinkies into the inside corners of her eyes, and then at the outside, to flick away the evidence of sentiment. "Time," she said. "It never goes backward. And nor does melody. When we are all dead and gone and those who are born to replace us are dead and gone, time will inch forward and the music of the world will play on, even when there are no human ears to hear it."

PREPARING TO LEAVE the next day, Rain accepted as traveling provisions such portions of monkey provender as her hosts could spare. Thilma and Agitor scurried about them like members of an inept staff. Getting underfoot, complicating matters. Jixiana had never left her post in that upstairs hallway and seemed satisfied with her lot. In the end, suffering a stomach ailment, Nanny decided against being lowered into the golden grove, so she waved from the window of her apartments as Rain was making her final goodbyes.

Chistery and Thilma walked Rain to the gate. Gardius shuffled behind, trying to worry off his proboscis the makeshift tin noseguard Agitor had cobbled up overnight and buckled in place under the dragon's chin.

"Do think about the Grimmerie," said Chistery, wringing his hands. "Perhaps this decay among our kind can yet be arrested. When you get your strength as a witch. It would be a kindness."

"I'm not taking on any more campaigns, not for myself or anyone else," said Rain. "But the Grimmerie is under the care of my father. Ready and waiting. If you could send a team of scouts to search for me beyond the Thousand Year Grasslands, you can locate Liir well enough. He's five, six days away on foot. There's a suspended walkway in need of repair. Round up a few monkeys who can still fly, it might be a matter of only a day or two." She told Chistery how to locate Nether How among the string of five lakes.

He wasn't paying much attention. "Liir's strengths aren't at magicking anything," said Chistery. "Nice boy and all that, but a plodder. No, the gift skipped him, mostly, whereas you've got it in spades."

"That's jumping to conclusions, just because I'm green. I ought to take offense."

"Think about it, anyway," Chistery begged her. "Come, Thilma. Let's let them slip away, if that's their only game."

He was a hunchbacked old primate now. As he disappeared among the columns of trees in the courtyard, she watched him grip his wings about him like the edges of a frayed bathrobe. The other monkeys, who seemed more comfortable in branches than at tables and chairs, were humming like bees, a sostenuto note just off-pitch enough to sound like all the glass in the world grinding in a mill, somewhere far away.

Thilma kept pace with Rain and the dwarf dragon as they marched across the drawbridge to the start of the downslope track. There it went: back to Red Windmill and the other hamlets, to the banks of the Vinkus River, and eventually to the Emerald City if you took the right turns and didn't change your mind. "You're not coming with us, Thilma," said Rain, partly a question and partly a prohibition.

"Thilma? Forget it." She huffed. She only seemed to want to be outside of the hearing of her clan. "Thilma doesn't volunteer for new mission to make Rain's life easier. Not again. Don't ask Thilma." She spit, which while a common enough activity for a flying monkey, at the moment seemed editorial punctuation.

"Oh, I know who got the spoiled egg for breakfast," said Rain, almost amused. "Can't let me go without reaming me out? What's your gripe?"

Thilma was a small flying monkey but a strong one. Her wings hadn't suffered the palsy that some of her clan experienced. She thumped the tips of her wings on the stony soil. "Thilma is at farmhouse when Lucikles returns from trip." She glowered at Rain.

"You said that. And that he's okay. You told me. He made it. On his bad foot. Am I supposed to ask another question?"

"Thilma see that Oena woman. See she broken. She learn fast that Lucikles take Rain for another wife."

"That's rich, even though it's none of your business. Anyway, you're wrong. Nothing like a marriage, Lucikles and me. We were traveling together. Things happen. Am I being scolded about human moral practices by a flying *monkey*?" Rain looked at Gardius, who appeared to be nodding. In agreement with Thilma's outrageous disapproval, maybe—it was hard to tell. Maybe the tin lid on his nose was chafing. Rain snapped, "I don't get it, Thilma."

"Rain doesn't see trouble this causes that family? To Oena, to children? To Lucikles too, beside himself with regret? This is real reason Thilma leave. Too sad for Thilma. That household. Crying, breaking up things, children terrified, grandmother angry. Wife despondent, husband hopeless. All from Rain and Lucikles to make reckless sleepy love."

"It meant nothing. If it was reckless, it was also pointless."

"What is point of pointlessness?"

"Um—search me. Distraction?"

"From what?"

That was the matter in a golden nutshell, wasn't it. "You should be haranguing Lucikles. He's the married one, not me. He had everything to lose. Me, I have nothing."

"That's Rain's excuse? Rain, Rain get her protection from that family. That wife and her creaky old motherly old mother take Rain in. Lucikles, yes, sure, Lucikles also foolish and wrong. Now Lucikles living with his wrong. Rain owns some of this wrong, too." She drew herself up, the silly little fur-capped creature. "Thilma give you no blessing for your journey."

"What do I need your blessing for? You're a flying monkey with a severe case of umbrage."

"From what Thilma hear," said her erstwhile rescuer, "Rain not worthy of color of her skin."

"How did you even find out about us?" asked Rain. A twinge of guilt, like a seed between the teeth. She wanted to worry it free and spit it out. "He was a fool to say anything at all when it meant—nothing."

"Nothing means nothing," said Thilma. "If it *meant* nothing, then when the surgeon-priests at the Groves of Salanx gave him tongue-freeing juniper juice, prior to the procedure, he'd have *said* nothing. Instead, truth rolled out his unguarded mouth when he was in fog of sedation. All about his boy, how he worries; all about his wife, how he worries. And about you, and the taint on his spirit of having taken you as a lover."

Rain said *ahhhh* with an open mouth, breath misting a mirror.

"Has he lost his whole foot?" But, turning back toward Kiamo Ko, Thilma shrugged noncommittally. "Thilma? Is he all right? Did he survive?" Thilma pretended not to hear, and didn't answer. When she got to the door cut in the stronghold gates, she slammed it behind her.

THE EMERALD CITY

1

In the past two years had Oz grown smaller. Or is it only the effect of travel, thought Rain. The breadth of the Nonestic Sea, the uncharted width of Maracoor Abiding on the other side, made omniscient Oz cringe a little on the map. Retract. When a place is no longer novel, one doesn't see it the same way.

The lower slopes of the Great Kells, the great yellow-foam crash of the Vinkus River. Villages, farms, foundries, windmills. The twisty tracks that used to run between Kellswater and Restwater, derived from deer runs at one point, were now beaten by commercial traffic into hard-packed thoroughfares served by the occasional inn and tavern. She supposed that Kellswater, its health revived, was teaming with fish and game birds. Attractive to settlers. Nothing stays the same while you go abroad.

Nanny's advice about a training noseguard for the dwarf dragon had been sound. Gardius scorched himself once, and once was enough. That evening Rain had to use a twig to pick out pellets of torched mucus from the sensitive nostrils. Not that he became an angel creature. When annoyed, he aired his opinions with a blast of smeltery breath. But he governed himself more strictly than before. She jettisoned the snout-helmet overnight.

During the days and nights that Rain and Gardius groped their way across Oz, they encountered the usual rabble. Some welcoming and some suspicious, some armed with stones and others with oven-warm bread, or beans from a roadside cook-fire. Rain accepted hospitality. She was pretty sure that her color, not to mention the awkward dragon lolloping alongside, gave her an advantage over the usual single woman trekking cross-country. Regardless, she kept to herself.

Nor did she rehearse strategies for what she would do when she arrived in the Emerald City. She would make an approach to Ozma. Probably. Wasn't that the plan. But what if when she got there, she discovered that she'd lost the appetite for an encounter whose nature she couldn't yet imagine. She wouldn't know till she arrived. One foot in front of the other, one padded paw in front of the other. Come on, Gardius.

She didn't browbeat or wheedle passersby for the scuttlebutt from the Emerald City. Somehow it was easier not to know. In her best days she'd never managed to be the sprightly girl-in-the-middle-of-a-chattering-circle. And over the past several years she'd perfected a kind of hulking presence, mostly stern and maybe censorious. A talent for unsettling. She gave people the creeps. She welcomed their silence. Why that, why did it matter. Maybe for fear of what such tongue-wagging might tell her. She didn't want to know—yet. Until there was no other way to sidestep it. Wasn't amnesia itself the greatest avoidance strategy of all.

Truth be told, she gave *herself* the creeps. She kept clear of reflective ponds and such mirrors as tinkers hang on the sides of caravans, for shaving. She began to wish she hadn't thrown away the tin lid for Gardius's nose. She might have been able to hammer it into a tin mask for herself.

Before too long—well, it had been long enough—she'd crossed the border of the Vinkus into the narrow stretch of Munchkinland that led to the Emerald City's southern gate, Munchkin Mousehole. The gleaming towers, the spires and domes of the capital city looked from this distance like a set of dials, some single coordinated machine of suspicious ambition. The clockwork mechanics of governmental power.

Rain saw hives of shanty settlements newly sprung up outside the gates. The spoils of peace, she supposed, now that reunification of Munchkinland and Loyal Oz was several years on. Gardius pretty much kept to her side, except for investigating road ditches to inspect the digestive expulsions of others roaming the territory.

Having little interest in townships or in crowds, she kept her head down. But she relished the hodgepodge blessing of accents. People speaking Ozish with a Quadling curl, a Munchkin broadness. Probably at Shiz Gate to the north you'd hear college tones and other upper-crust sonorities that flourished in the prosperous reaches of Gillikin country. The accents pleated across one another with ease, as if everyone had memorized their lines before leaving home this morning. Rain felt more tongue-tied by the day.

Then, there they were, the gates to the nation's capital, flung open in what looked like a permanent position. A token sentry languished in the guardhouse, smoking a cigarette and picking at a boil on his neck. She walked past without his noticing. She had worried that Gardius might draw attention, but the children in the alleys were only running in mock terror, and they circled back quickly. A pony dragon was more adorable than alarming, apparently.

Rain had known a few people in the Emerald City, back in the day, when the civil war had come to a head and her great-uncle Shell-of-God had abdicated the throne. First and foremost, her bosom companion, Brrr, the Cowardly Lion, who had ascended as regent while Ozma was being groomed for her elevation. The dwarf and his wife, Little Daffy. Dorothy too, for that matter, but she'd wafted off to some netherland or other, as was her habit. Most of Rain's circle didn't matter or had disappeared. In any case, even Rain's beloved Brrr, the Throne Minister at the time she had left two years ago—she didn't want to hear his silky lion's complaint. She only wanted Ozma. She supposed she'd have to go to the steps of the Palace.

One or two elderly people or Animals exclaimed "Elphaba!" as she crossed their paths. She didn't correct them. But when a rather squinty Quadling fellow, hawking beads on the pavement in front of a tonsorial parlor, followed that name with a "Praise be!" Rain relented. She couldn't accept reverence. Not after the dressing down that Thilma had delivered. Rain squatted on her haunches so she was eye to eye with the vendor and she said, "I'm not Elphaba, not even close."

"You're a good enough likeness, then. Acting her in some tragedy playhouse?"

"That would be a neat business to be in. No. I'm an anomaly. I just like the brass beads."

"Calcified milkweed pods; varnished, baked, and enhanced with highlights. Take them, on the house, please." She wouldn't. She threw him two coins that she'd purloined from Liir's desk. He asked, "If you're not Elphaba, who are you instead?"

"The Witch of Maracoor, will that do? Now listen. I want to know about Ozma."

"Don't ask me about Ozma. I've no opinion." He wasn't agnostic, he was skittish, clearly not wanting to be implicated in some factional divide. He tossed the coins back at her. "Keep the beads." He rolled up his carpet of wares and slung it over his shoulder and scurried off, leaving scattered items where they fell.

Curious. So that was it; she could avoid the subject no longer. Eventually remembering that people gather under bridges, she slipped into a group of itinerants and pickpockets reviewing their days' take. They threatened her until they saw Gardius furrow his brow. Then they opened their circle and gave her a scoop of dirty soup in a saucer, an adjacent crust of rye.

What her father had told her was true, apparently: Ozma hadn't yet ascended to the throne. The Cowardly Lion was still performing duties as the Regent Throne Minister. Where Ozma actually *was,* and why she hadn't claimed the crown due her by inheritance, these vagabonds couldn't say and they didn't care. They didn't much believe in Ozma, any more than they'd cottoned to that parody of brutal innocence, Dorothy of Kanzizz.

Rain sensed she oughtn't push them. Whatever was going on, it was a delicate moment for Ozma. Rain changed the subject to the activities of the domestic military who policed the underclasses. While the feisty crowd chattered their stories of sweet comeuppance, she plotted her tomorrow.

She slept with them. Think of it, a young woman on her own, and so on. In the dark, green skin became less obvious, so it served less well as a defense against unwanted advances. Gardius was a comfort and a protection.

2

When the town clocks had struck morning and the streets clattered with commerce, she thought she might get by without being noticed. Even the oddment of humanity can almost disappear if the crowd is full enough. She made her way up shady boulevards and across light-swept plazas, seeing with a new eye. The Emerald City was built of a different vernacular than the great capital city called Maracoor Crown. The hometown glories looked sprucer, perhaps glossier, like pastries coated with egg white before baking. But also cheaper for that. She couldn't have noticed this before. And so unlike Maracoor Crown, with its low, solid, columned blocks of sun-scrubbed pale granite and dark marble. Now was she growing homesick for the place that had put her on trial for sedition. What a basket case I am, she thought.

A kerchiefed cleaning woman heading for a staff entrance at the Palace frowned when Rain stopped her, saying, "I need you to bring a message to the Throne Minister: Rain in the forecast."

"Not my bailiwick, conveying threats," said the hard-bitten domestic, then, "but I would be obliged this time, miss," when Gardius backed Rain's request up with a fancy spray of fire droplets a little too close to the woman's ankles.

Rain contorted her fingers in a theatrical manner. Aiming at mystery, she suspected she only looked as if she was demonstrating muscular twitches for a class of medical students. "I'll come back for an answer, tomorrow, at this very hour. You or someone else will need to be here, or you'll learn what mischief I can make. I'm a certified trouble-maker. The Witch of Maracoor, in the flesh, as it happens." It felt okay to say it out loud.

When she returned to the Palace servants' entrance the next morning, the old scout with her mop and broom didn't show up. Rain loitered a while, conceding that she mustn't be very threatening as a witch after all. She was about to leave when the door opened and a younger woman peered out. For a brave and horrified instant Rain's heart leapt and fell simultaneously.

The recognition was wrong, though. A familiar face, just not the right one. "*Scarly?*" said Rain.

Scarly—the servant girl from St. Prowd's School in Shiz. Other than Tip, nearly the only friend her own age that Rain had ever made. Rain had taught her to read. "As I live and breathe," said Scarly, sounding like a middle-aged char, "it *is* you! I didn't believe it."

"Of course it's me, who else would it be?" She had one of the tarot cards ready to hand over, the one with the broom on it. "This is my calling card."

"Everybody en't been keeping their same shapes and forms, as *you* know. You en't never been green back in the day. Thought you might be some flitch of that old Elphaba. Had to come see for myself. It *is* you, just like a splinter in a sore place. Oh, Miss Rainary! Look, but you can't keep here. Now I seen you I'll have to say so. But you should go. It en't safe. And I daren't loiter."

Rain reached out to grab Scarly's wrist; at first the girl pulled back as if afraid of being burned. "Oh, it's not *that*," said Scarly, "I don't mean *that*. I'm just scared for you and not so happy for myself. There's a lot of thuggery skullduggery ranged against the Palace, and you showing up could kick up a coup. Can't you go back away wherever you went? You don't want to get nobody in trouble, do you?"

"Who could be in danger? Scarly, what are you talking about?"

"Not for me to say. Less said, less let loose." She twisted her wrist from Rain, not out of worry or anger, but so she could grip Rain's own hands in hers. "One day there'll be something like peace, you know. I believe that, I do! Meanwhile there's an awful handful of upkeep. I got my duster on. Don't come back, Miss Rainary, for everyone's good." She bobbed a curtsey.

"Don't you ever do that to me!" said Rain, nearly at a shout, and Gardius raised his eyebrows as if to defend his companion with a spittle of flame. "Wait! Where is Tip?"

Scarly put her finger to her lips and made a shushing sound, and then flapped her hands to shoo Rain away like a chicken. The maid disappeared behind a stoutly slammed utility door.

Rain and Gardius spent the day under a bandstand on the Royal Mall. Scarly had unnerved her—odd that it be done so easily, after all Rain had been through. But it couldn't come only to this, could it. Could it. She'd, what, she'd just walk away. Was that all. Really. Was that it then.

She was cowed, that much was true. Here she was in the shadows. Keeping her green skin hidden. She didn't know why, and was afraid to learn. Do they really burn witches in this modern day.

As evening fell, a troupe of unrepentant musicians came to the bandstand to practice their all-piccolo repertoire several times over. Rain lasted as long as she could stand it. By the time she and Gardius were driven from the shrieking overtones, shadows were settling beneath the great trees of the Mall. Rain decided to return to the servants' entrance at the Palace at dawn. Did Scarly think Rain would give up so easily. She was a witch, after all. She'd have Gardius torch the door if need be. She'd come all this way, via the otherworld and back, if you wanted to put it like that.

She didn't return the next morning, though, because sometime during the night, under the bridge, she was attacked by dark-clad thugs. She scarcely heard Gardius beginning a bark, and only began to apprehend the assault before a curtain of dark descended in her brain.

3

Rising to consciousness was like breasting the surface of the Nonestic Ocean after she'd fallen into it from a great height. A notion of movement but no light at the ceiling, no sense of when she might force her way through. If ever. The sensation more barometric than anything else.

Eventually, a warmth began to line the inside of her lids. A pale, colorless blush. She couldn't open her eyes. She moaned for Gardius but heard and felt no nearby stirring. The worst of the heaviness passed. She saw some dark shapes against darkness, some movement against stillness. Fell unconscious again. The sensation ebbed and flowed, until finally she could open her eyes and keep them open, and shift her gaze to see where she had been laid.

Though the place was nearly lightless, gradients of shadow suggested dimension. A large space, columns holding up a mezzanine along a far back wall. A high ornate ceiling curlicued around a recessed oval. Rain was lodged upon a platform along one end of the hall, looking into gloom, inert and sort of hesitant. Nearly morgue-like.

She thought she might be tied up but no, she *could* roll over, and, in a few moments, even pull herself to a sagging, half-upright position. She was on a settee of some sort.

The furniture became more convincing when a door opened. Light squared itself in, hurtful at first, softening. A person carrying a lamp paused, and lifted the apparatus high, the better to see across the boards.

"Scarly was right; it *is* you," said Ozma. "We thought it might be a ruse of some sort."

What was it that Rain recognized here. That Ozma's voice wasn't Tip's, not very; her presentation of herself was more . . . more curated. All these months, all those miles; and here she was, sedate as if swanning in from an afternoon of croquet and lemonade. Cool as an ornamental silk fan. Ozma's face was wary and perhaps kind; but then, Rain had never been good at nuances of expression.

When she found she could still speak, Rain said, "What happened and where am I? And where's the dragon?"

"I'll call for it. It's been kept downstairs in the joinery shop. It's all right. Jolly jumpy thing, trying to burn its way out to find you. Luckily there's a gate of iron bars, for air, don't you know; and the basement is built of granite block. Your companion couldn't burn through any of *that*." She stepped back through the doorway and spoke to an unseen accomplice. Returning, she continued, "I hardly have the right to pose a question of you. But I'll start anyway by asking if I may come closer."

"Not too close." At the flinch on Ozma's face, Rain added, "My head is pounding."

Ozma moved across the sloped flooring. A stage of some sort. Now Rain could see the wings. A network of perpendicular and angled ropes used to hoist and lower sets. Ropes that reminded her of sailing to Maracoor Crown with Lucikles from Maracoor Spot on the *Pious Enterprise*. "Can you turn up some lights?" asked Rain.

"The windows are draped as a matter of course, but extra bunting has been hung for increased security. It's safer to keep the house dark. No one is supposed to be here. It was the best we could think up at such short notice."

"Where in blazes are we?"

"The Lady's Mystique." Ah, Rain remembered it: a jewel box of a playhouse in the tony Emerald City neighborhood of Goldhaven. She groaned and felt her head.

"I've called for glasses of water. And your creature will be here shortly. Do you need anything else for right now? I'm sorry about the attack. It went rougher than planned because you awakened from some nightmare and you fought like a warrior goddess. Or so I'm told. We were trying to invite you to a midnight rendezvous. You weren't intended to be knocked on the head."

"I'm used to it. In fact, I'm nearly addicted to the occasional concussion."

Ozma's look was wintry. "Ever contrary, our Rain. And the side effects?"

"Distress and confusion. I don't know where I am. But I'm getting used to that feeling, too."

Ozma almost smiled. When there was a sound in the corridor, she went back. Rain watched her captor move across the floor, a shapely young woman in a becoming afternoon gown of plum moiré. White sleeves with shot cuffs, like a banker's clerk, and a gentleman's collar at the neck, but a comb with baroque flourish jabbed into her chignon, which listed off-center. The effect was arresting and also, Rain guessed, studied.

The princess royale returned with a beaker of water and a glass and set them down on a table next to the settee but returned to the doorway for a further consultation. Rain took in her jail cell. This whole setup made her feel as if she were appearing in some play of which she'd never been shown the script. Someone's impression of a salon, organized to be seen from the orchestra seats, the balconies and boxes. A room without solid walls, an imagined chamber hovering in the darkness. A carpet in bright greens and reds, and beyond, a lady's chair, and a wicker baby carriage filled with heaps of yarn bristling with knitting needles. Everything was a bit too big and bright and real. Those balls of yarn the size of cantaloupes. What was theater, thought Rain as she waited for Ozma, but legitimized spying on someone else's idea of the world.

Rain heard Ozma dismiss her chaperone, requiring the facto-tum to wait outside the building with the others. In the carriage yard. Until further notice. Maybe it was Scarly. Maybe not. Again Ozma came back. This time she carried a wicker basket on one arm and a leash looped in her hand. Gardius dragged backward on the lead until he saw Rain. Then he pulled out of Ozma's grip and tried to climb into Rain's lap. He had to settle for getting his paws and nose in her face. He licked her, and such was his new continence that his breath was almost cool, if malodorous.

"I know, I know, I missed you too," said Rain, chucking him under the chin. "Settle down now. Yes, you can come onto the settee." She pulled herself upright and put her feet on the floor. Gardius took up the rest of the seat, which remanded Ozma to the upholstered lady's chair flanked by an occasional table and the baby carriage. Ozma set the lidded basket in the baby carriage so Gardius wouldn't knock it over with his wagging tail.

Stalling, no way to start. How do you write your own life. "What's the show?" asked Rain finally, flicking a wrist at the decor.

"I caught a glimpse of a playbill tacked up backstage. It's called *The Revenge of Charity*, or something."

"Charity probably being the name of the heroine."

"That's all the virtue they ever credit us with."

The *us*, the *us* in that sentence: right away. Ozma staking her presence in simpatico with Rain, on the side of the female leads. The Tip in Ozma seemed in deep denial, maybe atrophied, maybe dissolved. Rain winced through a surge of grief, trying to keep it from showing. "Why are we here?" asked Rain. "I mean, not in this sorry hard life, but here in an empty hall all alone?"

Ozma turned her face to think how to answer. Glancing offstage, as it were. Giving Rain a chance to study her sharp profile. Rain etched the image with her fingertip into her opposite palm, to remember it feelingly if this was the last time.

"You know that there's opposition to my ascendance to the throne," Ozma said. Rain shrugged, not wanting to admit she hadn't stopped to collect the latest on the street. Ozma looked as if the Tip in her remembered how Rain could be. "You'll have sidestepped news of current events, I bet. But it's easy enough to understand. After the rush of celebration at my return from that sarcophagus of an endless boyhood, the usual suspects who trade in discord got together."

"Right away, I don't know what you mean. What usual suspects?"

"The cronies who supported Shell Thropp, the self-styled Emperor Apostle. Old Shell. Your great-uncle and our former Throne Minister. He may have fled into deep retirement as he promised, or be scheming a comeback. But his supporters—the barons and the princes of the factories, the men who benefited—they are appalled to have an Animal at the head of government. They find it insulting. A certain Lord Avaric bon Tenmeadows especially. They began to float the notion that I was an imposter. That old Mombey could never have bewitched an infant Ozma into a decades-long spell of childhood. The improbability of such events gave the grunts and groaners a platform on which to raise objection. Meanwhile Mombey has gone abroad and is unavailable for questioning. And I wasn't ready to put down an insurrection; I'm still not ready. I need political training and I need to grow up, too. To get used to this otherworldly status called womanhood. So I've gone into soft seclusion. And after a foiled attempt on my life, into deep hiding. All with the Regent Throne Minister's secret approval."

"Are you sure that old Brrr hasn't himself become power-mad? That his complicity with your plan isn't his own veiled grab for the throne of Oz? Might he have engineered a false attack on you to legitimize putting you into seclusion?"

"Oh, you're so cynical for one so young."

"I'm the same age as you—" But Ozma held up a finger and Rain backed off. Of course. Ozma had six or seven decades on Rain, even if it had been a somewhat catatonic, spell-bound life.

"Listen, Rain. Don't be a ninny. Of course Brrr is loyal and devoted. What Cowardly Lion wouldn't rather be back in Shiz, peddling antiques or writing sardonic sketches to perform in undergraduate common rooms? He keeps to his post out of regard for me, mostly. And because he thinks the revanchists who preferred your great-uncle Shell as Throne Minister would quickly install another puppet they could prop up and manipulate. Shell was good for the very rich in this city and in Gillikin, you know. Not so much for the working Animals and humans and the trodden and despondent."

"So—we're here because—?"

"When Brrr was slipped a note from Scarly that said you'd come back to the capital, he got word to me. We arranged that you'd be escorted to a safe zone."

"You're living here."

"Oh, no. I can't tell you where I stay. It would put you in danger to know. Not to mention me."

"Well, don't tell me then." Rain wrinkled her mouth for the first time. Attempting a smile, managing maybe a wince, at best. She thought it likely that she merely looked deranged. "The Lady's Mystique. Am I being obvious if I say this is a bit stagey?"

"I suppose it is over the top. But the theater is dark today, and it was the best we could think up at short notice. Look, I haven't much time. The place is surrounded by my plainclothes guards. Tell me why you've come back."

That was Tip in Ozma, certainly? More direct than Rain could have been. Or maybe Ozma had learned bluntness from Tip and she was now direct, as befits the head of a nation. Even if as yet uncrowned. "Tell me, Rain."

"I had to see you again," said Rain simply. "I went away to get away from you. I suffered amnesia by crashing into a—well, never mind—and now I wonder if that amnesia was partly willful. I didn't want to face you if you couldn't face me. I couldn't live in the world with you, or without you either. So I went out of the world, as far as I could go. Then I realized, I suppose, that I had no choice. If we were going to part, it had to be our own decision, together. An active choosing. Not forced upon us by magic spells dissolving or by the needs of state protocol. I came back to do this the right way."

"Well," said Ozma. "You've changed in two years. I see that."

"You mean besides the green?"

She flicked her fingers at that. "Makeup could do that if it wanted. That first year, when I was out and about the city more, I saw Elphabas going to fancy-dress balls three or four times a season. The ones I liked best were the rather beefy ones."

"You still have an eye for the ladies."

"Our situation is not to be mocked." She drew herself up; now she was both Tip and Ozma, decisive, inclined to correct and to be correct. "You *have* changed. You are harder."

"Is that such a bad thing?"

"Change is neither good nor bad; it matters how the change is used in the wicked world." Putting her hands together in her lap, Ozma lowered her chin so her eyes looked out from under the manicured brows. Her high-buttoned collars couldn't disguise a certain embonpoint. "I suspect you're more guarded. Probably more capable. And me? How do you find me?"

"That's a girly question and I've never been a girly girl."

"Well, for most of my life, neither was I."

They laughed at that, a genuine laugh—a tickling, stitch-ripping, time-shattering laugh. Nervous, self-conscious, but also a relief.

When she could catch her breath to continue, Rain said, "I mean, I was never good at asking myself questions about how I felt. Maybe because, like you, I was brought up in the disguise of a camouflage skin. I figured out that it was safer to leave all that stuff alone. I was skating on nerves and moxie, I was running my whole life. I didn't have the wherewithal to ask how I felt about anything. Even about you," she finished with a dry little gasp. "Tip."

"I'm not Tip," said Ozma in the smallest of voices, though in this room a spider up in the gods could have heard that.

"No part of you is left of the Tip that loved me?"

"The part of me that loves you wasn't dissolved when my disguise fell away," said Ozma.

Rain let Gardius lick the salt off her cheeks. When she could manage it, she muttered, "I don't know what to do with any of this. I don't know what country I live in or what life or what world. Why couldn't you have told me two years ago?"

"Told you what I didn't myself get yet? I was just waking up. From my own amnesia, a walking amnesia. Is amnesia just another term for the cluelessness of adolescence? Which we're barely out of, Rain. Besides, I didn't know—I don't know—what my— affection— could mean to you—other than sorrow and frustration and, I suppose, maybe an invitation to madness."

"Oh, I'm better than that," said Rain. "I can be utterly mad on my own coin, I don't need a prompt from you. I'm a witch now, do you get that? I mean, I pretend to be, but I suppose after a while the pretense drops away."

"Could you pretend to love me, then?" asked Ozma.

Rain shuddered. "I don't know. Couldn't we—somehow—maybe with the aid of the Grimmerie, which I can now read somewhat, and have accidentally kept safe from harm—couldn't we find a way to regress ourselves back to being boy Tip and thin colorless Rain?"

"If I understand what you mean," said Ozma softly, "this *is* the regression. Our truer selves. The others were the disguises. They can't hold." She stood up. "Do you think a knitting needle would puncture the hide of that scale-bound doggie?"

"No. And don't you dare. Whatever for—?"

"I would strongly like to persuade him to get off the chesterfield."

"Why?" said Rain. "We're not who we were. It's a play, a theater piece, a fakery. Suitable for this pretend parlor, maybe, but not for real. We'd be approaching each other under false pretenses. We can't make-believe at this kind of thing."

Ozma tilted her head and peered at Rain, trying to work something out. "I don't know what you've been up to for eighteen months or so, but it's been a tumble of sorts, hasn't it? You have the look of a much-traveled ambassador."

"My old friend," said Rain, "you have no idea. There and back again, just about."

"But it's brought you here. Can't you picture what we had, and wonder if it is available somehow still? Something like love was involved, if I'm not mistaken."

"Don't be dry and waspish. Ozma, while I was abroad—"

"Oh, *abroad*. My. An unappointed ambassador of the Palace, I presume?"

"You might say. But listen: I came across a concept called ephrarxis. If I understand it correctly, it means a nostalgia for something that might have been but never was. I take it to be a kind of sickness, frankly. Something that dissuades you from living in the present because the impossible other-history is so alluring."

"I have never heard of ephrarxis, but fear of its poisonous effect on healthy life seems to argue *for* me, not against me. Life as it really is, here, not as we imagined it earlier. Rain, there was a moment when you were pale and I was Tip, and we had never embraced anyone before, much less each other, but we took the risk. We—we clung. And first our world opened and then it broke. You survived whatever it is you went away to do, and you came back. And *now* you're unwilling to be held? You survived wars and famine and giant mosquitoes and boring little drinks parties, flew to the ends of the earth, and back, and *now* you're scared? How is this any different from when we braved our first contact? You're a new person and so am I. We're a little wiser and perhaps ought to be a little fiercer. What's the worst that can happen? That we're not right for each other? Isn't that what you came back to find out?"

Rain shoved Gardius to the carpet. Ozma moved over and sat down and took Rain in her arms. "When you first kissed Tip," she said, "you didn't know what that would be like. You didn't know you'd come to adore him. You're in the same moment now. Give us a go, will you?"

"When you first kissed Rain," began Rain, but, at that second, she didn't finish her thought.

NOTHING WAS CONCLUSIVE. Probably nothing could ever be conclusive. It was just where they were, now. It was intermission, in between Act One and Act Next. They had to make a plan, to buy themselves time. A day, or two, or three, till they were sure, till they could think, till they could come back to earth and breathe without panting. However long that would take.

Not a lifetime; they weren't thinking beyond the cast of their week. The local time, the time in which they were still together, before they broke apart. Whenever that would be—they couldn't read any cards about that.

"But I've told you," said Ozma, "the building is surrounded at the entrances by armed security forces dressed as laborers and locals. They're putting up a new bill on the marquee that they'll take down again as soon as I safely leave. A lot of effort for an hour's audience with you, but couldn't be helped. My personal team of guards has eyes everywhere. Under instructions from the Regent Throne Minister and his privy council, and with my blessing. The opposition leader, Lord Avaric, would choke on his own mustache in joy if I were apprehended by his goons. We have to take exquisite care."

"I'm a witch," said Rain. "I might not be much good at it, but I *can* rustle up a disguise."

"I've sent my attendants outside. So we're the only people in the building," said Ozma. "We can't leave like bored theatergoers waking up in their seats a day after the house lights were extinguished. But if we could . . ." She undid the remaining buttons of her snug plum waistcoat, which Rain had started on already. Underneath, the rest of a man's shirt. And when she hitched up her hems, she revealed a pair of men's black afternoon trousers. "My butler's. He doesn't know I borrowed them."

"*You're* the witch, now. Precisely what did you come prepared for, Ozma?"

"Whatever I found."

The princess picked up her basket as she and Rain went to rummage around backstage. They came upon a wardrobe and dressing room hung with dusty costuming. A stiff gentleman's hat that could settle and center upon Ozma's chignon. She hung her plum dress upon a hook. "Unless you want to try it on?" she asked Rain.

"Haven't got that far yet," said Rain. "I'll just take this greasy beggar's shawl. More my style, the last few years."

They inspected the basement for possible secret exits that the security forces might not know about. Nothing. "We haven't much time," said Ozma. "My people won't think me to be in danger as long as the perimeters of the theater aren't breached, but they will be coming to collect me shortly. I told them an hour. If we want to escape their notice and buy ourselves some time to—to—"

"To stop faffing about? Upstairs, then."

With Gardius behind them, sniffing at the remains of theater mice, they climbed wooden staircases to where roustabouts made magic happen in their own way. Up here, through angled glass, light fell upon dingy flats and flies suspended till needed in the limelights. A yellow brick road, a boarding school dormitory, a throne room. Rain passed them by. "I suppose the skylights are also guarded?"

"Yes. The roof is staffed with its own detail." But Ozma grinned at Rain.

"What?"

"I was remembering our escape from St. Prowd's through a skylight."

"You're right. We're practiced at this." Saying *we* at this point was in itself a new country to Rain, as unexplored as Maracoor had been. Sweet Oz, was it possible she was blushing?

They arrived at a warren of small rooms halfway down the stairs on the far side of the stage. The water closet was rank and fetid—no useful window. Then a staff lunchroom. An iron stove, probably for keeping cast and crew alive during winter performances, was capped with an exhaust pipe. It fed itself through a hole sealed over with a square of wood. A vertical trapdoor hammered shut. Flush in the brick wall, no purchase. No prying it away. "This will lead outside, it has to," said Rain. "It's where the smoke goes."

"A spell would come in handy now," said Ozma.

"You be the Queen of Bossiness, I'll be the witch? Is that it? Gardius," said Rain. "We are in need of your help."

The dwarf dragon paced forward and studied the two young

women quizzically. Rain spoke to him with her hands on his cheeks, and then turned his head to the wooden hatch in the brick. Gardius emitted a small stream of flame, thin as a child's chalk. "He's going to burn the place down, not a good plan," said Ozma. "Stop him."

"He knows what he's doing," said Rain. "Even if I don't."

The creature kept up the jet of gold until the board had a blackened side, like toast too near the flame. When enough of it had smoked through, Rain and Ozma used a stove poker to pry the rest away. A moldy old patch job, it splintered apart. They broke it into fragments and shoved them in the stove. The light of outside—it was late afternoon—gave them their first daylight view of each other. Ozma was a pearl against a pearly sky; and Rain felt freshened as spring growth.

Sections of the stovepipe outside the building rose above the rooftop. It was affixed to the exterior walls by a series of iron rings. While it listed dreadfully after Gardius's labors, it hadn't collapsed into the alley. The noise would have drawn attention to their efforts. Ozma scrabbled to the top of the cold stove and peered over the edge of the makeshift sill. "We're in luck," she said.

"For the first time in our lives," said Rain.

"No, second. The first was meeting each other at St. Prowd's. From which we fled thanks to the skylight, the roofs, the shadows. As you remember. We've got this down cold. Climb up, there's room. I'll squinch over. Look, I think in order to jury-rig this venting apparatus here, ironmongers had to pound a few prongs of iron into the mortar between the bricks. See? From the alley below. So they could get up here. Then there was no reason to take the posts down, because the wall was sealed, and anyway one day the stovepipe might need repairing." She craned and looked skyward. "The footholds don't continue to the roof. So I don't think the security detail will have considered this a possible escape route even if they noticed it. Though they *ought* to have noticed it. What are we paying them for?"

"Shut up," said Rain. "Can we get out this way?"

Ozma jumped to the floor and glanced around. A clipboard and a cast list, and a pencil attached on a string. She turned the paper over and scrawled. *Ozma leaves willingly in her own custody, unimperiled. She will communicate in time.* She made a mark that Rain guessed must be a signature scrawl, meaning *by Ozma's hand attesting.* She hung the clipboard on a nail next to the opening they'd kicked out of the wall. Couldn't be missed. "For Brrr, so he doesn't have Lord Avaric arrested for kidnapping. Though Avaric is guilty of other sedition. Shall we?" As if about to enter a ballroom for a state occasion.

The aperture was wide enough for Gardius to get through. He launched clumsily from the pedestal of the potbellied stove and nearly slammed into the wall of the building across the alley, but curveted up into safer skies. No doubt he'd be drawing attention of men on the ground. They'd be racing inside now and discovering the princess's absence from the stage. Then combing the building.

Ozma handed Rain the wicker basket and climbed out the hatch. Some muscle memory of being boy may have helped; or maybe that didn't enter into it. Rain passed the basket through once Ozma was steady outside and ready to grab it, and then Rain followed her. Quick work to descend, like climbing down a tree.

SCARLY HAD RETREATED to a nook in the alley to indulge in a cigarette. She was hanging back because Palace help were forbidden to be seen with smoke or drink in public. An alley could scarcely be deemed a public thoroughfare, but she didn't want to push the matter. The matron of the salon staff was already on Scarly's case for speaking before being spoken to. Scarly needed to keep her nose clean and her breath sweet, so she had sprigs of mintgrass and lemon parsley in her apron pocket, at the ready to obliterate traces of her disobedience.

She was grinding the butt against a paving stone and preparing to continue her circuit around the perimeter of the theater when she heard a hushed giggling above her. She ducked back into the shadow of the stage door overhang but peered out. The princess royale and the self-advertising Witch of Maracoor were straddling some hitherto unnoticed windowsill and kicking themselves free into the air. Scarly thought Rain looked like a salamander upon the red brick, making her way down the outside wall on iron brackets hammered in place by someone in the building trades. Struts for a ladder devoid of the parallel uprights. And the uninstalled Throne Minister, dressed as a man no less, followed the witch. Scarly drew in her breath.

All her life she'd been the sideline pair of hands, the silent observer, the hauler of coal shuttles, the collector of pails of ash and buckets of night slop, until at last she'd graduated to supervising the gloves of Palace guests, their parasols and sometimes their pistols. Scarly's poise was improved and she'd learned to hold her chin level and not to duck her eyes floorward as often. But though Rain had once taught Scarly to read, the parlor maid's tongue had proved uneducable. Accents are disguisable only through silence. By remaining mute she'd encouraged palace operatives to believe she might be either simple or perhaps somewhat deaf. So Scarly kept her own counsel and she heard more than she understood. And forgot very little of it.

What the disappearance of Ozma might mean to the delicate balance of powers within the Palace was certain—total mayhem and nothing less. Unless senior staff collaborated on some fiction of Ozma's being indisposed, truth would out. Maybe Scarly could buy the princess royale some time to get to wherever she seemed intent in going as she descended the iron rungs on the building's back wall. When the disappearance was noticed, Scarly could invent some tissue of possibility, some unverifiable lie—she'd seen Ozma jump in a carriage and order the driver to take her . . . somewhere. But without knowing where Ozma and Rain might be headed, anyplace Scarly could suggest to divert the inevitable posse might be too close to the actual destination. She'd keep quiet and listen—she was used to that.

More to the point, Scarly had only a few minutes to decide if she wanted to become implicated in this breakout without being invited to be a collaborator. Her fondness for Rain derived from the days at St. Prowd's, when the scholar child was pale and incidental—a poor girl, let's face it, nearly as poor as Scarly but set up with a firmer backbone—a witch in embryo even then.

And Scarly had hidden behind her professional backstairs reticence when she first encountered Tip as a boy. Once able to imagine a turn in Tip's path, she'd daydreamed about his recognizing little scullery maid Scarly as his True Only One. But she'd found herself turning even shyer when he became tricked out as Ozma. Scarly had felt bewildered and, perhaps, betrayed. She'd felt obscurely insulted, as if he'd done it to avoid having to disappoint her. Even though she knew Tip and Rain had become heartbeats-in-tandem, one to the other.

Skeins of memory whirled around her like cigarette smoke, unstable and pungent. Her rheumy distractible mother and her barleycorn father, and all those siblings who thought she was putting on Palace affectations when she came home once a season with city treats. Her voice, comically rustic in the Emerald City, was now deemed posh and artificial when heard again at the family kitchen yard. She had no cool mattress where she could lie down as herself, unmocked and serene. She couldn't win with anyone, in any place.

So did that make Scarly more or less likely to see Rain and Ozma, nearly as homeless as herself but for different reasons, as an item to be cherished or as yet another indignity, this time something she could eradicate? She'd stood at Ozma's side with distant affection, and now Ozma appeared to be skiving off without signing the register. It didn't seem fair—and yet when had life ever been fair, only in children's stories and sometimes not even then.

WHEN OZMA AND RAIN hit the yard by the stage door, they sized one another up. Rain corrected the angle of Ozma's stiff and outlandish hat. Ozma wet her hand and began to thumb away the soot from Rain's cheek. "Hey, blend it in more," said Rain, "it'll just increase the disguise."

"What will they think, a young gentleman dallying in an alley at this hour with a woman not of his class," said Ozma.

"They'll think what they always think, and they'll be partly right. Shall I take the basket, as I'm the female lead, at least to the audience in the street?" It was too weighty for a loaf of bread, and a heaviness rolled inside it. "What you got in here, firearms?" asked Rain, switching the basket to her other hand.

"Not today. No, it's Tay. Your rice otter. You left him for me, remember? I was going to give him back to you if—if we were goodbyeing." She glanced sideways at Rain. "Now you can't have him back. You can only borrow him. For the next few days anyway—who knows how long this exeat will last."

Rain's fever broke just about then. All her clothes went damp on the inside.

They passed within a foot of Scarly in shadow. In shadow and holding her breath.

Into Goldhaven Square, which was busying itself of an autumn evening, the well-heeled on their evening strolls, regarding the shop windows and one another. Ozma offered Rain her arm. Rain took it. Gardius would track them from rooftops, no doubt. A child rolled a hoop across a street; a nanny scolded such impertinence. A soprano began to do scales in an upstairs window. Leaves shivered in a sudden breath of wind, and a few yellow tags fell to the pavement. Unutterably ordinary.

4

They muttered with their heads close together, walking in the dusk along the Royal Mall, toward the Ozma Fountain and the Shiz Road.

"You've shrunk, as a woman," said Rain. "You used to be three inches taller than me, when you were Tip."

"I don't think so," said Ozma. "More likely you've had a growth spurt."

"Are we going anyplace special or are we just out on a stroll until we get picked up by your security detail?"

"You don't think my disguise as a man is convincing? After all those decades of practice? I'm shattered."

"Be serious. I didn't go through hellwater to joke right now."

Ozma shrugged. "Brrr will quietly put out teams to hunt for the green girl, guessing I'll be with you. So we daren't go back to Kiamo Ko. I think even Shiz, where we met, would be dicey. We could head to your father's home."

"Nether How? No. I don't want to draw him into this. He'll tell the truth if he's approached, so best not to involve him."

"What about the mucklands of Quadling Country. Isn't that where your mother is from?"

"Not an option," said Rain firmly. "And I don't suppose we should stay here."

"Too risky, you're right. So where?"

For now, they settled on where they'd be least suspected of going—the heart of Gillikin Country. Shiz, the provincial capital, proved a great temptation as a hideout, because that was where Tip and Rain had first met. But it seemed smart to resist, to keep west of those haunts—the fleshpots of ephrarxia! Safer to head into the Pertha Hills. True, that was home territory of the industrial barons, those reactionaries who wanted to find Shell Thropp and return him to the throne, or some parallel boss. But for just that reason, the north would seem an unlikely place for Ozma to secret herself. Estates and farms and lots of rolling meadow and woodland. Fox hunting country. Enough ornamental and native greenery to cloak Rain, too. Perfect.

Glinda's old stomping grounds, as it happened.

Whatever would Glinda think of all that had happened? Or, come to consider it, Elphaba herself? Where was she now?

Wherever, Rain hoped that they might both be proud of her. Not that she'd do anything differently if they weren't. She'd moved on from the payment of dues.

Becoming aware, perhaps, of a new course of talent in her. Something not like flying, not at all. Neither was it like being able to spit up spells and tame the moment. It was more like—she was able to think of it now without getting angry at herself—more like being able to hold a hypothesis about how something *seemed*. Not what it was or wasn't, but how it impressed itself upon her.

This was a new notion. Perhaps other kids got this at seven. She was a late developer. The cultivation of the emotions—not just feeling, but registering the feeling.

Perhaps there was no use, really, for noticing the nuances of emotion. But it reminded her she had survived all this. She was still alive. Despite everything.

"Moongirl," said Ozma, "you'd better watch that gap in the paving. You'll break your ankle and then I'll have to carry you."

"Or leave me behind."

"That's not in the cards, either. If I don't have you, there's no reason to abandon my position in the Palace."

"Why haven't you taken the throne yet? You're not a minor."

"You talked about amnesia. I suppose my being magicked into the form of Tip was another sort of amnesia. I never knew I was living decades as a lad. Part of Mombey's spell, maybe. Also, we moved every few years. If I happened to make friends in any new quarter, we left before I could notice that they were growing up and I wasn't. Oz is big that way. We also went north—some time in Fliaan, some time in Quox. Mombey could shape-shift somewhat, but she didn't age either, or she kept coming back to her preferred form, which was somewhat slinky. Since she was my only benchmark, and I had no real education, I just floated along like a fish, getting older but getting no wiser."

"Who says fish don't get wiser?"

"Don't change the subject. What happens now if I step forward and release Brrr from his regency and become the Throne Minister? There are some who will never believe I am Ozma. Why should they—some days I can hardly believe it myself. There'll be cries for me to assert myself. And in those decades of a somewhat mothy, protracted boyhood, I learned nothing about our nation's history. So in order to be qualified as a head of state, I've been studying up. The Ozmas! Endless. I will be grilled on them, and I'll need to prove my stuff. Ozma the Bilious, Ozma the Scarcely Beloved, Ozma the Librarian, Ozma Contortia, Ozma Glikkusia. That's the one who annexed the Glikkus from the dwarves."

"I didn't know the Glikkus was annexed."

"Right. And that brings up the current political situation internationally. Leave aside the likes of Lord Avaric and your great-uncle, Shell Thropp. In the past two years, they've discovered poxite in the Scalps. The dwarves were always so drunk with ambition for their diamonds that they never noticed poxite. Which is used in explosives, did you know that? Firearms and worse. Now the Nome King is showing signs of wanting to press a prior claim on that part of Oz, liberate it from colonial oppression. Whoever is going to argue for military action to prevent it has to know the history of the conflict and the region. I've been up to my ladylike eyelashes boning up on matters of state. If I'm going to do this, I'm going to do it when I'm ready. I'm not ready yet. My duties are clear, and I accept that; but can't I allow myself to recognize my life as open-ended and—and *mine*—at the same time?" Ozma clutched Rain's arm harder. "Because there is this, too. I wasn't ready, and I wasn't going to be ready, until I knew better where this—this between us—where it stood."

"After you figure it out, will you be ready to take a husband?"

Ozma laughed. "Who knows. Would you be ready to take a wife?"

GARDIUS HAD BEEN smart enough to keep his distance until Ozma and Rain had cleared the walls of the Emerald City. How much easier this, thought Rain, than sneaking out of the gates of Maracoor Crown not so long ago! Beyond the Shiz Gate, the dwarf dragon came bouncing down to earth, cheery and ready to play fetch. He'd mastered the art of not roasting the stick he wanted Rain to throw. But by the time they'd reached a more rural district northwest of the walls of the Emerald City, it seemed prudent to send Gardius away. However docile he was trying to be, he was too roguishly himself to be able to pass in society as a dog. He wouldn't accede to Rain's repeated request of him to piss off until finally she had to buy a loaf tin in a country store and threaten to muzzle him again.

She took the tarot card with a picture of a book on it, and in the white space of the sky around the image, she inscribed the words

Don't worry. Where am I now? Not gone. Then, so the card couldn't fall out, she wrapped it in a length torn from her apron strings. She tied the ends of the apron string around Gardius's neck like a collar.

Leading him out behind a carriage house where they'd stopped for the night, she held his nose between her hands. She let the dragon lick her nose and ears and mouth. She licked him back. Then she said:

> *Have I come to think in questions?*
> *Have I come to make suggestions?*
> *Scaeti scaetiri, periouranos.*
> *We break ourselves out of our prison.*
> *You go back to Liir and Trism.*
> *Scaeti scaetiri, periouranos.*

At first Gardius looked as if he intended to buck the requirements of enchantment. He had the strength of will to pull it off. But perhaps seeing Rain use a skill of which she was still so clearly frightened made his dwarf dragon heart tender.

Or, more probably, thought Rain, he leaves of his own free will.

She watched him lumber into the sky, a great flying lummox the size of a waffle cart. As a kind of departing signal he flared a few bursts of flame to say goodbye. Not a great move, Ozma opined, for anyone who might be watching and taking notes. We better duck for cover. Come here, shelter with me. Mmm.

THEY'D GOT AN EARLY START next morning. Rain had taken from Ozma those gentleman's gloves and covered her green hands with them, and she dragged her shawl around her brow. She'd perfected this hooded maneuver while escaping the city of Maracoor

Crown. Then she blued her green nose and chin with pollen from the flowers Lucikles had given her in Ithira Strand. It wasn't an absolute makeover but she could pass more easily.

Those flowers, they had not yet faded. Maybe they never would. Maybe she would give them to Ozma someday.

Producing a staggering clutch of banknotes from a leather fold, Ozma practiced deepening her voice, and she approached a local stable. And my, the carriage that such cash could secure. Silvered handles on the lockable door. Dark drapes. They reveled in the privacy, lying back in blankets upon the leathery banquette, though they didn't dare to act out the parts of a randy bon vivant dragging his woman away for a weekend in the playgrounds of the Pertha Hills.

But no carriage driver or ostler could be trusted for long, since cash worked in more than one direction. So outside of a town called East Spillabout, Ozma dismissed the conveyance. Following a hearty lunch of sausages and onion porridge, they left the public house out a back door. The sky was newly washed after a passing autumn shower. A washerwoman smoked a pipe while she wrung out bar cloths; two children played catch with a rolled-up ball of stockings. Life had its little continuities that knew nothing of a fleeing potentate and a curiously colored young witch. And how good that was to realize.

Ozma and Rain continued on foot for a while, skirting the center of town. Out of sight of villagers, Rain could lower her shawl and be somewhat green in the light. Ozma could remove her top hat and even loosen the chignon a little.

Tay perched on Rain's shoulder as if a day hadn't gone by.

"We should probably come up with a new name for you," said Rain. "*Ozma* is going to prove something of a liability if we're trying to pass unnoticed."

"Any ideas?"

Rain thought. "I've been away, and met some folks. There's Tesasi. You could be Tesasi. Or maybe Scyrilla. Or Poena?"

"Those sound too foreign. Better an everyday name, like Maretta or Chane. A scrub girl's name, familiar in any schoolyard."

"So not Dorothy, then."

"Ha! No, thank you. What about Tippa? Too weird?"

"Almost. But we can give it a go." Rain took her hand, Ozma's hand, to see if it was Tippa's hand. Maybe it was.

They paused on the grassy verge of the periphery road. Which way to go? To the north, they could make out the slopes of the Pertha Hills. Stockbroker Stables, some called it. To the east, rain showers smeared the horizon. The fugitives wouldn't think south; for now, they'd left the Emerald City behind. While from the west, immediately above a sloping cornfield, a pair of flying creatures made an elegant descent to examine the late harvest. They dropped slanting through the air like two soft rags of paper. "Herons?" asked Ozma— asked Tippa—pointing.

"Or cranes?" said Rain. Well, they might be. They could be. Iskinaary's twin crossbreed children? Hatched and on their own already? She sighed. "There's a lot yet to do, you know. Orphan children on the edge of the wilderness, just for a start. Who knows if Iskinaary has survived? I rather think not. We don't all have Nanny's improbable constitution. But there's work to be done."

"Work to be done, whether on the throne or in the farmer's field," said Tippa. "Stay alive today, and plan for tomorrow. Keeping faith with life. Shall we snitch some corn?"

"Gardius would have been useful for roasting dinner."

"Do you know what we are doing tomorrow?"

"You're asking me, my lady liege?"

Tippa tackled Rain for her insolence and brought her into the grass. They sat up after a while, panting. "Seriously," said Tippa. "I can see the sense of hiding in plain sight, in this part of Oz that no one would seriously think I'd dare to go. But for how long? And what next?"

"We can't do *next* yet, we can barely do *now*."

"But we have to think. Not just feel, Rain—we must consider."

Rain was silent, rubbing the grass with one hand and the fur around the neck of the otter with the other. The arithmetic of justice was beyond her ability to decipher. But just to get here, to this day on the edge of a field, had taken two years. She had wandered away, comatose as a calabash, and eventually flown away across the sea. In her despair and anger she'd jettisoned the Grimmerie, and look what that had done. Sure, maybe some good, in that it helped liberate Maracoor from the danger posed by the Fist of Mara. But that had been accidental benefit. And accidental cost, oh, as bad or worse, in the deaths of Moey and of King Copperas, not to mention Skedelander military men and civilians of Maracoor Abiding. She had a debt she would have to service until she was no longer alive to make payment.

"We can't repair the world, just the two of us," she said softly. "I tried to do that alone, by sinking the Grimmerie, and look what happened."

"You do something else instead, then. A swap. A moral swap. No?" asked Tippa. "At my side as I try to keep the place from rotting—isn't that worth doing?"

Rain didn't answer, just closed her eyes. Then she smiled. Though she didn't yet say anything to Tippa, she'd thought of aging Iskinaary on his own, out on a desolate farm, trying to supervise Aubiano and a bunch of orphans. Whose disappeared parents were not Rain's fault. "Well, all right, maybe," she said, more to herself than to Tippa.

"Maybe what?"

"Maybe this," she said, and kissed Tippa. "Come, we have to find a place for the night. That rain is moving west. There's bound to be an inn of some sort in that settlement beyond the meadow."

Done with the broom, done with the book. The last card left, just a welcome blank. We should be so lucky, the unpredicted life. So they moved on, emulating the only forward-leaning impulses they could rely upon: time and melody.

Though they were shielded by tall greenery, their passage rustled the stalks and disturbed other scavengers, who rose complaining at being displaced from the eternal corn. At first Rain sensed that it was the spirit-guests of Moey and Asparine, those harpies who had escorted Rain to her farthest point away before she was ready to turn back toward home. Could they have followed her back to Oz?

She didn't know, but to this she could attest: above the wind-whistled meadow lifted an arpeggio of fretful crows. A flinging of dark notes liberated from the strict rules of a lined page. Notes and ghost notes, statements and harmonic echoes. The scoring of an unsingable aria against the fretless heaven.

IN THE MIDDLE of the night, a quiet storm broke over the world. In her blankets, Rain stirred and put the back of her hand against the cheek of whoever this was next to her. She drifted in that universal and solitary sea, an unmooring allowed by midnight. Not quite certain with whom she slept, not quite sure who she was, or where. The rain fell upon the shed dormer of the attic room they'd negotiated to hire. It splashed over the sill. Tay lifted its head, twitched its whiskers in appetite for submersion, but settled again—it was all or nothing for the rice otter. The rain slid in sheets along cedar roof tiles, and in currents, gurgling, through tin gutters. The sound was near and far at once.

The rain fell upon trees and roofs and upon domestic animals standing in pastures. It counted the countless blades of grass upon the world and numbered each one with its touch. The district around East Spillabout allowed for the drenching, church and schoolyard and meadow alike. What choice did it have. The rain considered the reaches of southern Gillikin as far as the Emerald City, and farther beyond. It rained upon the two-umbrella home of Candle Osqa'ami, Rain's mother, in distant Quadling Country. It rained upon the roofs of Mockbeggar Hall in Munchkinland, where Rain had come to consciousness of self under the watch of Lady Glinda. It rained upon the Palace of the Emerald City, and the Lion heard it but paid it no attention, too busy fretting, as he tossed in his royal bed, about how to keep the disappearance of Ozma secret from political adversaries. It rained upon the dormitory where Scarly lay awake in bitter torment, wondering what to say to Brrr should their paths cross in the Palace corridors tomorrow. It rained upon the tent of Avaric bon Tenmeadows, where with a retinue of thirty he was engaged on an illegal hunt of tree elves in the Sleeve of Ghastille. Upon the barn at Nether How, and Gardius fretted, for weather upset his canny olfactory alert system; upon the roofs at Nether How, but Trism and Liir slept on, encoiled. It fell upon the conical lids of the towers at Kiamo Ko. In the courtyard, the golden trees shivered in the downpour; in her swaddlings, Nanny dreamed uneasily of a tornado intending to make a return appearance. Out in the west, rain in the grasslands, rain in the desert, and rain then upon the Nonestic Sea.

Too much to continue? But rain obeys no authorial management. It rained across the sea, though none could chart it. It rained upon the temple roof of Maracoor Spot, and in the morning the brides of Maracoor would find their sandals floated sideways on the stone porch. Upon the sails of trading ships and the roofs of monkey islands of pirate ships it fell, and down to decks it slipped, and out the slits beneath the rails it slid; the sea accepted the tribute and made no comment. It's just possible that Mee-rahn-nah and clan didn't register the rain at all, any more than a house registers spiders on the roof.

Across Maracoor Abiding, as far north as we have heard about, it rained in the blue-flowered graveyard of Ithira Strand and upon other islands famous or nameless; and as far south, Skedelandia, it rained, the same rain, at the same moment though not the same hour, given how far west Maracoor lay. Across the great ennobled city of Maracoor Crown the rain darkened marble pediments and red-clay pantiles and it gave wet shoulders to the figures of deity and it washed pigeon shit off the stone-laureled heads of patrons and magistrates standing on their plinths. It freshened garden patches of basil and mint, and filled cisterns usefully. Up the pastures and spinneys of High Chora sloped the same rain, muddying the roadways, sending highwaymen scurrying into their dry hideaways, teasing the forests and tangling the overgrowth into knottier knots. Upon the farmstead of Mia Zephana the rain fell, and it had no apprehension of who lay sleepless under those gables, nor what their own stormy moods might be doing, slackening or strengthening.

Upon the pond beyond the farm the rain fell as if in penitence, and though no one saw it, the form of Relexis Kee stretched his godly limbs upon the Throne Tree and closed his eyes and took off his golden torque and bathed in superior nudity.

In some stretch of landscape that cannot be named, the blue Wolf, Artoseus, disappeared, because though rain reveals some spirits it camouflages others, and Artoseus was prone to invisibility even at the driest of times.

Into the waters of the great Seethe dropped the rain, increasing the force of its meander through regions as yet uncharted. Upon the tribe of the Arborians it fell, and the Arborians took it as their due but were nonetheless grateful. Hidden deep in the Walking Mountains stood the tower of an old Oracle, and whether the rain dripped through the ceiling of a newly departed soul or upon the head of an old geezer alive enough to complain about the indignity, it is too dark to be sure. Safely below, Cossy slept, for rain is mother to the young. Tesasi, the queen of the Caryatids, sat in a doorway stretching her ancient wooden ankles in the slipstream, to keep herself supple for another millennium or so. And still the rain fell, and still it fell, until the rain fell still.

Here concludes Volume Three of
Another Day.

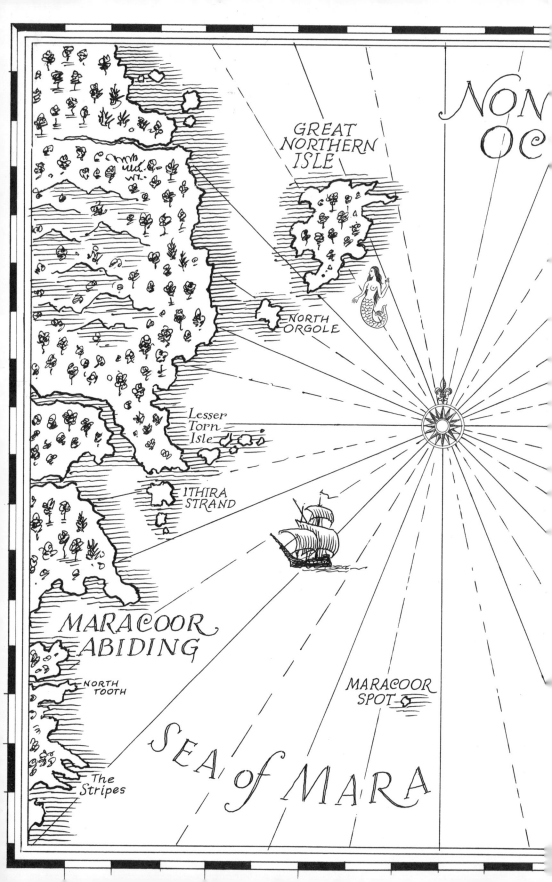